THE
COLD STORM

A THRILLER

JOHN ETTERLEE

Independently published

ISBN: 9780578537023

www.johnetterleebooks.com

INDEX OF FIRST LINES AND TITLES

Where titles differ from first lines they are shown in italic. An asterisk indicates English singing translations of the Irish hymns.

Author/Translator	Hymn No.	Text used by permission of
Jabusch, W. F.	29	
Kaan, F. H.	32, 114	Oxford University Press
	119, 121	Stainer & Bell Ltd.
Kendrick, G.	23, 47, 56, 58, 71, 74, 81, 107	Thankyou Music
Kyle, P.	52	Thankyou Music
Lafferty, K.	77	Word (UK) Ltd.
Marshall-Taylor, G.	87	Jubilee Hymns/© G. Marshall-Taylor
McAuley, J. P.	76	Curtis Brown (Australia) Pty. Ltd/© Mrs N. McAuley
Mowbray, D.	14	Stainer & Bell Ltd.
	111	Jubilee Hymns/© D. Mowbray
Nystrom, M.	5	Restoration Music Ltd.
O'Driscoll, T. H.	98	
Old, M.	79	Scripture Union
Owens, J. & C.	28	Music Publishing International Ltd.
Peacey, J. R.	34	Ms M. J. Hancock
Perry, M. A.	118, 129	Jubilee Hymns/© M. Perry
Porteous, C.	103	Jubilee Hymns/© C. Porteous
Prebble, S.	117	Thankyou Music
Quinn, J.	11, 21, 90, 128	Geoffrey Chapman Ltd.
	19	International Commission on English in the Liturgy Inc.
Ruston, R.	72	McCrimmon Publishing Co. Ltd.
Saward, M. J.	13	Jubilee Hymns/© M. Saward
Scott, L.	44	Mrs V. Leonard Williams
Seddon, J. E.	33, 84	Jubilee Hymns/© Mrs M. Seddon
Simms, G. O.	138*, 139*, 141*	
Smith, L. Jnr.	42	Thankyou Music
Stevenson, L.	15*	Oxford University Press
Strover, M. C. T.	37	Jubilee Hymns/© C. Strover
Struther, J.	53	Oxford University Press
Temple, S.	57	Franciscan Communications, USA
Timms, G. B.	83	Oxford University Press
Toolan, S.	104	GIA Publications Inc., USA
Verrall, P.	100	Herald Music Services
Westendorf, O.	116	Archdiocese of Philadelphia, USA
	124	World Library Publications Inc., USA
Winslow, J. C.	67	Mrs J. Tyrrell
Wren, B. A.	12, 88, 105	Oxford University Press

ACKNOWLEDGEMENTS

The Hymnal Revision Committee of the Church of Ireland and Oxford University Press thank the following who have given permission for copyright material to be included. Every effort has been made to trace copyright owners, and the compilers apologize to anyone whose rights have inadvertently not been acknowledged. A blank in the third column indicates that permission has been granted by the author or translator. Particulars of copyright music will be found in the music edition.

An asterisk indicates a translation.

Author/Translator	Hymn No.	Text used by permission of
Alternative Prayer Book 1984	127, 131	© 1984, the General Synod of the Church of Ireland, published by Collins
Appleford, P.	113	© Josef Weinberger Ltd.
Barker, O.	41	Thankyou Music
Bayly, A. F.	54, 68	Oxford University Press
Bilbrough, D.	49	Thankyou Music
Blakeley, P.	27	A. & C. Black (Publishers) Ltd., from Someone's Singing, Lord
Bowers, J. E.	102	
Brooks, R. T.	80	Hope Publishing Company, USA
Burns, E. J.	93	
Carter, S.	43, 70, 97	Stainer & Bell Ltd.
Chisholm, T. O.	36	Hope Publishing Company, USA
Clark, H.	117	Thankyou Music
Coelho, T.	18	Word (UK) Ltd.
Colvin, T.	46	Hope Publishing Company, USA
Connaughton, L.	109	McCrimmon Publishing Co. Ltd.
Courtney, R.	65	
Cross, S.	16	Exors. of Stewart Cross
Darling, E. F.	126	Oxford University Press/© E. F. Darling
Davison, W. D.	140*	Oxford University Press/© W. D. Davison
Downey, P.	138*	
Dudley-Smith, T.	9, 17, 25, 51, 61, 64, 75, 78, 94, 95, 115, 130, 136, 137	
Dunn, F.	135	Thankyou Music
Ellis, C.	125	Oxford University Press
Evans, D.	7	Thankyou Music
Farjeon, E.	59	David Higham Associates
Fishel, D.	1, 82	The Word of God, USA
Foley, J. B.	24, 122	North American Liturgy Resources, USA
Foley, W. B.	40	Faber Music Ltd.
Gaunt, H. C. A.	73, 123	Oxford University Press
Gillard, R.	99	Thankyou Music
Gillman, B.	10	Thankyou Music
Green, F. Pratt	22, 30, 48, 50, 63, 96, 110	Stainer & Bell Ltd.
Green, M.	86	Cherry Lane Music Ltd.
Hewlett, M.	106	Oxford University Press
Hine, S. K.	66*	Thankyou Music
Houghton, F.	55	Overseas Missionary Fellowship/this version Jubilate Hymns
Hyde, D.	140	D. Sealy
Icarus, P.	85	McCrimmon Publishing Co. Ltd.
Idle, C. M.	38, 132, 133	Jubilate Hymns/© C. M. Idle
ICET	134	Copyright © 1970, 1971, 1975, International Consultation on English Texts

145

1 Take my life, and let it be
consecrated, Lord, to thee;
take my moments and my days,
let them flow in ceaseless praise.

2 Take my hands, and let them move
at the impulse of thy love;
take my feet, and let them be
swift and beautiful for thee.

3 Take my voice, and let me sing
always, only, for my King;
take my intellect and use
every power as thou shalt choose.

4 Take my will, and make it thine;
it shall be no longer mine;
take my heart, it is thine own;
it shall be thy royal throne.

5 Take my love; my Lord, I pour
at thy feet its treasure store:
take myself, and I will be
ever, only, all, for thee.

Frances Ridley Havergal (1836–79)

146

1 What a friend we have in Jesus
all our sins and griefs to bear,
what a privilege to carry
everything to God in prayer;
O what peace we often forfeit,
O what needless pain we bear,
all because we do not carry
everything to God in prayer!

2 Have we trials and temptations,
is there trouble anywhere?
We should never be discouraged:
take it to the Lord in prayer.
Can we find a friend so faithful
who will all our sorrows share?
Jesus knows our every weakness:
take it to the Lord in prayer.

3 Are we weak and heavy-laden,
cumbered with a load of care?
Jesus is our only refuge:
take it to the Lord in prayer.
Do your friends despise, forsake you?
Take it to the Lord in prayer;
in his arms he'll take and shield you,
you will find a solace there.

Joseph Medlicott Scriven (1819–86), altd.

6 In your hearts enthrone him; there let him subdue
all that is not holy, all that is not true;
crown him as your captain in temptation's hour,
let his will enfold you in its light and power.

7 With his Father's glory, Jesus comes again,
angel hosts attend him and announce his reign;
for all wreaths of empire meet upon his brow,
and our hearts confess him King of glory now.

Caroline Maria Noel (1817–77)
and in this version Jubilate Hymns

144

1 O for a thousand tongues to sing
my dear Redeemer's praise,
the glories of my God and King,
the triumphs of his grace!

2 Jesus! The name that charms our fears,
that bids our sorrows cease;
'tis music in the sinner's ears,
'tis life, and health, and peace.

3 He speaks, and, listening to his voice,
new life the dead receive,
the mournful, broken hearts rejoice,
the humble poor believe.

4 Hear him, ye deaf; his praise, ye dumb,
your loosened tongues employ:
ye blind, behold your Saviour come;
and leap, ye lame, for joy.

5 My gracious Master and my God,
assist me to proclaim,
to spread through all the world abroad,
the honours of thy name.

Charles Wesley (1707–88)

3 God's great goodness aye endureth,
deep his wisdom, passing thought:
splendour, light, and life attend him,
beauty springeth out of naught.
Evermore
from his store
new-born worlds rise and adore.

4 Daily doth the almighty giver
bounteous gifts on us bestow;
his desire our soul delighteth,
pleasure leads us where we go.
Love doth stand
at his hand;
joy doth wait on his command.

5 Still from man to God eternal
sacrifice of praise be done,
high above all praises praising
for the gift of Christ his Son.
Christ doth call
one and all:
ye who follow shall not fall.

Joachim Neander (1650–80)
tr. Robert Bridges (1844–1930)

143

1 At the name of Jesus every knee shall bow,
every tongue confess him King of glory now;
'tis the Father's pleasure we should call him Lord,
who from the beginning was the mighty Word.

2 At his voice creation sprang at once to sight,
all the angel faces, all the hosts of light;
thrones and dominations, stars upon their way,
all the heavenly orders, in their great array.

3 Humbled for a season, to receive a name
from the lips of sinners unto whom he came;
faithfully he bore it spotless to the last,
brought it back victorious when from death he passed.

4 Bore it up triumphant with its human light,
through all ranks of creatures to the central height;
to the eternal Godhead, to the Father's throne,
filled it with the glory of his triumph won.

5 Name him, Christians, name him, with love strong as death,
but with awe and wonder, and with bated breath;
he is God the Saviour, he is Christ the Lord,
ever to be worshipped, trusted and adored.

2 'Sé Íosa mo ríse, mo chara is mo ghrá;
   'sé Íosa mo dhídean ar pheacaí is ar bhás;
   'sé Íosa mo aoibhneas, mo scáthán de ghnáth;
   is a Íosa, 'Dhé dhílis, ná scar uaim go brách.

3 Bí, a Íosa, go síoraí im chroí is im bhéal,
   bí, a Íosa, go síoraí im thuigse mar an gcéann',
   bí, a Íosa, go síoraí im mheabhair mar léann,
   's ó, a Íosa, 'Dhé dhílis, ná fág mé liom féin.

*Anon. (from a manuscript
found in Ulster by Douglas Hyde)*

*1 O Jesus, ev'ry moment be in my heart and mind;
   O Jesus, stir my heart with sorrow for my sins;
   O Jesus, fill my heart with never-failing love;
   O Jesus, sweet Master, never part from me.*

*2 O Jesus is my king, my friend, and my love;
   O Jesus is my shelter from sinning and from death;
   O Jesus, my gladness, my mirror all my days;
   O Jesus, my dearest Lord, never part from me.*

*3 O Jesus, be for ever in my heart and my mouth;
   O Jesus, be for ever in my thought and my prayer;
   O Jesus, be for ever in my quiet mind;
   O Jesus, my sweet Lord, do not leave me alone.*

tr. George Otto Simms (b. 1910)

142

1 All my hope on God is founded;
   he doth still my trust renew,
   me through change and chance he guideth,
   only good and only true,
   God unknown,
   he alone
   calls my heart to be his own.

2 Pride of man and earthly glory,
   sword and crown betray his trust;
   what with care and toil he buildeth,
   tower and temple, fall to dust.
   But God's power,
   hour by hour,
   is my temple and my tower.

140

1 Álainn farraige spéirghlas,
  álainn uisceacha ciúin',
  álainn taitneamh na gréine
  ar na tonnta tá fúinn;
  faoileáin 'g eiteal 'sna spéartha,
  teas le héirí an lae;
  Ó! nach álainn an saol!
  Ó! nach álainn, a Dhé!
  Siúd uait amharc na sléibhte
  barr' á bhfolach fá cheo,
  caoirí ciúin' ar a dtaobha,
  síth is sonas is só.

2 Tógfad suas mo chroíse,
  tógfad suas mo ghlór,
  molfad eisean achoíche
  fá gach iontas mór;
  ardaigh feasta mo smaointe
  mar na sléibhte san aer,
  ciúnaigh feasta mo chroíse
  mar an t-uisce soiléir;
  éist lem achainí, a Thiarna,
  tar is cónaigh im chléibh,
  réitigh m'anam; 's im intinn
  déansa t'áras, a Dhé.

1 *Beautiful the green-blue sea*
  and the quiet waters,
  beautiful the shining sun
  on the waves below;
  seagulls flying above
  as warmth returns with the day;
  O, how lovely the world is!
  O, how lovely, O God!
  See the hills beyond,
  their summits covered in mist,
  and quiet sheep on their sides,
  O peace, contentment and joy!

2 *I will lift up my heart to God,*
  I will lift up my voice,
  I will praise him evermore
  for his wonderful world;
  like the water clear
  my heart will now be calm,
  like the hills in the air
  my thoughts will now arise,
  hear my prayer, O Lord,
  O come, within me dwell,
  prepare my soul, O God,
  and make your home in my mind.

Douglas Hyde (An Craoibhin)
(1860–1949)

tr. Anon.
adpt. Donald Davison

*At this point the line order differs from
that in the original.

141

1 Bí, a Íosa, im chroíse i gcuimhne gach uair,
  bí, a Íosa, in chroíse le haithrí go luath,
  bí, a Íosa, im chroíse le cumann go buan,
  ó, a Íosa, 'Dhé dhílis, ná scar thusa uaim.

138

1 Dia do bheath' a naoidhe naoimh,
'sa mhainséar cé taoi bocht
meadhrach saibhir a tá tú
's glórmhar id dhún féin anocht.

1 *All hail and welcome, holy child,*
you poor babe in the manger.
So happy and rich it is you are
tonight inside your castle.

2 Dia do bheath' a Íosa 'rís!
'Do bheatha, i gclí on Óigh!
A Ghnuís is áille ná'n ghrian,
na mílte fáilte 'do Dhia óg!

2 *God bless you, Jesus, once again!*
Your life in its young body,
your face more lovely than the sun—
a thousand welcomes, Baby!

3 Míle fáilte 'nocht i gclí
le mo chroíse dom Rí fial,
i ndá nádur 'do chuaigh, póg
is fáilte uaim do Dhia!

3 *Tonight we greet you in the flesh;*
my heart adores my young King.
You came to us in human form—
I bring you a kiss and a greeting.

Aodh Mac Cathmhaoil
(1571–1626)
adpt. Peter Downey (b. 1956)

tr. George Otto Simms
(b. 1910)

139

1 Ag Críost an síol;
ag Críost an fómhar.
In iothlainn Dé
go dtugtar sinn.

1 *The seed is Christ's,*
and his the sheaf;
within God's barn
may we be stored.

2 Ag Críost an mhuir;
ag Críost an t-iasc.
I líonta Dé
go gcastar sinn.

2 *The sea is Christ's;*
and his the fish;
in the nets of God
may we be caught.

3 Ó fhás go haois,
is ó aois go bás,
do dhá láimh, a Críost,
anall tharainn.

3 *From birth to youth,*
and from youth till death,
your two hands, O Christ,
stretch over us.

4 Ó bhás go críoch,
ní críoch ach athfhás,
i bParthas na nGrást
go rabhaimid.

4 *From death—the end?*
No end—but new life
in sweet Paradise
may we be found.

Anon.

tr. George Otto Simms
(b. 1910)

136

1 Tell out, my soul, the greatness of the Lord:
unnumbered blessings, give my spirit voice;
tender to me the promise of his word;
in God my Saviour shall my heart rejoice.

2 Tell out, my soul, the greatness of his name:
make known his might, the deeds his arm has done;
his mercy sure, from age to age the same;
his holy name, the Lord, the Mighty One.

3 Tell out, my soul, the greatness of his might:
powers and dominions lay their glory by;
proud hearts and stubborn wills are put to flight,
the hungry fed, the humble lifted high.

4 Tell out, my soul, the glories of his word:
firm is his promise, and his mercy sure.
Tell out, my soul, the greatness of the Lord
to children's children and for evermore.

Timothy Dudley-Smith (b. 1926)
based on the Magnificat

137

1 Living Lord, our praise we render!
His the blood for sinners shed.
In the Father's power and splendour
Christ is risen from the dead.

2 Death's dominion burst and broken
by that Life which no more dies;
we to whom the Lord has spoken,
one with Christ, in freedom rise.

3 One with Christ, both dead and risen;
dead to self and Satan's claim,
raised from death and sin's dark prison,
life is ours through Jesus' name.

Timothy Dudley-Smith (b. 1926)
based on the Easter Anthems

4 Christ, at God's right hand victorious,
you will judge the world you made:
Lord, in mercy help your servants
for whose freedom you have paid:
raise us up from dust to glory,
guard us from all sin today;
King enthroned above all praises,
save your people, God, we pray.

Christopher Martin Idle (b. 1938)
based on the Te Deum

134

Holy, holy, holy Lord,
God of power and might,
Holy, holy, holy Lord,
God of power and might,
heav'n and earth are full of your glory.
Hosanna in the highest.

*Blessed is he who comes in the name of the Lord.
Hosanna in the highest.

Sanctus (International Consultation on English Texts)

* The Benedictus ('Blessed is he') may be omitted if desired.

135

Jubilate, ev'rybody,
serve the Lord in all your ways,
and come before his presence singing:
enter now his courts with praise.
For the Lord our God is gracious,
and his mercy everlasting.
Jubilate, jubilate, jubilate Deo!

from Psalm 100 (the Jubilate)
para. Fred Dunn

132

1 Glory in the highest to the God of heaven!
  Peace to all your people through the earth be given:
  mighty God and Father, thanks and praise we bring,
  singing alleluias to our heavenly King.

2 Jesus Christ is risen, God the Father's Son:
  with the Holy Spirit, you are Lord alone!
  Lamb once killed for sinners, all our guilt to bear,
  show us now your mercy, now receive our prayer.

3 Christ the world's true Saviour, high and holy one,
  seated now and reigning from your Father's throne:
  Lord and God, we praise you; highest heaven adores:
  in the Father's glory, all the praise be yours!

Christopher Martin Idle (b. 1938)
based on the Gloria in Excelsis

133

1 God, we praise you! God, we bless you!
  God, we name you sovereign Lord!
  Mighty King whom angels worship,
  Father, by your Church adored:
  all creation shows your glory,
  heaven and earth draw near your throne,
  singing, 'Holy, holy, holy,
  Lord of hosts, and God alone!'

2 True apostles, faithful prophets,
  saints who set their world ablaze,
  martyrs, once unknown, unheeded,
  join one growing song of praise,
  while your Church on earth confesses
  one majestic Trinity:
  Father, Son, and Holy Spirit,
  God, our hope eternally.

3 Jesus Christ, the King of glory,
  everlasting Son of God,
  humble was your virgin mother,
  hard the lonely path you trod:
  by your cross is sin defeated,
  hell confronted face to face,
  heaven opened to believers,
  sinners justified by grace.

130

1 Faithful vigil ended,
watching, waiting cease:
Master, grant your servant
his discharge in peace.

2 All your Spirit promised,
all the Father willed,
now these eyes behold it
perfectly fulfilled.

3 This your great deliverance
sets your people free;
Christ their light uplifted
all the nations see.

4 Christ, your people's glory!
Watching, doubting cease:
grant to us your servants
our discharge in peace.

Timothy Dudley-Smith (b. 1926)
based on the Nunc Dimittis

131

1 Glory and honour and power:
are yours by right, O Lord our God.

2 For you created all things:
and by your will they have their being.

3 Glory and honour and power:
are yours by right, O Lamb for us slain;

4 for by your blood you ransomed men* for God:
from ev'ry race and language,
from ev'ry people and nation,

5 to make them* a kingdom of priests:
to stand and serve before our God.

6 To him who sits on the throne and to the Lamb:
be praise and honour, glory and might
for ever and ever. Amen.

from the Alternative Prayer Book (1984)

* The word 'us' may be substituted for 'men'
and 'them' where indicated, if desired.

3 Of old you gave your solemn oath
  to Father Abraham;
  whose seed a mighty race should be
  and blest for evermore.
  You vowed to set your people free
  from fear of every foe,
  that we might serve you all our days
  in goodness, love, and peace.

4 O tiny child, your name shall be
  the prophet of the Lord;
  the way of God you will prepare
  to make God's coming known.
  You shall proclaim to Israël
  salvation's dawning day,
  when God shall wipe away all sins
  with mercy and with love.

5 The rising sun shall shine on us
  to bring the light of day
  to all who sit in darkest night
  and shadow of the grave.
  Our footsteps God shall safely guide
  to walk the ways of peace,
  whose name for evermore be blest,
  who lives and loves and saves.

James Quinn (b. 1919), altd. 1985
based on the Benedictus

129

1 Come, worship God who is worthy of honour,
  enter his presence with thanks and a song!
  He is the rock of his people's salvation,
  to whom our jubilant praises belong.

2 Ruled by his might are the heights of the mountains,
  held in his hands are the depths of the earth;
  his is the sea, his the land, for he made them,
  king above all gods, who gave us our birth.

3 We are his people, the sheep of his pasture,
  he is our maker and to him we pray;
  gladly we kneel in obedience before him—
  great is the God whom we worship this day!

4 Now let us listen, for God speaks among us,
  open our hearts and receive what he says:
  peace be to all who remember his goodness,
  trust in his promises, walk in his ways!

Michael Arnold Perry (b. 1942)
based on Psalm 95; 1–7

127

1 Bless the Lord, the God of our fathers:*
Sing his praise and exalt him for ever.

2 Bless his holy and glorious name:

3 Bless him in his holy and glorious temple:

4 Bless him who beholds the depths:

5 Bless him seated between the cherubim:

6 Bless him on the throne of his kingdom:

7 Bless him in the heights of heav'n:

8 Bless the Father, the Son, and the Holy Spirit:

from the Alternative Prayer Book (1984)

* The word 'forebears' may be substituted for 'fathers'
if desired.

128

1 Blest be the God of Israël,
the everlasting Lord.
You come in power to save your own,
your people Israël.
For Israël you now raise up
salvation's tower on high
in David's house who reigned as king
and servant of the Lord.

2 Through holy prophets did you speak
your word in days of old,
that you would save us from our foes
and all who bear us ill.
On Sinaï you gave to us
your covenant of love;
so with us now you keep your word
in love that knows no end.

3 The Lord is here—inviting us to go
   and share the news with people everywhere.
   He waits outside in need and help alike,
   the Spirit moves through deed as well as prayer.

4 So let us go, intent to seek and find,
   living this hope that God is always near.
   Sharing and trusting, let us live his love,
   that all the world may say—'The Lord is here.'

Christopher Ellis (b. 1949)

126

1 All created things, bless the Lord;
   all you heavens, bless the Lord;
   all you angels, bless the Lord;
   sing to God and praise his name.

2 Sun and moon and stars of heaven,
   rain and dew and winds that blow,
   fire and heat and ice and snow,
   sing to God and praise his name.

3 Bless the Lord, you nights and days;
   light and darkness, praise him too;
   clouds and lightnings in the sky,
   sing to God and praise his name.

4 Hills and mountains, bless the Lord;
   flowing rivers with the seas,
   flying birds and earthly beasts,
   sing to God and praise his name.

5 All who dwell upon the earth,
   priests and servants of the Lord,
   humble people, holy ones,
   sing to God and praise his name.

6 Bless the Father, bless the Son,
   bless the Spirit, Three in One;
   sound his glory all your days;
   give to God exalted praise.

Edward Flewett Darling (b. 1933)
based on the Benedicite

3 Send us forth alert and living,
   sins forgiven, wrongs forgiving,
   in your Spirit strong and free.
   Finding love in all creation,
   bringing peace in every nation,
   may we faithful followers be.

Howard Charles Adie Gaunt (1902–83)

124

1 Sent forth by God's blessing, our true faith confessing,
   the people of God from his dwelling take leave.
   The supper is ended; O now be extended
   the fruits of his service in all who believe.
   The seed of his teaching, our hungry souls reaching,
   shall blossom in action for God and for all.
   His grace shall incite us, his love shall unite us
   to further God's kingdom and answer his call.

2 With praise and thanksgiving to God who is living,
   the tasks of our everyday life we will face.
   Our faith ever sharing, in love ever caring,
   we claim as our neighbour all those of each race.
   One bread that has fed us, one light that has led us
   unite us as one in his life that we share.
   Then may all the living with praise and thanksgiving
   give honour to Christ and his name that we bear.

Omer Westendorf (b. 1916), altd.

125

1 The Lord is here—he finds us as we seek
   to learn his will and follow in his way.
   He gives himself just as he gave his Word,
   the God of promise greets us ev'ry day.

2 The Lord is here—he meets us as we share—
   this is the life he calls us now to live;
   in offered peace, in shared-out bread and wine,
   our God is gift and calls us now to give.

3 To fill each human house with love,
   it is the sacrament of care;
   the work that Christ began to do
   we humbly pledge ourselves to share.

4 Then give us courage, Father God,
   to choose again the pilgrim way,
   and help us to accept with joy
   the challenge of tomorrow's day.

Frederik Herman Kaan (b. 1929)

122

One bread, one body, one Lord of all,
one cup of blessing which we bless;
and we, though many, throughout the earth,
we are one body in this one Lord.

1 Gentile or Jew,
   servant or free,
   woman or man,
   no more.

2 Many the gifts,
   many the works,
   one in the Lord
   of all.

3 Grain for the fields,
   scattered and grown,
   gathered to one,
   for all.

John B. Foley
based on 1 Corinthians 10: 16–17, 12: 4;
Galatians 3: 28; The Didache, 9

123

1 Praise the Lord, rise up rejoicing,
   worship, thanks, devotion voicing:
   glory be to God on high!
   Christ, your cross and passion sharing,
   by this Eucharist declaring
   yours the eternal victory.

2 Scattered flock, one Shepherd sharing,
   lost and lonely, one voice hearing,
   ears are open to your word;
   by your blood new life receiving,
   in your body firm, believing,
   we are yours, and you the Lord.

2 For the sacramental breaking,
  for the honour of partaking,
  for your life our lives remaking,
  young and old, we praise your name.

3 From the service of this table
  lead us to a life more stable;
  for our witness make us able;
  blessing on our work we claim.

4 Through our calling closely knitted,
  daily to your praise committed,
  for a life of service fitted,
  let us now your love proclaim.

Frederik Herman Kaan (b. 1929)

120

1 For the bread which you have broken,
  for the wine which you have poured,
  for the words which you have spoken,
  now we give you thanks, O Lord.

2 By these pledges that you love us,
  by your gift of peace restored,
  by your call to heaven above us,
  hallow all our lives, O Lord.

3 In your service, Lord, defend us,
  in our hearts keep watch and ward;
  in the world to which you send us
  let your kingdom come, O Lord.

Louis Fitzgerald Benson (1855–1930)

121

1 Now let us from this table rise
  renewed in body, mind and soul;
  with Christ we die and live again,
  his selfless love has made us whole.

2 With minds alert, upheld by grace,
  to spread the Word in speech and deed,
  we follow in the steps of Christ,
  at one with all in hope and need.

3 Let kindred voices join,
  honouring the Lamb of God
  who teaches us by bread and wine
  the mystery of his body.

4 Pour out your Spirit on us,
  empowering us to live as one,
  to carry your redeeming love
  to a world enslaved by sin.

Sherrell Prebble and Howard Clark

118

Alleluia, alleluia!

1 As we walk along beside you,
  and we hear you speak of mercy,
  then it seems our hearts are burning
  for we find you in the sharing of the word.

2 As we ask that you stay with us
  and we watch what you are doing,
  then our eyes begin to open
  for we see you in the breaking of the bread.

3 As we reach for you believing
  and we go to love and serve you,
  then our lives will be proclaiming
  that we know you in the rising from the dead.

  Lord, alleluia!

Michael Arnold Perry (b. 1942)
based on Luke 24: 13–35

119

1 Father, who in Jesus found us,
  God, whose love is all around us,
  who to freedom new unbound us,
  keep our hearts with joy aflame.

116

You satisfy the hungry heart
with gift of finest wheat;
come, give to us, O saving Lord,
the bread of life to eat.

1 As when the shepherd calls his sheep,
   they know and heed his voice;
   so when you call your fam'ly, Lord,
   we follow and rejoice.

2 With joyful lips we sing to you
   our praise and gratitude,
   that you should count us worthy, Lord,
   to share this heav'nly food.

3 Is not the cup we bless and share
   the blood of Christ outpoured?
   Do not one cup, one loaf declare
   our oneness in the Lord?

4 The myst'ry of your presence, Lord,
   no mortal tongue can tell:
   whom all the world cannot contain
   comes in our hearts to dwell.

5 You give yourself to us, O Lord;
   then selfless let us be,
   to serve each other in your name
   in truth and charity.

Omer Westendorf (b. 1916)

117

Alleluia! Alleluia!
Opening our hearts to him,
singing alleluia!
Alleluia! Jesus is our King!

1 Create in us, O God,
   a humble heart that sets us free
   to proclaim the wondrous majesty
   of our Father in heaven.

2 We bear the name of Christ.
   Justified, we meet with him.
   His words and presence calm our fear,
   revealing God, our Father, here.

114

1 Put peace into each other's hands
and like a treasure hold it,
protect it like a candle-flame,
with tenderness enfold it.

2 Put peace into each other's hands
with loving expectation;
be gentle in your words and ways
in touch with God's creation.

3 Put peace into each other's hands,
like bread we break for sharing;
look people warmly in the eye:
our life is meant for caring.

4 As at communion, shape your hands
into a waiting cradle;
the gift of Christ receive, revere,
united round the table.

5 Put Christ into each other's hands,
he is love's deepest measure;
in love make peace, give peace a chance
and share it like a treasure.

Frederik Herman Kaan (b. 1929)

115

1 We come as guests invited
when Jesus bids us dine,
his friends on earth united
to share the bread and wine;
the bread of life is broken,
the wine is freely poured,
for us, in solemn token
of Christ our dying Lord.

2 We eat and drink, receiving
from Christ the grace we need,
and in our hearts believing
on him by faith we feed;
with wonder and thanksgiving
for love that knows no end,
we find in Jesus living
our ever-present friend.

3 One bread is ours for sharing,
one single fruitful vine,
our fellowship declaring
renewed in bread and wine—
renewed, sustained and given
by token, sign and word,
the pledge and seal of heaven,
the love of Christ our Lord.

Timothy Dudley-Smith (b. 1926)

3 Christ the living bread from heaven,
Christ whose blood is drink indeed,
here by faith and with thanksgiving
in our hearts on you we feed.

4 By your death for sin atoning,
by your resurrection-life,
hold us fast in joyful union,
strengthen us to face the strife.

5 While afar in solemn radiance
shines the feast that is to come—
after conflict, heaven's glory,
your great feast of love and home.

Constance Coote (1844–1936)

113

1 Lord Jesus Christ, you have come to us,
you are one with us, Mary's son—
cleansing our souls from all their sin,
pouring your love and goodness in;
Jesus, our love for you we sing, living Lord.

2 Lord Jesus Christ, now and every day
teach us how to pray, Son of God.
You have commanded us to do
this, in remembrance, Lord, of you;
into our lives your power breaks through, living Lord.

3 Lord Jesus Christ, you have come to us,
born as one of us, Mary's son—
led out to die on Calvary,
risen from death to set us free;
living Lord Jesus, help us see you are Lord.

4 Lord Jesus Christ, we would come to you,
live our lives for you, Son of God;
all your commands we know are true;
your many gifts will make us new;
into our lives your power breaks through, living Lord.

Patrick Robert Norman Appleford (b. 1925)

3 And after supper he washed their feet,
  for service, too, is sacrament.
  In him our joy shall be made complete—
  sent out to serve, as he was sent.

  (*Organ introduction*)

4 No end there is: we depart in peace.
  He loves beyond our uttermost:
  in every room in our Father's house
  he will be there, as Lord and host.

Frederick Pratt Green (b. 1903)

111

1 At the supper, Christ the Lord
  gathered friends and said the blessing;
  bread was broken, wine was poured,
  faith in Israel's God expressing:
  signs of the forthcoming passion,
  tokens of a great salvation.

2 After supper, Jesus knelt,
  taking towel and bowl of water;
  washing the disciples' feet,
  servant now as well as master:
  'You,' said he, 'have my example—
  let your way of life be humble!'

3 In the fellowship of faith
  Christ himself with us is present;
  supper of the Lord in truth,
  host and master all-sufficient!
  From this table, gladly sharing,
  send us, Lord, to love and caring.

David Mowbray (b. 1938)

112

1 In the quiet consecration
  of this glad communion hour,
  here we rest in you, Lord Jesus,
  taste your love and touch your power.

2 Here we learn through sacred symbol
  all your grace can be and do,
  by this wonderful indwelling—
  you in us, and we in you.

2 Love is his way, love is his mark,
   sharing his last Passover feast.
   Christ at his table, host to the twelve,
   love, only love, is his mark:

3 Love is his mark, love is his sign,
   bread for our strength, wine for our joy,
   'This is my body, this is my blood'—
   love, only love, is his sign:

4 Love is his sign, love is his news,
   'Do this,' he said, 'lest you forget
   all my deep sorrow, all my dear blood'—
   love, only love, is his news:

5 Love is his news, love is his name,
   we are his own, chosen and called,
   family, brethren, cousins and kin,
   love, only love, is his name:

6 Love is his name, love is his law,
   hear his command, all who are his:
   'Love one another, I have loved you'—
   love, only love, is his law.

7 Love is his law, love is his word:
   love of the Lord, Father and Word,
   love of the Spirit, God ever one,
   love, only love, is his word:

Luke Connaughton (1917–79)

110

1 An upper room did our Lord prepare
   for those he loved until the end:
   and his disciples still gather there,
   to celebrate their risen friend.

2 A lasting gift Jesus gave his own—
   to share his bread, his loving cup.
   Whatever burdens may bow us down,
   he by his cross shall lift us up.

107

1 Jesus, stand among us
at the meeting of our lives,
be our sweet agreement
at the meeting of our eyes;

O Jesus, we love you,
so we gather here,
join our hearts in unity
and take away our fear.

2 So to you we're gathering
out of each and every land,
Christ the love between us
at the joining of our hands;

3 Jesus stand among us
at the breaking of the bread,
join us as one body
as we worship you, our head.

Graham Kendrick (b. 1950)
based on Matthew 18: 20

108

1 Let us break bread together, we are one;
let us break bread together, we are one;

We are one as we stand*
with our face to the risen Son,
O Lord, have mercy on us.

2 Let us drink wine together . . . (*etc.*)

3 Let us praise God together . . . (*etc.*)

American Traditional Folk Hymn

*The word 'kneel' may be substituted
for 'stand' when appropriate.

109

1 Love is his word, love is his way,
feasting with friends, fasting alone,
living and dying, rising again,
love, only love, is his way:

Richer than gold is the love of my Lord,
better than splendour and wealth.

2 I come with Christians far and near
  to find, as all are fed
  the new community of love
  in Christ's communion bread.

3 As Christ breaks bread and bids us share,
  each proud division ends.
  The love that made us, makes us one,
  and strangers now are friends.

4 And thus with joy we meet our Lord.
  His presence, always near,
  is in such friendship better known,
  we see and praise him here.

5 Together met, together bound,
  we'll go our different ways,
  and as his people in the world
  we'll live and speak his praise.

Brian Arthur Wren (b. 1936)

106

1 Jesus, our Master, on the night that they came
  to take you to prison, to death and to shame,
  you called to your table the friends that you knew,
  and asked them to do this in remembrance of you.

2 Still through the ages your new friends draw near,
  and know when they do so, that you will be here;
  we know you are present, though just out of view,
  to meet those who gather in remembrance of you.

3 When it is over, and all gone away,
  come back to our thoughts for the rest of the day,
  and stay with us always, who met here to do
  the thing you commanded, in remembrance of you.

Michael Edward Hewlett (b. 1916)

104

1 'I am the Bread of Life;
   he who comes to me shall not hunger;
   he who believes in me shall not thirst.
   No one can come to me
   unless the Father draw him.'

   *'And I will raise him up, and I will raise him up,
   and I will raise him up on the last day.'*

2 'The bread that I will give
   is my flesh for the life of the world,
   and he who eats of this bread,
   he shall live for ever,
   he shall live for ever.'

3 'Unless you eat
   of the flesh of the Son of Man,
   and drink of his blood,
   and drink of his blood
   you shall not have life within you.'

4 'I am the Resurrection,
   I am the Life.
   He who believes in me,
   even if he die,
   he shall live for ever.'

5 Yes Lord, we believe
   that you are the Christ,
   the Son of God
   who has come
   into the world.

Suzanne Toolan (b. 1927)
based on John 6

105

1 I come with joy to meet my Lord,
   forgiven, loved, and free,
   in awe and wonder to recall
   his life laid down for me.

4 On the evening of his passion
  Jesus gave the wine and bread,
  so that all who love and serve him
  shall for evermore be fed.
  Taste and see the Lord is gracious,
  feed upon the living bread.

John Edward Bowers (b. 1923)

103

1 He gave his life in selfless love,
  for sinners once he came;
  he had no stain of sin himself,
  but bore our guilt and shame:
  he took the cup of pain and death,
  his blood was freely shed;
  we see his body on the cross,
  we share the living bread.

2 He did not come to call the good
  but sinners to repent;
  it was the lame, the deaf, the blind
  for whom his life was spent:
  to heal the sick, to find the lost—
  it was for such he came,
  and round his table all may come
  to praise his holy name.

3 They heard him call his Father's name—
  then 'Finished!' was his cry;
  like them we have forsaken him
  and left him there to die:
  the sins that crucified him then
  are sins his blood has cured;
  the love that bound him to a cross
  our freedom has ensured.

4 His body broken once for us
  is glorious now above;
  the cup of blessing we receive,
  a sharing of his love:
  as in his presence we partake,
  his dying we proclaim
  until the hour of majesty
  when Jesus comes again.

Christopher Porteous (b. 1935)
and in this version Jubilate Hymns

101

1 Break thou the bread of life,
   dear Lord, to me,
   as thou didst break the loaves
   beside the sea;
   beyond the sacred page
   I seek thee, Lord,
   my spirit longs for thee,
   O living Word.

2 Bless thou the truth, dear Lord,
   to me, to me,
   as thou didst bless the bread
   by Galilee;
   then shall all bondage cease,
   all fetters fall,
   and I shall find my peace,
   my all in all.

Mary Artemisia Lathbury
(1841–1913)

102

1 Christians, lift your hearts and voices,
   let your praises be outpoured;
   come with joy and exultation
   to the table of the Lord;
   come believing, come expectant,
   in obedience to his word.

2 See, presiding at his table,
   Jesus Christ our great high priest;
   where he summons all his people,
   none is greatest, none is least;
   graciously he bids them welcome
   to the eucharistic feast.

3 Lord, we offer in thanksgiving
   life and work for you to bless;
   yet unworthy is the offering,
   marred by pride and carelessness;
   so, Lord, pardon our transgressions,
   plant in us true holiness.

3 I will hold the Christ-light for you
in the night-time of your fear;
I will hold my hand out to you,
speak the peace you long to hear.

4 I will weep when you are weeping;
when you laugh I'll laugh with you.
I will share your joy and sorrow
'til we've seen this journey through.

5 When we sing to God in heaven
we shall find such harmony,
born of all we've known together
of Christ's love and agony.

6 Won't you let me be your servant,
let me be as Christ to you?
Pray that I may have the grace
to let you be my servant, too.

Richard Gillard

100

1 Would you walk by on the other side,
when someone called for aid?
Would you walk by on the other side,
and would you be afraid?

> *Cross over the road, my friend,*
> *ask the Lord his strength to lend,*
> *his compassion has no end,*
> *cross over the road.*

2 Would you walk by on the other side,
when you saw a loved one stray?
Would you walk by on the other side,
or would you watch and pray?

3 Would you walk by on the other side,
when starving children cried?
Would you walk by on the other side,
and would you not provide?

Pamela Verrall
based on Luke 10: 30–7

98

1 Who are we who stand and sing?
We are God's people.
What this bread and wine we bring?
Food for God's people.
As once with twelve Christ spake,
poured wine, and bread did break;
he now of us will make
a faithful people.

2 What command does Christ impart
to us his people?
Soul and strength and mind and heart;
serve me, my people.
As he in love came low,
our world and work to know;
to life he bids us go
to be his people.

3 Who are we who say one creed?
We are God's people.
What the word we hear and read?
Word of God's people.
Through time, in every race,
from earth to farthest space,
we'll be, with Christ's good grace,
a faithful people.

Thomas Herbert O'Driscoll (b. 1928)

99

1 Brother, sister, let me serve you,
let me be as Christ to you.
Pray that I may have the grace
to let you be my servant, too.

2 We are pilgrims on a journey,
and companions on the road;
we are here to help each other
walk the mile and bear the load.

3 Come, Holy Spirit, aid us
  to keep the vows we make;
  this very day invade us,
  and every bondage break;
  come, give our lives direction,
  the gift we covet most—
  to share the resurrection
  that leads to Pentecost.

Frederick Pratt Green (b. 1903)

97

1 When I needed a neighbour, were you there,
  were you there?
  When I needed a neighbour, were you there?

  And the creed and the colour and the name
  won't matter,
  were you there?

2 I was hungry and thirsty, were you there,
  were you there?
  I was hungry and thirsty, were you there?

3 I was cold, I was naked, were you there,
  were you there?
  I was cold, I was naked, were you there?

4 When I needed a shelter, were you there,
  were you there?
  When I needed a shelter, were you there?

5 When I needed a healer, were you there,
  were you there?
  When I needed a healer, were you there?

6 Wherever you travel, I'll be there,
  I'll be there,
  Wherever you travel, I'll be there,

  And the creed and the colour and the name
  won't matter,
  I'll be there.

Sydney Carter (b. 1915)
based on Matthew 25: 31–46

2 We trust in Christ to save;
in him new life begins:
who by his cross a ransom gave
for all our sins.
Our spirits' strength and stay
who when all flesh is dust
will keep us in that final day,
in him we trust.

3 We would be true to him
till earthly journeys end,
whose love no passing years can dim,
our changeless friend.
May we who bear his Name
our faith and love renew,
to follow Christ our single aim,
and find him true.

Timothy Dudley-Smith (b. 1926)

95

1 When God the Spirit came
upon his Church outpoured
in sound of wind and sign of flame
they spread his truth abroad,
and filled with the Spirit
proclaimed that Christ is Lord.

2 What courage, power and grace
that youthful Church displayed!
To those of every tribe and race
they witnessed unafraid,
and filled with the Spirit
they broke their bread and prayed.

3 They saw God's word prevail,
his kingdom still increase,
no part of all his purpose fail,
no promised blessing cease,
and filled with the Spirit
knew love and joy and peace.

4 Their theme was Christ alone,
the Lord who lived and died,
who rose to his eternal throne
at God the Father's side,
and filled with the Spirit
the Church was multiplied.

5 So to this present hour
our task is still the same,
in pentecostal love and power
his gospel to proclaim,
and filled with the Spirit,
rejoice in Jesus' name.

Timothy Dudley-Smith (b. 1926)
based on Acts 2

96

1 When Jesus came to Jordan
to be baptized by John,
he did not come for pardon,
but as his Father's Son.
He came to share repentance
with all who mourn their sins,
to speak the vital sentence
with which good news begins.

2 He came to share temptation,
our utmost woe and loss;
for us and our salvation
to die upon the cross.
So when the Dove descended
on him, the Son of Man,
the hidden years had ended,
the age of grace began.

93

1 We have a gospel to proclaim,
   good news for all throughout the earth;
   the gospel of a Saviour's name:
   we sing his glory, tell his worth.

2 Tell of his birth at Bethlehem,
   not in a royal house or hall
   but in a stable dark and dim:
   the Word made flesh, a light for all.

3 Tell of his death at Calvary,
   hated by those he came to save;
   in lonely suffering on the cross
   for all he loved, his life he gave.

4 Tell of that glorious Easter morn:
   empty the tomb, for he was free;
   he broke the power of death and hell
   that we might share his victory.

5 Tell of his reign at God's right hand,
   by all creation glorified;
   he sends his Spirit on his Church
   to live for him, the Lamb who died.

6 Now we rejoice to name him King;
   Jesus is Lord of all the earth:
   this gospel-message we proclaim,
   we sing his glory, tell his worth.

Edward Joseph Burns (b. 1938)

94

1 We turn to Christ anew
   who hear his call today,
   his way to walk, his will pursue,
   his word obey.
   To serve him as our king
   and of his kingdom learn,
   from sin and every evil thing
   to him we turn.

91

1 This is the day that the Lord has made.
We will rejoice and be glad in it.

2 This is the day when he rose again.
We will rejoice and be glad in it.

3 This is the day when the Spirit came.
We will rejoice and be glad in it.

based on Psalm 118: 24

92

1 To God be the glory! Great things he hath done!
So loved he the world that he gave us his Son;
who yielded his life an atonement for sin,
and opened the life gate that all may go in.

Praise the Lord! Praise the Lord! Let the earth hear his voice!
Praise the Lord! Praise the Lord! Let the people rejoice!
O come to the Father, through Jesus the Son:
and give him the glory! Great things he hath done!

2 O perfect redemption, the purchase of blood!
To every believer the promise of God;
the vilest offender who truly believes,
that moment from Jesus a pardon receives.

3 Great things he hath taught us, great things he hath done,
and great our rejoicing through Jesus the Son;
but purer, and higher, and greater will be
our wonder, our rapture, when Jesus we see.

Frances van Alstyne (1820–1915)

2 Lo, Jesus meets us, risen from the tomb;
   lovingly he greets us, scatters fear and gloom;
   let the Church with gladness hymns of triumph sing,
   for her Lord now liveth, death hath lost its sting:

3 No more we doubt thee, glorious Prince of Life;
   life is nought without thee: aid us in our strife;
   make us more than conquerors through thy deathless love;
   bring us safe through Jordan to thy home above:

Edmond Louis Budry (1854–1932)
tr. Richard Birch Hoyle (1875–1939)

90

1 'This is my will,
   my one command,
   that love should dwell
   among you all.
   This is my will,
   that you should love
   as I have shown
   that I love you.

2 No greater love
   can be than this:
   to choose to die
   to save one's friends.
   You are my friends
   if you obey
   what I command
   that you should do.

3 I call you now
   no longer slaves;
   no slave knows all
   his master does.
   I call you friends,
   for all I hear
   my Father say
   you hear from me.

4 You chose not me,
   but I chose you,
   that you should go
   and bear much fruit.
   I chose you out
   that you in me
   should bear much fruit
   that will abide.

5 All that you ask
   my Father dear
   for my name's sake
   you shall receive.
   This is my will,
   my one command,
   that love should dwell
   in each, in all.'

James Quinn (b. 1919)
based on John 15: 12–17

88

1 There's a spirit in the air,
   telling Christians everywhere:
   'Praise the love that Christ revealed,
   living, working, in our world.'

2 Lose your shyness, find your tongue,
   tell the world what God has done:
   God in Christ has come to stay.
   Live tomorrow's life today!

3 When believers break the bread,
   when a hungry child is fed,
   praise the love that Christ revealed,
   living, working, in our world.

4 Still his Spirit gives us light,
   seeing wrong and setting right:
   God in Christ has come to stay.
   Live tomorrow's life today!

5 When a stranger's not alone,
   where the homeless find a home,
   praise the love that Christ revealed,
   living, working, in our world.

6 May the Spirit fill our praise,
   guide our thoughts and change our ways.
   God in Christ has come to stay.
   Live tomorrow's life today!

7 There's a Spirit in the air,
   calling people everywheré:
   praise the love that Christ revealed,
   living, working, in our world.

Brian Arthur Wren (b. 1936)

89

1 Thine be the glory, risen, conquering Son,
   endless is the victory thou o'er death hast won;
   angels in bright raiment rolled the stone away,
   kept the folded grave-clothes where thy body lay:

   Thine be the glory, risen, conquering Son,
   endless is the victory thou o'er death hast won.

86

1 There is a Redeemer,
Jesus, God's own Son,
precious Lamb of God, Messiah,
Holy One.

Thank you, O my Father,
for giving us your Son,
and leaving your Spirit
till the work on earth is done.

2 Jesus my Redeemer,
Name above all names,
precious Lamb of God, Messiah,
O for sinners slain.

3 When I stand in glory
I will see his face,
and there I'll serve my King for ever,
in that holy place.

Melody Green
based on Isaiah 47: 4; Acts 1: 8;
Philippians 2: 9; Revelation 22: 3–4

87

1 There is singing in the desert, there is laughter in the skies,
there are wise men filled with wonder, there are shepherds with surprise,
you can tell the world is dancing by the light that's in their eyes,
for Jesus Christ is here.

Come and sing aloud your praises,
come and sing aloud your praises,
come and sing aloud your praises,
for Jesus Christ is here.

2 He hears deaf men by the lakeside, he sees blind men in the streets,
he goes up to those who cannot walk, he talks to all he meets,
touching silken robes or tattered clothes, it's everyone he greets,
for Jesus Christ is here.

Geoffrey Marshall-Taylor (b. 1943)

3 He bids us live together
in unity and peace,
employ his gifts in blessing
and let base passions cease:
we should not grieve the Spirit
by open sin or shame,
nor let our words and actions
deny his holy name.

4 The word, the Spirit's weapon,
will bring all sin to light;
and prayer, by his directing,
will add new joy and might:
be filled then with his Spirit,
live out God's will and word;
rejoice with hymns and singing,
make music to the Lord!

James Edward Seddon (1915–83)

85

1 The voice of God goes out to all the world;
his glory speaks across the universe.
The great King's herald cries from star to star:
with power, with justice, he will walk his way.

2 The Lord has said: 'Receive my messenger,
my promise to the world, my pledge made flesh,
a lamp to every nation, light from light':
with power, with justice, he will walk his way.

3 The broken reed he will not trample down,
nor set his heel upon the dying flame.
He binds the wounds, and health is in his hand:
with power, with justice, he will walk his way.

4 Anointed with the Spirit and with power,
he comes to crown with comfort all the weak,
to show the face of justice to the poor:
with power, with justice, he will walk his way.

5 His touch will bless the eyes that darkness held,
the lame shall run, the halting tongue shall sing,
and prisoners laugh in light and liberty:
with power, with justice, he will walk his way.

Peter Icarus

2 Uprising from the waters there,
the voice from heaven did witness bear
that he, the Son of God, had come
to lead his scattered people home.

3 Above him see the heavenly Dove,
the sign of God the Father's love,
now by the Holy Spirit shed
upon the Son's anointed head.

4 How blest that mission then begun
to heal and save a race undone;
straight to the wilderness he goes
to wrestle with his people's foes.

5 Dear Lord, let those baptized from sin
go forth with you, a world to win;
and send the Holy Spirit's power
to shield them in temptation's hour.

6 On you shall all your people feed
and know you are the Bread indeed,
who gives eternal life to those
that with you died, and with you rose.

George Boorne Timms (b. 1910)

84

1 The Spirit came, as promised,
in God's appointed hour;
and now to each believer
he comes in love and power:
and by his Holy Spirit
God seals us as his own,
and through his Son and Spirit
makes access to his throne.

2 The Spirit makes our bodies
the temple of the Lord;
he binds us all together
in faith and true accord:
the Spirit in his greatness
brings power from God above
and with the Son and Father
dwells in our hearts in love.

3 For each child is special,
accepted and loved,
a love gift from Jesus
to his Father above.

4 And now he is giving
his gifts to us all,
for no one is worthless
and each one is called.

5 The Spirit's anointing
on all flesh comes down,
and we shall be channels
for works like his own.

6 We come now believing
your promise of power,
for we are your people
and this is your hour.

7 The King is among us,
his Spirit is here;
let's draw near and worship,
let songs fill the air.

Graham Kendrick (b. 1950)

82

The light of Christ has come into the world;
the light of Christ has come.

1 We must all be born again to see the kingdom of God;
the water and the Spirit bring new life in God's love.

2 God gave up his only Son out of love for the world,
so that all who believe in him will live for ever.

3 The light of Christ has come to us so that we might have salvation;
from the darkness of our sins we walk into glory with Christ Jesus.

Donald Fishel (b. 1928)
based on John 3

83

1 The sinless one to Jordan came
to share our fallen nature's blame;
God's righteousness he thus fulfilled
and chose the path his Father willed.

80

1 Thanks to God whose Word was spoken
in the deed that made the earth.
His the voice that called a nation,
his the fires that tried her worth.
God has spoken:
praise him for his open Word.

2 Thanks to God whose Word incarnate
glorified the flesh of man.
Deeds and words and death and rising
tell the grace in heaven's plan.
God has spoken:
praise him for his open Word.

3 Thanks to God whose Word was written
in the Bible's sacred page,
record of the revelation
showing God to every age.
God has spoken:
praise him for his open Word.

4 Thanks to God whose Word is published
in the tongues of every race.
See its glory undiminished
by the change of time or place.
God has spoken:
praise him for his open Word.

5 Thanks to God whose Word is answered
by the Spirit's voice within.
Here we drink of joy unmeasured,
life redeemed from death and sin.
God is speaking:
praise him for his open Word.

Reginald Thomas Brooks (1918–85)

81

1 The King is among us,
his Spirit is here;
let's draw near and worship,
let songs fill the air.

2 He looks down upon us,
delight in his face,
enjoying his children's love,
enthralled by our praise.

78

1 'Set your troubled hearts at rest'—
hear again the word divine;
all our Father does is best;
let his peace be yours and mine.

2 Trusting still in God above,
set your troubled hearts at rest;
find within a Father's love
comfort for a soul distressed.

3 When you come to make request
know that God will answer prayer;
set your troubled hearts at rest,
safe within a Father's care.

4 Be at peace, then, and rejoice,
loved and comforted and blessed;
hear again the Saviour's voice:
'Set your troubled hearts at rest.'

Timothy Dudley-Smith (b. 1926)
based on John 14: 1

79

Spirit of God, unseen as the wind,
gentle as is the dove;
teach us the truth and help us believe,
show us the Saviour's love.

1 You spoke to us long, long ago,
gave us the written word;
we read it still, needing its truth,
through it God's voice is heard.

2 Without your help we fail our Lord,
we cannot live his way;
we need your power, we need your strength,
following Christ each day.

Margaret Old (b. 1932)

76

Seek, O seek the Lord, while he is near;
trust him, speak to him in prayer,
and he will hear.

1 God be with us in our lives,
  direct us in our calling;
  break the snares the world contrives,
  keep us from falling.

2 God, increase in us the life
  that Christ by dying gave us:
  though we faint in mortal strife
  his blood will save us.

3 Strengthen in our hearts the love
  we owe to one another;
  how can we love God above
  and not our brother?

James Phillip McAuley (1917–76)
based on Isaiah 55

77

1 Seek ye first the kingdom of God,
  and his righteousness,
  and all these things shall be added unto you;
  Allelu-, alleluia:

  Alleluia, alleluia, alleluia, alleluia!

2 Ask, and it shall be given unto you;
  seek, and ye shall find;
  knock, and the door shall be opened unto you;
  Allelu-, alleluia:

3 Man shall not live by bread alone,
  but by every word
  that proceeds from the mouth of the Lord;
  Allelu-, alleluia:

Karen Lafferty
based on Matthew 6: 33 and 7: 7,
and Deuteronomy 8: 3

75

1 Safe in the shadow of the Lord
   beneath his hand and power,
   I trust in him,
   I trust in him,
   my fortress and my tower.

2 My hope is set on God alone
   though Satan spreads his snare,
   I trust in him,
   I trust in him,
   to keep me in his care.

3 From fears and phantoms of the night,
   from foes about my way,
   I trust in him,
   I trust in him,
   by darkness as by day.

4 His holy angels keep my feet
   secure from every stone;
   I trust in him,
   I trust in him,
   and unafraid go on.

5 Strong in the Everlasting Name,
   and in my Father's care,
   I trust in him,
   I trust in him,
   who hears and answers prayer.

6 Safe in the shadow of the Lord,
   possessed by love divine,
   I trust in him,
   I trust in him,
   and meet his love with mine.

Timothy Dudley-Smith (b. 1926)
based on Psalm 91

3 Word of God's forgiveness granted
to the wild or guilty soul,
word of love that works undaunted,
changes, heals, and makes us whole.

4 Speak to us, O Lord, believing,
as we hear, the sower sows;
may our hearts, your word receiving,
be the good ground where it grows.

Howard Charles Adie Gaunt (1902–83)

74

Rejoice! Rejoice! Christ is in you,
the hope of glory in our hearts.
He lives! He lives! His breath is in you,
arise a mighty army, we arise.

1 Now is the time for us
to march upon the land,
into our hands
he will give the ground we claim.
He rides in majesty
to lead us into victory,
the world shall see
that Christ is Lord!

2 God is at work in us
his purpose to perform,
building a kingdom
of power not of words,
where things impossible
by faith shall be made possible;
let's give the glory
to him now.

3 Though we are weak, his grace
is everything we need;
we're made of clay
but this treasure is within.
He turns our weaknesses
into his opportunities,
so that the glory
goes to him.

Graham Kendrick (b. 1950)
based on 1 Corinthians 4: 20;
2 Corinthians 4: 7; 12: 10; Colossians 1: 27

3 O Lord, dark powers are poised to flood
  our streets with hate and fear;
  we must awaken!
  O Lord, let love reclaim the lives
  that sin would sweep away
  and let your kingdom come.

4 Yet, O Lord, your glorious cross shall tower
  triumphant in this land,
  evil confounding.
  Through the fire your suff'ring Church display
  the glories of her Christ:
  praises resounding!

Graham Kendrick (b. 1950)
based on Isaiah 58: 6–9; Amos 5: 24

72

1 Promised Lord and Christ is he,
  May we soon his kingdom see.

   Come, O Lord, quickly come.
   Come in glory,
   come in glory,
   come in glory,
   quickly come.

2 Teaching, healing, once was he.
  May we soon his kingdom see.

3 Dead and buried once was he.
  May we soon his kingdom see.

4 Risen from the dead is he.
  May we soon his kingdom see.

5 Soon to come again is he.
  May we soon his kingdom see.

Roger Ruston

73

1 Rise and hear! The Lord is speaking,
  as the gospel words unfold;
  we, in all our agelong seeking,
  find no firmer truth to hold.

2 Word of goodness, truth, and beauty,
  heard by simple folk and wise,
  word of freedom, word of duty,
  word of life beyond our eyes.

2 Round the corner of the world I turn,
more and more about the world I learn;
all the new things that I see
you'll be looking at along with me:

3 As I travel through the bad and good,
keep me travelling the way I should;
where I see no way to go
you'll be telling me the way, I know:

4 Give me courage when the world is rough,
keep me loving though the world is tough;
leap and sing in all I do,
keep me travelling along with you:

5 You are older than the world can be,
you are younger than the life in me;
ever old and ever new,
keep me travelling along with you:

Sydney Carter (b. 1915)

71

1 O Lord, the clouds are gathering,
the fire of judgement burns,
how we have fallen!
O Lord, you stand appall'd to see
your laws of love so scorn'd
and lives so broken.

> *Have mercy, Lord,*
> *forgive us, Lord,*
> *restore us, Lord,*
> *revive your Church again.*
> *Let justice flow like rivers*
> *and righteousness like a*
> *never failing stream.*

2 O Lord, over the nations now
where is the dove of peace?
Her wings are broken.
O Lord, while precious children starve
the tools of war increase;
their bread is stolen.

69

1 O sing a song of Bethlehem,
   of shepherds watching there,
   and of the news that came to them
   from angels in the air:
   the light that shone on Bethlehem
   fills all the world today;
   of Jesus' birth and peace on earth
   the angels sing alway.

2 O sing a song of Nazareth,
   of sunny days of joy,
   O sing of fragrant flowers' breath
   and of the sinless boy:
   for now the flowers of Nazareth
   in every heart may grow;
   now spreads the fame of his dear name
   on all the winds that blow.

3 O sing a song of Galilee,
   of lake and woods and hill,
   of him who walked upon the sea
   and bade its waves be still:
   for though, like waves on Galilee,
   dark seas of trouble roll,
   when faith has heard the Master's word,
   falls peace upon the soul.

4 O sing a song of Calvary,
   its glory and dismay;
   of him who hung upon the tree,
   and took our sins away:
   for he who died on Calvary
   is risen from the grave,
   and Christ our Lord, by heaven adored,
   is mighty now to save.

Louis Fitzgerald Benson (1855–1930)

70

1 One more step along the world I go,
   one more step along the world I go:
   from the old things to the new
   keep me travelling along with you:

   And it's from the old I travel to the new;
   keep me travelling along with you.

3 O Lord of all wisdom, I give you my mind,
 rich truth that surpasses our knowledge to find;
 what eye has not seen and what ear has not heard
 is taught by your Spirit and shines from your Word.

4 O Lord of all bounty, I give you my heart;
 I praise and adore you for all you impart,
 your love to inspire me, your counsel to guide,
 your presence to shield me, whatever betide.

5 O Lord of all being, I give you my all;
 if I ever disown you, I stumble and fall;
 but, led in your service your word to obey,
 I'll walk in your freedom to the end of the way.

Jack Copley Winslow (1882–1974), altd.

68

1 O Lord of every shining constellation
 that wheels in splendour through the midnight sky:
 grant us your Spirit's true illumination
 to read the secrets of your work on high.

2 You, Lord, have made the atom's hidden forces;
 your laws its mighty energies fulfil:
 teach us, to whom you give such rich resources,
 in all we use, to serve your holy will.

3 O Life, awaking life in cell and tissue;
 from flower to bird, from beast to brain of man:
 help us to trace, from birth to final issue,
 the sure unfolding of your ageless plan.

4 You, Lord, have stamped your image on your creatures
 and, though they mar that image, love them still:
 lift up our eyes to Christ, that in his features
 we may discern the beauty of your will.

5 Great Lord of nature, shaping and renewing,
 you made us more than nature's sons to be;
 you help us tread, with grace our souls enduing,
 the road to life and immortality.

Albert Frederick Bayly (1901–84)

66

1 O Lord my God! When I in awesome wonder
consider all the works thy hand hath made,
I see the stars, I hear the mighty thunder,
thy pow'r throughout the universe display'd:

Then sings my soul, my Saviour God, to thee,
How great thou art! How great thou art!
Then sings my soul, my Saviour God, to thee,
How great thou art! How great thou art!

2 When through the woods and forest glades I wander,
and hear the birds sing sweetly in the trees;
when I look down from lofty mountain grandeur,
and hear the brook, and feel the gentle breeze:

3 And when I think that God his Son not sparing,
sent him to die—I scarce can take it in.
That on the cross my burden gladly bearing,
he bled and died to take away my sin:

4 When Christ shall come with shout of acclamation
and take me home—what joy shall fill my heart!
Then I shall bow in humble adoration
and there proclaim, my God, how great thou art!

Russian hymn, tr. Stuart K. Hine (b. 1899)
based on Psalm 8; Romans 5: 9–11;
1 Thessalonians 4: 16–17

67

1 O Lord of creation, to you be all praise!
Most mighty your working, most wondrous your ways!
Your glory and might are beyond us to tell,
and yet in the heart of the humble you dwell.

2 O Lord of all power, I give you my will,
in joyful obedience your tasks to fulfil.
Your bondage is freedom; your service is song;
and, held in your keeping, my weakness is strong.

2 O Christ the same, the friend of sinners sharing
our inmost thoughts, the secrets none can hide,
still as of old upon your body bearing
the marks of love, in triumph glorified—
O Son of Man, who stooped for us from heaven,
O Prince of life, in all your saving power,
O Christ the same, to whom our hearts are given,
we bring our thanks to you for this the present hour.

3 O Christ the same, secure within whose keeping
our lives and loves, our days and years remain,
our work and rest, our waking and our sleeping,
our calm and storm, our pleasure and our pain—
O Lord of love, for all our joys and sorrows,
for all our hopes, when earth shall fade and flee,
O Christ the same, beyond our brief tomorrows,
we bring our thanks to you for all that is to be.

Timothy Dudley-Smith (b. 1926)
based on Hebrews 13: 8

65

O let us spread the pollen of peace
throughout our land,
let us spread the pollen of peace
throughout our land.
Let us spread the pollen of peace,
and make all hatred cease;
let us spread the pollen of peace
throughout our land.

1 Oh Christ has sown the seeds of love;
Christ has launched the wingèd dove.
Let us make the flower grow
and let the people know
that Christ has sown the seeds of love.

2 All it needs is our love to make it grow;
all it needs is our hopefulness to show,
and tell those who are choked with fear
that the Prince of Peace is here;
all it needs is our love to make it grow.

Roger Brian Courtney (b. 1954)
written for the Corrymeela Community

3 O Breath of love, come breathe within us,
  renewing thought and will and heart;
  come, love of Christ, afresh to win us,
  revive your Church in every part.

4 Revive us, Lord! Is zeal abating
  while harvest fields are vast and white?
  Revive us, Lord, the world is waiting,
  equip your Church to spread the light.

Elizabeth (Bessie) Ann Porter Head (1850–1936)

63

1 O Christ, the healer, we have come
  to pray for health, to plead for friends.
  How can we fail to be restored
  when reached by love that never ends?

2 From every ailment flesh endures
  our bodies clamour to be freed;
  yet in our hearts we would confess
  that wholeness is our deepest need.

3 In conflicts that destroy our health
  we recognize the world's disease;
  our common life declares our ills.
  Is there no cure, O Christ, for these?

4 Grant that we all, made one in faith,
  in your community may find
  the wholeness that, enriching us,
  shall reach and prosper humankind.

Frederick Pratt Green (b. 1903)

64

1 O Christ the same, through all our story's pages,
  our loves and hopes, our failures and our fears;
  eternal Lord, the King of all the ages,
  unchanging still, amid the passing years—
  O living Word, the source of all creation,
  who spread the skies, and set the stars ablaze,
  O Christ the same, who wrought our whole salvation,
  we bring our thanks to you for all our yesterdays.

5 May his beauty rest upon me
 as I seek to make him known;
 so that all may look to Jesus,
 seeing him alone.

6 May I run the race before me
 strong and brave to face the foe,
 looking only unto Jesus
 as I onward go.

Katie Barclay Wilkinson (1859–1928), altd.

61

1 Not for tongues of heaven's angels,
 not for wisdom to discern,
 not for faith that masters mountains,
 for this better gift we yearn:
 May love be ours, O Lord.

2 Love is humble, love is gentle,
 love is tender, true and kind;
 love is gracious, ever-patient,
 generous of heart and mind:
 May love be ours, O Lord.

3 Never jealous, never selfish,
 love will not rejoice in wrong;
 never boastful nor resentful,
 love believes and suffers long:
 May love be ours, O Lord.

4 In the day this world is fading
 faith and hope will play their part;
 but when Christ is seen in glory
 love shall reign in every heart:
 May love be ours, O Lord.

Timothy Dudley-Smith (b. 1926)
based on 1 Corinthians 13

62

1 O Breath of life, come sweeping through us,
 revive your Church with life and power.
 O Breath of life, come, cleanse, renew us,
 and fit your Church to meet this hour.

2 O Wind of God, come, bend us, break us,
 till humbly we confess our need;
 then in your tenderness re-make us,
 revive, restore, for this we plead.

59

1 Morning has broken
like the first morning;
blackbird has spoken
like the first bird.
Praise for the singing!
Praise for the morning!
Praise for them, springing
fresh from the Word!

2 Sweet the rain's new fall
sunlit from heaven,
like the first dewfall
on the first grass.
Praise for the sweetness
of the wet garden,
sprung in completeness
where his feet pass.

3 Mine is the sunlight!
Mine is the morning
born of the one light
Eden saw play!
Praise with elation,
praise every morning,
God's re-creation
of the new day!

Eleanor Farjeon (1881–1965)

60

1 May the mind of Christ my Saviour
live in me from day to day,
by his love and power controlling
all I do and say.

2 May the word of God enrich me
with his truth from hour to hour,
so that all may see I triumph
only through his power.

3 May the peace of God my Father
in my life for ever reign,
that I may be calm to comfort
those in grief and pain.

4 May the love of Jesus fill me
as the waters fill the sea,
him exalting, self abasing—
this is victory!

2 Make me a channel of your peace:
where there's despair in life let me bring hope,
where there is darkness, only light,
and where there's sadness, ever joy:
    O Master, grant . . .

3 Make me a channel of your peace:
it is in pardoning that we are pardoned,
in giving of ourselves that we receive,
and in dying that we're born to eternal life.

Sebastian Temple
based on the Prayer of St Francis

58

1 Meekness and majesty,
manhood and deity,
in perfect harmony,
the man who is God.
Lord of eternity
dwells in humanity,
kneels in humility
and washes our feet.

Oh, what a mystery,
meekness and majesty,
bow down and worship,
for this is your God.

2 Father's pure radiance,
perfect in innocence,
yet learns obedience
to death on a cross.
Suffering to give us life,
conquering through sacrifice;
and as they crucify
prays 'Father, forgive.'

3 Wisdom unsearchable,
God the invisible;
love indestructible
in frailty appears.
Lord of infinity
stooping so tenderly
lifts our humanity
to the heights of his throne.

Graham Kendrick (b. 1950)
based on John 3: 13–16,
Philippians 2: 6–11

56

1 Lord, the light of your love is shining
in the midst of the darkness, shining;
Jesus, Light of the world, shine upon us,
set us free by the truth you now bring us,
shine on me, shine on me.

> *Shine, Jesus, shine,*
> *fill this land with the Father's glory;*
> *blaze, Spirit, blaze,*
> *set our hearts on fire.*
> *Flow, river, flow,*
> *flood the nations with grace and mercy;*
> *send forth your word, Lord,*
> *and let there be light.*

2 Lord, I come to your awesome presence,
from the shadows into your radiance;
by the blood I may enter your brightness,
search me, try me, consume all my darkness.
Shine on me, shine on me.

3 As we gaze on your kingly brightness,
so our faces display your likeness,
ever changing from glory to glory,
mirrored here may our lives tell your story.
Shine on me, shine on me.

Graham Kendrick (b. 1950)
based on John 1: 1–5; 3: 19–21;
2 Corinthians 3: 18; 1 John 1: 7

57

1 Make me a channel of your peace:
where there is hatred let me bring your love,
where there is injury, your pardon, Lord,
and where there's doubt, true faith in you:
O Master, grant that I may never seek
so much to be consoled as to console;
to be understood as to understand,
to be loved, as to love with all my soul!

54

1 Lord of the home, your only Son
received a mother's tender love,
and from an earthly father won
his vision of your home above.

2 Help us, O Lord, our homes to make
your Holy Spirit's dwelling place;
our hands' and hearts' devotion take
to be the servants of your grace.

3 Teach us to keep our homes so fair
that, were our Lord a child once more,
he might be glad our hearth to share,
and find a welcome at our door.

4 Lord, may your Spirit sanctify
each household duty we fulfil;
may we our Master glorify
in glad obedience to your will.

Albert Frederick Bayly (1901–84)

55

1 Lord, you were rich beyond all splendour,
yet, for love's sake, became so poor;
leaving your throne in glad surrender,
sapphire-paved courts for stable floor:
Lord, you were rich beyond all splendour,
yet, for love's sake, became so poor.

2 You are our God beyond all praising,
yet, for love's sake, became a man
stooping so low, but sinners raising
heavenwards, by your eternal plan:
you are our God, beyond all praising,
yet, for love's sake, became a man.

3 Lord, you are love beyond all telling,
Saviour and King, we worship you;
Emmanuel, within us dwelling,
make us and keep us pure and true:
Lord, you are love beyond all telling,
Saviour and King, we worship you.

Frank Houghton (1894–1972)
and in this version Jubilate Hymns

52

Lord Jesus, we enthrone you,
we proclaim you our King.
Standing here in the midst of us
we raise you up with our praise,
and as we worship build a throne,
and as we worship build a throne,
and as we worship build a throne,
come Lord Jesus and take your place.

Paul Gilbert Kyle (b. 1953)
based on Psalm 22: 3

53

1 Lord of all hopefulness, Lord of all joy,
   whose trust, ever childlike, no cares could destroy,
   be there at our waking, and give us, we pray,
   your bliss in our hearts, Lord, at the break of the day.

2 Lord of all eagerness, Lord of all faith,
   whose strong hands were skilled at the plane and the lathe,
   be there at our labours, and give us, we pray,
   your strength in our hearts, Lord, at the noon of the day.

3 Lord of all kindliness, Lord of all grace,
   your hands swift to welcome, your arms to embrace,
   be there at our homing, and give us, we pray,
   your love in our hearts, Lord, at the eve of the day.

4 Lord of all gentleness, Lord of all calm,
   whose voice is contentment, whose presence is balm,
   be there at our sleeping, and give us, we pray,
   your peace in our hearts, Lord, at the end of the day.

Jan Struther (Joyce Placzek) (1901–53)

4 Journey ends: where afar
   Bethlem shines, like a star,
   stable door stands ajar.
   Unborn Son of Mary,
   Saviour, do not tarry.

     Ring bells, ring, ring, ring!
     Sing, choirs, sing, sing, sing!
     Jesus comes,
     Jesus comes:
     we will make him welcome.

   Frederick Pratt Green (b. 1903)

51

1 Lord, for the years your love has kept and guided,
   urged and inspired us, cheered us on our way;
   sought us and saved us, pardoned and provided,
   Lord of the years, we bring our thanks today.

2 Lord, for that word, the word of life which fires us,
   speaks to our hearts and sets our souls ablaze;
   teaches and trains, rebukes us and inspires us,
   Lord of the word, receive your people's praise.

3 Lord, for our land, in this our generation,
   spirits oppressed by pleasure, wealth and care;
   for young and old, for this and every nation,
   Lord of our land, be pleased to hear our prayer.

4 Lord, for our world, when we disown and doubt him,
   loveless in strength, and comfortless in pain;
   hungry and helpless, lost indeed without him,
   Lord of the world, we pray that Christ may reign.

5 Lord, for ourselves; in living power remake us—
   self on the cross and Christ upon the throne—
   past put behind us, for the future take us,
   Lord of our lives, to live for Christ alone.

   Timothy Dudley-Smith (b. 1926)

48

1 Let every Christian pray,
this day, and every day,
come, Holy Spirit, come.
Was not the Church we love
commissioned from above?
Come, Holy Spirit, come.

2 The Spirit brought to birth
the Church of Christ on earth
to seek and save the lost:
never has he withdrawn,
since that tremendous dawn,
his gifts at Pentecost.

3 Age after age, he strove
to teach her how to love:
come, Holy Spirit, come;
age after age, anew
she proved the gospel true:
come, Holy Spirit, come.

4 Only the Spirit's power
can fit us for this hour:
come, Holy Spirit, come;
instruct, inspire, unite;
and make us see the light:
come, Holy Spirit, come.

Frederick Pratt Green (b. 1903)

49

Let there be love shared among us,
let there be love in our eyes,
may now your love sweep this nation,
cause us O Lord to arise,
give us a fresh understanding
of brotherly love that is real,
let there be love shared among us,
let there be love.

Dave Bilbrough

50

1 Long ago, prophets knew
Christ would come, born a Jew,
come to make all things new,
bear his people's burden,
freely love and pardon.

Ring, bells, ring, ring, ring!
Sing, choirs, sing, sing, sing!
When he comes,
when he comes,
who will make him welcome?

2 God in time, God in man,
this is God's timeless plan:
he will come, as a man,
born himself of woman,
God divinely human:

3 Mary hail! Though afraid,
she believed, she obeyed.
In her womb God is laid,
till the time expected,
nurtured and protected:

46

Jesu, Jesu,
fill us with your love,
show us how to serve
the neighbours we have from you.

1 Kneels at the feet of his friends,
   silently washes their feet,
   master who acts as a slave to them.

2 Neighbours are rich folk and poor,
   neighbours are black, brown and white,
   neighbours are nearby and far away.

3 These are the ones we should serve,
   these are the ones we should love.
   All these are neighbours to us and you.

4 Loving puts us on our knees,
   serving as though we were slaves,
   this is the way we should live with you.

Tom Colvin (c. 1965) and the people of Ghana

47

1 Led like a lamb to the slaughter,
   in silence and shame,
   there on your back you carried a world
   of violence and pain.
   Bleeding, dying, bleeding, dying.

   You're alive, you're alive, you have risen,
   Alleluia!
   And the power and the glory is given,
   Alleluia,
   Jesus to you.

2 At break of dawn, poor Mary,
   still weeping she came,
   when through her grief she heard your voice
   now speaking her name.
   *Mary! Master! Mary! Master!

3 At the right hand of the Father,
   now seated on high,
   you have begun your eternal reign
   of justice and joy.
   Glory, glory, glory, glory.

Graham Kendrick (b. 1950)

*It is effective if the men sing 'Mary!' and the women reply 'Master!'

44

1 I sing a song of the saints of God,
   patient and brave and true,
   who toiled and fought and lived and died
   for the Lord they loved and knew;
   and one was a doctor, and one was a queen,
   and one was a shepherdess on the green:
   they were all of them saints of God; and I mean,
   God helping, to be one too.

2 They loved their Lord so good and dear,
   and his love made them strong;
   and they followed the right, for Jesus' sake,
   the whole of their good lives long;
   and one was a soldier, and one was a priest,
   and one was slain by a fierce wild beast:
   and there's not any reason, no, not the least,
   why I shouldn't be one too.

3 They lived not only in ages past,
   there are hundreds of thousands still;
   the world is bright with the joyous saints
   who love to do Jesus' will;
   you can meet them in school, or in lanes, or at sea,
   in church, or in trains, or in shops, or at tea:
   for the saints of God are just like me,
   and I mean to be one too.

Lesbia Scott (1898–1986)

45

I will enter his gates with thanksgiving in my heart;
I will enter his courts with praise;
I will say this is the day that the Lord has made;
I will rejoice for he has made me glad.

He has made me glad, he has made me glad,
I will rejoice for he has made me glad.
He has made me glad, he has made me glad,
I will rejoice for he has made me glad.

based on Psalm 118: 19, 24

5 Out from the tomb he came with grace and majesty,
  he is alive, he is alive.
  God loves us so, see here his hands, his feet, his side,
  yes, we know he is alive.
    He is alive! (4 times)

6 How lovely on the mountains are the feet of him
  who brings good news, good news,
  announcing peace, proclaiming news of happiness:
  our God reigns, our God reigns!
    Our God reigns! (4 times)

Leonard Smith Jnr.

43

1 I danced in the morning
  when the world was begun,
  and I danced in the moon
  and the stars and the sun,
  and I came down from heaven
  and I danced on the earth;
  at Bethlehem I had my birth.

   Dance then wherever you may be;
   I am the Lord of the Dance, said he,
   and I'll lead you all, wherever you may be,
   and I'll lead you all in the dance, said he.

2 I danced for the scribe
  and the pharisee,
  but they would not dance
  and they wouldn't follow me;
  I danced for the fishermen,
  for James and John;
  they came with me
  and the dance went on.

3 I danced on the Sabbath
  and I cured the lame:
  the holy people
  said it was a shame.
  They whipped and they stripped
  and they hung me high,
  and they left me there
  on a cross to die.

4 I danced on a Friday
  when the sky turned black;
  it's hard to dance
  with the devil on your back.
  They buried my body
  and they thought I'd gone;
  but I am the dance
  and I still go on.

5 They cut me down
  and I leap up high;
  I am the life
  that'll never, never die;
  I'll live in you
  if you'll live in me:
  I am the Lord
  of the Dance, said he.

Sydney Carter (b. 1915)

42

1 How lovely on the mountains are the feet of him
who brings good news, good news,
announcing peace, proclaiming news of happiness:
our God reigns, our God reigns!
Our God reigns! (4 times)

POPULAR VERSION

2 You watchmen, lift your voices joyfully as one,
shout for your king, your king.
See eye to eye the Lord restoring Zion:
your God reigns, your God reigns!
Your God reigns! (4 times)

3 Waste places of Jerusalem, break forth with joy,
we are redeemed, redeemed.
The Lord has saved and comforted his people:
your God reigns, your God reigns!

4 Ends of the earth, see the salvation of your God,
Jesus is Lord, is Lord.
Before the nations he has bared his holy arm:
your God reigns, your God reigns!

ORIGINAL VERSION

2 He had no stately form, he had no majesty,
that we should be drawn to him.
He was despised and we took no account of him,
yet now he reigns with the most high.
Now he reigns (3 times)
with the most high!

3 It was our sin and guilt that bruised and wounded him,
it was our sin that brought him down.
When we like sheep had gone astray, our shepherd came
and on his shoulders bore our shame.
On his shoulders (3 times)
he bore our shame.

4 Meek as a lamb that's led out to the slaughterhouse,
dumb as a sheep before its shearer,
his life ran down upon the ground like pouring rain,
that we might be born again.
That we might be (3 times)
born again.

40

1 Holy Spirit, come, confirm us
in the truth that Christ makes known;
we have faith and understanding
through your helping gifts alone.

2 Holy Spirit, come, console us,
come as advocate to plead,
loving Spirit from the Father,
grant in Christ the help we need.

3 Holy Spirit, come, renew us,
come yourself to make us live,
holy through your loving presence,
holy through the gifts you give.

4 Holy Spirit, come, possess us,
you the love of Three in One,
Holy Spirit of the Father,
Holy Spirit of the Son.

William Brian Foley (b. 1919)

41

1 How beautiful the morning and the day;
my heart abounds with music, my lips can only say:
how beautiful the morning and the day.

2 How glorious the morning and the day;
my heart is still and listens, my soul begins to pray
to him who is the glory of the day.

3 How bountiful the blessings that he brings
of peace and joy and rapture that makes my spirit sing:
how bountiful the blessings that he brings.

4 How merciful the workings of his grace,
arousing faith and action my soul would never face
without his matchless mercy and his grace.

5 How barren was my life before he came,
supplying love and healing; I live now to acclaim
the majesty and wonder of his name.

Owen Barker

3 Gone is their thirst and no more shall they hunger,
  God is their shelter, his power at their side:
  sun shall not pain them, no burning will torture;
  Jesus the Lamb is their shepherd and guide.

4 He will go with them to clear living water
  flowing from springs which his mercy supplies:
  gone is their grief, and their trials are over;
  God wipes away every tear from their eyes.

5 Blessing and glory and wisdom and power
  be to the Saviour again and again;
  might and thanksgiving and honour for ever
  be to our God: Alleluia! Amen.

Christopher Martin Idle (b. 1938)
based on Revelation 7

39

1 He is Lord, he is Lord;
  he is risen from the dead, and he is Lord;
  every knee shall bow, every tongue confess
  that Jesus Christ is Lord.

2 He is King, he is King;
  he will draw all nations to him, he is King;
  and the time shall be when the world shall sing
  that Jesus Christ is King.

3 He is love, he is love;
  he has shown us by his life that he is love;
  all his people sing with one voice of joy
  that Jesus Christ is love.

4 He is life, he is life;
  he has died to set us free and he is life;
  and he calls us all to live evermore,
  for Jesus Christ is life.

Anon.

3 Pardon for sin and a peace that endureth,
   thine own dear presence to cheer and to guide;
   strength for today and bright hope for tomorrow,
   blessings all mine, with ten thousand beside!

Thomas Obediah Chisholm (1866–1960)

37

1 Have you heard the raindrops drumming on the rooftops?
   Have you heard the raindrops dripping on the ground?
   Have you heard the raindrops splashing in the streams
   and running to the rivers all around?

> *There's water, water of life,*
> *Jesus gives us the water of life:*
> *There's water, water of life,*
> *Jesus gives us the water of life.*

2 There's a busy workman digging in the desert,
   digging with a spade that flashes in the sun:
   soon there will be water rising in the wellshaft,
   spilling from the bucket as it comes.

3 Nobody can live who hasn't any water,
   when the land is dry then nothing much grows:
   Jesus gives us life if we drink the living water,
   sing it so that everybody knows.

Martin Christian Tinn Strover (b. 1932)

38

1 Here from all nations, all tongues, and all peoples,
   countless the crowd but their voices are one;
   vast is the sight and majestic their singing—
   'God has the victory: he reigns from the throne!'

2 These have come out of the hardest oppression;
   now they may stand in the presence of God,
   serving their Lord day and night in his temple,
   ransomed and cleansed by the Lamb's precious blood.

35

Go, tell it on the mountain,
over the hills and ev'rywhere.
Go, tell it on the mountain
that Jesus Christ is born.

1 While shepherds kept their watching
   o'er silent flocks by night,
   behold throughout the heavens
   there shone a holy light.

2 The shepherds feared and trembled
   when lo, above the earth
   rang out the angel chorus
   that hailed the Saviour's birth.

3 Down in a lowly manger
   our humble Christ was born;
   and God sent us salvation
   that blessèd Christmas morn.

North American traditional Spiritual

36

1 Great is thy faithfulness, O God my Father,
   there is no shadow of turning with thee;
   thou changest not, thy compassions they fail not,
   as thou hast been thou for ever wilt be.

   Great is thy faithfulness!
   Great is thy faithfulness!
   Morning by morning new mercies I see;
   all I have needed thy hand hath provided—
   great is thy faithfulness, Lord, unto me!

2 Summer and winter, and spring-time and harvest,
   sun, moon and stars in their courses above,
   join with all nature in manifold witness
   to thy great faithfulness, mercy and love.

3 Go forth and tell! Where still the darkness lies
in wealth or want, the sinner surely dies:
give us, O Lord, concern of heart and mind,
a love like yours which cares for humankind.

4 Go forth and tell! The doors are open wide:
share God's good gifts—let no one be denied;
live out your life as Christ your Lord shall choose,
your ransomed powers for his sole glory use.

5 Go forth and tell! O Church of God, arise!
Go in the strength which Christ your Lord supplies;
go till all nations his great name adore
and serve him, Lord and King for evermore.

James Edward Seddon (1915–83)

34

1 Go forth for God; go forth to the world in peace;
be of good courage, armed with heavenly grace,
in God's good Spirit daily to increase,
till in his kingdom we behold his face.

2 Go forth for God; go forth to the world in strength;
hold fast the good, be urgent for the right,
render to no one evil; Christ at length
shall overcome all darkness with his light.

3 Go forth for God; go forth to the world in love;
strengthen the faint, give courage to the weak,
help the afflicted; richly from above
his love supplies the grace and power we seek.

4 Go forth for God; go forth to the world in joy,
to serve God's people every day and hour,
and serving Christ, our every gift employ,
rejoicing in the Holy Spirit's power.

5 Sing praise to him who brought us on our way,
sing praise to him who bought us with his blood,
sing praise to him who sanctifies each day,
sing praise to him who reigns one Lord and God.

John Raphael Peacey (1896–1971) and others

32

1 God of Eve and God of Mary,
   God of love and mother-earth,
   thank you for the ones who with us
   shared their life and gave us birth.

2 As you came to earth in Jesus,
   so you come to us today;
   you are present in the caring
   that prepares us for life's way.

3 Thank you, that the Church, our mother,
   gives us bread and fills our cup,
   and the comfort of the Spirit
   warms our hearts and lifts us up.

4 Thank you for belonging, shelter,
   bonds of friendship, ties of blood,
   and for those who have no children,
   yet are parents under God.

5 God of Eve and God of Mary,
   Christ our brother, human Son,
   Spirit, caring like a mother,
   take our love and make us one!

Frederik Herman Kaan (b. 1929)

33

1 Go forth and tell! O Church of God, awake!
   God's saving news to all the nations take:
   proclaim Christ Jesus, Saviour, Lord, and King,
   that all the world his worthy praise may sing.

2 Go forth and tell! God's love embraces all;
   he will in grace respond to all who call:
   how shall they call if they have never heard
   the gracious invitation of his word?

3 Here our children find a welcome
in the Shepherd's flock and fold,
here, as bread and wine are taken,
Christ sustains us, as of old.
Here the servants of the Servant
seek in worship to explore
what it means in daily living
to believe and to adore.

4 Lord of all, of Church and Kingdom,
in an age of change and doubt
keep us faithful to the gospel,
help us work your purpose out.
Here, in this day's dedication,
all we have to give, receive.
We, who cannot live without you,
we adore you, we believe.

Frederick Pratt Green (b. 1903)

31

1 God is love—his the care,
tending each, everywhere;
God is love—all is there!
Jesus came to show him,
that we all might know him:

Sing aloud, loud, loud;
sing aloud, loud, loud:
God is good,
God is truth, God is beauty—praise him!

2 Jesus shared all our pain,
lived and died, rose again,
rules our hearts, now as then—
for he came to save us
by the truth he gave us:

3 To our Lord praise we sing—
light and life, friend and king,
coming down love to bring,
pattern for our duty,
showing God in beauty:

Percy Dearmer (1867–1936)
(omitting former verse 2)

29

God has spoken to his people, hallelujah!
And his words are words of wisdom, hallelujah!
God has spoken to his people, hallelujah!
And his words are words of wisdom, hallelujah!

1 Open your ears, O Christian people,
   open your ears and hear good news.
   Open your hearts, O royal priesthood,
   God has come to you. (*twice*)

2 They who have ears to hear his message,
   they who have ears, then let them hear.
   They who would learn the way of wisdom,
   let them hear God's word. (*twice*)

3 Israel comes to greet the Saviour,
   Judah is glad to see his day.
   From east and west the peoples travel,
   he will show the way. (*twice*)

Willard Francis Jabusch (b. 1930)

30

1 God is here; as we his people
   meet to offer praise and prayer,
   may we find in fuller measure
   what it is in Christ we share.
   Here, as in the world around us,
   all our varied skills and arts
   wait the coming of his Spirit
   into open minds and hearts.

2 Here are symbols to remind us
   of our lifelong need of grace;
   here are table, font and pulpit,
   here the cross has central place;
   here in honesty of preaching,
   here in silence as in speech,
   here in newness and renewal
   God the Spirit comes to each.

27

1 Give to us eyes
that we may truly see,
flight of a bird,
the shapes in a tree,
curve of a hillside,
colours in a stone,
give to us seeing eyes, O Lord.

2 Give to us ears
that we may truly hear,
music in birdsong,
rippling water clear,
whine of the winter wind,
laughter of a friend,
give to us hearing ears, O Lord.

3 Give to us hands
that we may truly know,
patterns in tree bark,
crispness of the snow,
smooth feel of velvet,
shapes in a shell,
give to us knowing hands, O Lord.

Peggy Blakeley

28

1 God forgave my sin in Jesus' name;
I've been born again in Jesus' name,
and in Jesus' name I come to you
to share his love as he told me to.

He said:
Freely, freely you have received,
freely, freely give;
go in my name and because you believe,
others will know that I live.

2 All power is given in Jesus' name,
in earth and heaven in Jesus' name;
and in Jesus' name I come to you
to share his power as he told me to.

Jimmy and Carol Owens

3 Rooted deep in Christ our master,
Christ our pattern and our goal,
teach us, as the years fly faster,
goodness, faith and self-control.

4 Fruitful trees, the Spirit's tending,
may we grow till harvests cease;
till we taste, in life unending,
heaven's love and joy and peace.

Timothy Dudley-Smith (b. 1926)
based on Galatians 5: 22–3

26

1 Give me oil in my lamp, keep me burning,
give me oil in my lamp, I pray;
give me oil in my lamp, keep me burning,
keep me burning till the break of day.

Sing hosanna, sing hosanna,
sing hosanna to the King of kings!
Sing hosanna, sing hosanna,
sing hosanna to the King!

2 Give me joy in my heart, keep me praising,
give me joy in my heart, I pray;
give me joy in my heart, keep me praising,
keep me praising till the break of day.

3 Give me peace in my heart, keep me loving,
give me peace in my heart, I pray;
give me peace in my heart, keep me loving,
keep me loving till the break of day.

4 Give me love in my heart, keep me serving,
give me love in my heart, I pray;
give me love in my heart, keep me serving,
keep me serving till the break of day.

Traditional

The first verse may be omitted if desired.

24

For you are my God;
you alone are my joy.
Defend me, O Lord.

1 You give marvellous comrades to me:
the faithful who dwell in your land.
Those who choose alien gods
have chosen an alien band.

2 You are my portion and cup;
it is you that I claim for my prize.
Your heritage is my delight,
the lot you have given to me.

3 Glad are my heart and my soul;
securely my body shall rest.
For you will not leave me for dead,
nor lead your beloved astray.

4 You show me the path for my life;
in your presence the fulness of joy.
To be at your right hand for ever
for me would be happiness always.

John B. Foley
based on Psalm 16

25

1 Fruitful trees, the Spirit's sowing,
may we ripen and increase,
fruit to life eternal growing,
rich in love and joy and peace.

2 Laden branches freely bearing
gifts the Giver loves to bless;
here is fruit that grows by sharing,
patience, kindness, gentleness.

2 In the just reward of labour,
God's will is done;
in the help we give our neighbour,
God's will is done;
in our worldwide task of caring
for the hungry and despairing;
in the harvests we are sharing,
God's will is done.

3 For the harvests of the Spirit,
thanks be to God!
For the good we all inherit,
thanks be to God!
For the wonders that astound us,
for the truths that still confound us;
most of all, that love has found us,
thanks be to God!

Frederick Pratt Green (b. 1903)

23

1 From heav'n you came, helpless babe,
enter'd our world, your glory veil'd;
not to be served but to serve,
and give your life that we might live.

*This is our God, the Servant King,
he calls us now to follow him,
to bring our lives as a daily offering
of worship to the Servant King.*

2 There in the garden of tears,
my heavy load he chose to bear;
his heart wth sorrow was torn,
'Yet not my will but yours,' he said.

3 Come see his hands and his feet,
the scars that speak of sacrifice,
hands that flung stars into space
to cruel nails surrendered.

4 So let us learn how to serve,
and in our lives enthrone him;
each other's needs to prefer,
for it is Christ we're serving.

Graham Kendrick (b. 1950)

21

1   Forth in the peace of Christ we go;
    Christ to the world with joy we bring;
    Christ in our minds, Christ on our lips,
    Christ in our hearts, the world's true King.

2   King of our hearts, Christ makes us kings;
    kingship with him his servants gain;
    with Christ, the Servant-Lord of all,
    Christ's world we serve to share Christ's reign.

3   Priests of the world, Christ sends us forth
    this world of time to consecrate,
    our world of sin by grace to heal,
    Christ's world in Christ to re-create.

4   Prophets of Christ, we hear his word:
    he claims our minds, to search his ways,
    he claims our lips, to speak his truth,
    he claims our hearts, to sing his praise.

5   We are his Church, he makes us one:
    here is one hearth for all to find,
    here is one flock, one Shepherd-King,
    here is one faith, one heart, one mind.

James Quinn (b. 1919)

22

1   For the fruits of his creation,
    thanks be to God!
    For his gifts to every nation,
    thanks be to God!
    For the ploughing, sowing, reaping,
    silent growth while we are sleeping;
    future needs in earth's safe keeping,
    thanks be to God!

19

1 Father of mercy, God of consolation,
look on your people, gathered here to praise you,
pity our weakness, come in power to aid us,
source of all blessing.

2 Son of the Father, Lord of all creation,
come as our Saviour, Jesus, friend of sinners,
grant us forgiveness, lift our downcast spirit,
heal us and save us.

3 Life-giving Spirit, be our light in darkness,
come to befriend us, help us bear our burdens,
give us true courage, breathe your peace around us,
stay with us always.

4 God in Three Persons, Father, Son and Spirit,
come to renew us, fill your Church with glory,
grant us your healing, pledge of resurrection,
foretaste of heaven.

James Quinn (b. 1919)

20

1 Finished the strife of battle now,
gloriously crowned the victor's brow:
sing with gladness, hence with sadness:

Alleluia, alleluia!

2 After the death that him befell,
Jesus Christ has harrowed hell:
songs of praising we are raising:

3 On the third morning he arose,
shining with victory o'er his foes;
earth is singing, heaven is ringing:

4 Lord, by your wounds on you we call:
now that from death you've freed us all:
may our living be thanksgiving:

Latin hymn, ? 17th cent.
tr. John Mason Neale (1818–66)

3 Holy Spirit, rushing, burning
wind and flame of Pentecost,
fire our hearts afresh with yearning
to regain what we have lost.
May your love unite our action,
nevermore to speak alone:
God, in us abolish faction,
God, through us your love make known.

Stewart Cross (1928–89)

17

1 Father, now behold us
and this child, we pray:
in your love enfold us,
wash our sins away.

2 Christ's eternal blessing
for this life we claim:
faith, by ours, professing;
signed in Jesus' Name.

3 By the Spirit tended
childhood grow to youth,
from all ill defended,
full of grace and truth.

4 God of all creation,
stoop from heaven's throne,
and by Christ's salvation
make this child your own.

Timothy Dudley-Smith (b. 1926)

18

1 Father, we adore you,
lay our lives before you:
how we love you!

2 Jesus, we adore you,
lay our lives before you:
how we love you!

3 Spirit, we adore you,
lay our lives before you:
how we love you!

Terrye Coelho

3 Fair are the flowers,
  fairer still the children,
  in all the freshness of youth arrayed:
  yet is their beauty
  fading and fleeting;
  my Jesus, yours will never fade.

4 Fair is the sunshine,
  fairer still the moonlight
  and fair the twinkling starry host.
  Jesus shines brighter,
  Jesus shines clearer
  than all the stars that heaven can boast.

5 All fairest beauty.
  heavenly and earthly,
  wondrously, Jesus, in you I see;
  none can be nearer,
  fairer or dearer,
  than you, my Saviour, are to me.

from the German (Münster, 1677)
tr. Lilian Sinclair Stevenson (1870–1960)
and others

16

1 Father, Lord of all creation,
  ground of being, life and love;
  height and depth beyond description
  only life in you can prove:
  you are mortal life's dependence:
  thought, speech, sight are ours by grace;
  yours is every hour's existence,
  sovereign Lord of time and space.

2 Jesus Christ, the Man for others,
  we, your people, make our prayer:
  help us love—as sisters, brothers—
  all whose burdens we can share.
  Where your name binds us together
  you, Lord Christ, will surely be;
  where no selfishness can sever
  there your love the world may see.

2 Poet, painter, music-maker
all your treasures bring;
craftsman, actor, graceful dancer
make your offering;
join your hands in celebration:
let creation
shout and sing!

3 Word from God eternal springing
fill our minds, we pray;
and in all artistic vision
give integrity:
may the flame within us burning
kindle yearning
day by day.

4 In all places and forever
glory be expressed
to the Son, with God the Father
and the Spirit blessed:
in our worship and our living
keep us striving
for the best.

David Mowbray (b. 1938)

15

1 Fairest Lord Jesus,
Lord of all creation,
Jesus, of God and Mary the Son;
you will I cherish,
you will I honour,
you are my soul's delight and crown.

2 Fair are the meadows,
fairer still the woodlands,
robed in the verdure and bloom of spring.
Jesus is fairer,
Jesus is purer,
he makes the saddest heart to sing.

13

1 Christ triumphant, ever reigning,
Saviour, Master, King!
Lord of heaven, our lives sustaining,
hear us as we sing:

Yours the glory and the crown,
the high renown, th'eternal name!

2 Word incarnate, truth revealing,
Son of Man on earth!
Power and majesty concealing
by your humble birth:

3 Suffering servant, scorned, ill-treated,
victim crucified!
Death is through the cross defeated,
sinners justified:

4 Priestly king, enthroned for ever
high in heaven above!
Sin and death and hell shall never
stifle hymns of love:

5 So, our hearts and voices raising
through the ages long,
ceaselessly upon you gazing,
this shall be our song:

Michael John Saward (b. 1932)

14

1 Come to us, creative Spirit,
in our Father's house;
every human talent hallow,
hidden skills arouse,
that within your earthly temple,
wise and simple
may rejoice.

3 Christ be in all hearts
thinking about me,
Christ be on all tongues
telling of me.
Christ be the vision
in eyes that see me,
in ears that hear me,
Christ ever be.

James Quinn (b. 1919)
adapted from 'St Patrick's Breastplate'

12

1 Christ is alive! Let Christians sing;
the cross stands empty to the sky;
let streets and homes with praises ring;
love drowned in death shall never die.

2 Christ is alive! No longer bound
to distant years in Palestine;
but saving, healing, here and now,
and touching every place and time.

3 Not throned afar, remotely high,
untouched, unmoved by human pains,
but daily, in the midst of life,
our Saviour in the Godhead reigns.

4 In every insult, rift and war,
where colour, scorn or wealth divide,
he suffers still, yet loves the more,
and lives where even hope has died.

5 Christ is alive, and comes to bring
new life to this and every age,
till earth and all creation ring
with joy, with justice, love, and praise.

Brian Arthur Wren (b. 1936)

10

Bind us together, Lord,
bind us together
with cords that cannot be broken.
Bind us together, Lord,
bind us together,
O bind us together with love.

1 There is only one God.
  There is only one King.
  There is only one body;
  that is why we sing.

2 Made for the glory of God,
  purchased by his precious Son.
  Born with the right to be clean,
  for Jesus the victory has won.

3 You are the family of God.
  You are the promise divine.
  You are God's chosen desire.
  You are the glorious new wine.

Bob Gillman

11

1 Christ be beside me,
  Christ be before me,
  Christ be behind me,
  King of my heart.
  Christ be within me,
  Christ be below me,
  Christ be above me,
  never to part.

2 Christ on my right hand,
  Christ on my left hand,
  Christ all around me,
  shield in the strife.
  Christ in my sleeping,
  Christ in my sitting,
  Christ in my rising,
  light of my life.

4 Be still, my soul: the hour is hastening on
  when we shall be forever with the Lord,
  when disappointment, grief, and fear are gone,
  sorrow forgot, love's purest joys restored.
  Be still, my soul: when change and tears are past,
  all safe and blessèd we shall meet at last.

Katharina von Schlegel (1697–?)
tr. Jane Laurie Borthwick (1813–97)

9

1 Be strong in the Lord
  in armour of light!
  With helmet and sword,
  with shield for the fight;
  on prayer be dependent,
  be belted and shod,
  in breastplate resplendent—
  the armour of God.

2 Integrity gird
  you round to impart
  the truth of his word
  as truth in your heart:
  his righteousness wearing
  as breastplate of mail,
  his victory sharing,
  be strong to prevail.

3 With eagerness shod
  stand firm in your place,
  or go forth for God
  with news of his grace:
  no foe shall disarm you
  nor force you to yield,
  no arrow can harm you
  with faith as your shield.

4 Though Satan presume
  to test you and try,
  in helmet and plume
  your head shall be high:
  beset by temptation
  be true to your Lord,
  your helmet salvation
  and scripture your sword.

5 So wield well your blade,
  rejoice in its powers!
  Fight on undismayed
  for Jesus is ours!
  Then in him victorious
  your armour lay down,
  to praise, ever glorious,
  his cross and his crown.

Timothy Dudley-Smith (b. 1926)
based on Ephesians 6: 10–18

7

1 Be still, for the presence of the Lord, the Holy One is here.
   Come, bow before him now, with reverence and fear.
   In him no sin is found, we stand on holy ground.
   Be still, for the presence of the Lord, the Holy One is here.

2 Be still, for the glory of the Lord is shining all around;
   he burns with holy fire, with splendour he is crowned.
   How awesome is the sight, our radiant King of light!
   Be still, for the glory of the Lord is shining all around.

3 Be still, for the power of the Lord is moving in this place,
   he comes to cleanse and heal, to minister his grace.
   No work too hard for him, in faith receive from him;
   be still, for the power of the Lord is moving in this place.

Dave Evans
based on Exodus 3: 1–6

8

1 Be still, my soul: the Lord is on thy side;
   bear patiently the cross of grief or pain;
   leave to thy God to order and provide;
   in every change he faithful will remain.
   Be still, my soul: thy best, thy heavenly friend
   through thorny ways leads to a joyful end.

2 Be still, my soul: thy God doth undertake
   to guide the future as he has the past.
   Thy hope, thy confidence let nothing shake;
   all now mysterious shall be bright at last.
   Be still, my soul: the waves and winds still know
   his voice who ruled them while he dwelt below.

3 Be still, my soul: when dearest friends depart,
   and all is darkened in the vale of tears,
   then shalt thou better know his love, his heart,
   who comes to soothe thy sorrow and thy fears.
   Be still, my soul: thy Jesus can repay,
   from his own fullness, all he takes away.

5

1 As the deer pants for the water,
  so my soul longs after you.
  You alone are my heart's desire
  and I long to worship you.

> *You alone are my strength, my shield,*
> *to you alone may my spirit yield.*
> *You alone are my heart's desire*
> *and I long to worship you.*

2 I want you more than gold or silver,
  only you can satisfy.
  You alone are the real joy-giver
  and the apple of my eye.

3 You're my friend and you are my brother,
  even though you are a king.
  I love you more than any other,
  so much more than anything.

Martin Nystrom

6

1 Awake, awake to love and work!
  The lark is in the sky,
  the fields are wet with diamond dew,
  the world's awake to cry
  their blessings on the Lord of life,
  as he goes meekly by.

2 Come, let thy voice be one with theirs,
  shout with their shout of praise;
  see how the giant sun soars up,
  great lord of years and days;
  so let the love of Jesus come,
  and set thy soul ablaze.

3 To give, and give, and give again,
  what God has given thee;
  to spend thyself, nor count the cost;
  to serve right gloriously
  the God who gave all worlds that are
  and all that are to be.

Geoffrey Anketell Studdert-Kennedy (1883–1929)

3

1　And can it be that I should gain
　　an interest in the Saviour's blood?
　　Died he for me, who caused his pain?
　　For me, who him to death pursued?
　　Amazing love! how can it be　　　} *twice (etc.)*
　　that thou, my God, shouldst die for me! }

2　He left his Father's throne above—
　　so free, so infinite his grace—
　　emptied himself of all but love,
　　and bled for Adam's helpless race.
　　'Tis mercy all, immense and free;
　　for, O my God, it found out me!

3　Long my imprisoned spirit lay
　　fast bound in sin and nature's night;
　　thine eye diffused a quickening ray—
　　I woke, the dungeon flamed with light;
　　my chains fell off, my heart was free.
　　I rose, went forth, and followed thee.

4　No condemnation now I dread;
　　Jesus, and all in him, is mine!
　　Alive in him, my living head,
　　and clothed in righteousness divine,
　　bold I approach the eternal throne,
　　and claim the crown, through Christ, my own.

Charles Wesley (1707–88)

4

A new commandment I give unto you,
that you love one another as I have loved you,
that you love one another as I have loved you.
By this shall all know that you are my disciples,
if you have love one to another.
By this shall all know that you are my disciples,
if you have love one to another.

John 13: 34–5

1

Alleluia, alleluia, give thanks to the risen Lord!
Alleluia, alleluia, give praise to his name.

1 Jesus is Lord of all the earth.
He is the King of creation.

2 Spread the good news through all the earth,
Jesus has died and has risen:

3 We have been crucified with Christ—
now we shall live for ever:

4 God has proclaimed the just reward—
life for the world, alleluia!

5 Come, let us praise the living God,
joyfully sing to our Saviour!

Donald Fishel (b. 1928)

2

1 Amazing grace (how sweet the sound!)
that saved a wretch like me!
I once was lost, but now am found;
was blind, but now I see.

2 'Twas grace that taught my heart to fear,
and grace my fears relieved;
how precious did that grace appear
the hour I first believed!

3 Through many dangers, toils and snares
I have already come;
'tis grace has brought me safe thus far,
and grace will lead me home.

4 The Lord has promised good to me,
his word my hope secures;
he will my shield and portion be
as long as life endures.

5 Yes, when this flesh and heart shall fail,
and mortal life shall cease,
I shall possess within the veil
a life of joy and peace.

John Newton (1725–1807)

FOREWORD

by the Archbishop of Armagh and Primate of All Ireland,
The Most Reverend R. H. A. Eames

I have pleasure in commending this collection of hymns for use throughout the Church of Ireland. It is obvious that a great deal of thought and research has gone into its preparation, and I hope the book will be used regularly and widely in all our churches.

The Church of Ireland has a long and illustrious musical tradition. Many of our hymn-writers have found international acceptance and approval. The depth of spirituality, which has long been an integral part of our ethos, has been evident in the hymns used in parish churches throughout Ireland. But passing years have produced different attitudes to the ways in which we express our love for God in worship. This book takes account of such developments, and in it you will find hymns from a wide range of different sources. It is helpful to have some of the most popular of modern hymns included in one book. I am sure their use will add to the contemporary expression of the Faith we hold.

The House of Bishops welcomes the publication of this book and believes that clergy and parishioners alike will find in it much to enrich and renew their worship.

✠ ROBERT ARMAGH

CONTENTS

Jointly published by
Association for Promoting Christian Knowledge, Dublin
and
Oxford University Press, Walton Street, Oxford OX2 6DP

Oxford New York Toronto
Delhi Bombay Calcutta Madras Karachi
Petaling Jaya Singapore Hong Kong Tokyo
Nairobi Dar es Salaam Cape Town
Melbourne Auckland
and associated companies in
Berlin Ibadan

Oxford is a trade mark of Oxford University Press

© *The Church of Ireland 1990*

For sale in the Republic of Ireland and Northern Ireland only

First printed in 1990
Reprinted in 1990 (twice)

ISBN 0 19 148151 3

Origination by Barnes Music Engraving Ltd.
Printed in Scotland

A Music Edition is also available

This collection of hymns was compiled by a committee set up by resolution of the General Synod of the Church of Ireland in 1987, following a suggestion from the Association for Promoting Christian Knowledge that the *Irish Church Hymnal* should be revised to meet the present needs of the Church. The Committee included nominees of the Standing Committee of the General Synod and of the APCK. The 1988 General Synod accepted the recommendation of the Committee that a broadly-based supplement to the *Irish Church Hymnal* should be compiled, submitted to the House of Bishops for approval, and published as soon as practicable, without prejudice to the later revision of the Hymnal.

IRISH CHURCH PRAISE

An Authorized Supplement
to the 1960 Edition of the
Irish Church Hymnal

WORDS EDITION

ASSOCIATION FOR
PROMOTING CHRISTIAN KNOWLEDGE

OXFORD UNIVERSITY PRESS

1990

For my wife, Elizabeth, who supports every step of my creative process. You're the best! For all U.S. service members, past and present, who put themselves in harms way to defend freedom. For members of the elite United States Special Operations and Special Forces units. As a disabled and retired U.S. Army Veteran, I have deep respect for you guys. Last, but certainly not least, for my late grandfather, Buck, who the main character's grandfather is loosely based on. I wish we had more time. I miss you.

CONTENTS

"Better to die standing than to live on your knees."

—Ernesto "Che" Guevara

CHAPTER 1

THE BEGINNING

IF HE'D ONLY KNOWN it would be their last winter together that year. It was mid-December, 1995. Roger was young way back then—too inexperienced to know how cruel life could be at times, particularly for a child who'd hardly begun to relish life.

But, he still vividly remembered the scent of pine needles in the air. The bliss of being dozens of miles from the streets where grown-ups didn't trust you to explore on your own. Out there, in the Montana wilderness, he could be a child, without having to concern himself with the distractions of everyday life.

Together, with his best friend, life was complete. Roger would have stayed there all year round if he could. It had become a ritual. Being in the mountains elicited a total peace within him that, to this day, he could never explain. It was a shame that, sometimes, that peace could be shattered through unforeseeable events.

Those hills were undeniably beautiful in the wintertime. Their wildlife and succulent mountain streams were the epitome of the outdoor lifestyle. Displaying the perfect backdrop against the broad, Montana plains, it was the ideal setting for a child's fairy tale. But, fairy tales could be deceiving. A future that no one could have predicted.

Stretching his camouflage beanie securely over his head, Roger tip-toed through the middle of the extensive hardwoods, every inch of ground covered in a solid layer of white. He was looking, listening, and waiting for any sign of movement in the trees above him. It was the only life for an active boy from Montana. Seeing the edge of the peaks from his back porch in Bozeman, he had always dreamt, as boys sometimes do, of one-day making life up there.

As Roger made his way further down the slope from the cabin, his ears remained wary to any and every sound around him. Suddenly, a rustle coming from high overhead. Peeping skyward toward the remaining sunlight, starting to disappear behind the heavy clouds, he detected a gray flurry scampering up a nearby tree. Its profile shown correctly against the gloomy sky.

Removing the weapon from his back, he held it snugly against his shoulder.

"Hold still, you," he said to himself, glancing down the sights of the rifle that grandad had given to him for his birthday that year.

The flurry began to pick up as he hunted the animal the length of a football field, lifting his knees in the high snow and hearing it crackle with every stride forward.

"Come on," Roger said to himself. "Just give me one second."

The animal sprang from limb to limb, swirling around the massive tree before running down the trunk and coming to a standstill on top of a rotten, hollow log.

"Breathe in, exhale, pause," Roger continued, quietly. "There you go. That's perfect."

As he squeezed the trigger, the shot blasted through the dense forest canopy, echoing as it sent flocks of birds hurling toward the sky.

"Got you!" he said excitedly.

The sounds of wildlife reoccurred throughout the mountainside as Roger trampled through the thick brush to retrieve his kill, his .22 rifle hung over his shoulder.

"Beautiful," he said, grinning as he put the animal into his bag.

He was proud of himself. He knew that granddaddy would also be proud of what he had learned. Now he was hurrying back to the house before the weather got too heavy, toting his small satchel and tracking the smoke billowing from the top of the chimney as the wind howled. It had been an exceptionally harsh winter up in the Montana Mountains. Indeed, heavy winters there was nothing new. But, this one was unusually brutal.

Roger was spending Christmas break at his grandpa Buck's little mountain cabin, a simple wooden house reminiscent of a simpler time and way of life. The place evoked a certain rustic charm that seemed to be straight out of the old, American frontier. Over the fireplace mantle, an old, crisply folded American flag stood erect next to a wooden display case.

'Staff Sergeant John, "Buck" O'Neil, U.S. Army,' the tag said, below a set of old military medals that included the Purple Heart and the Bronze Star. Buck was a nickname given to him during the war for being the "young buck" in his Army unit. The name had stuck with him throughout his many years.

After closing the front door, Roger tossed his hooded, striped flannel jacket onto the wall hook and knocked the snow off of his beige cargo pants and black winter boots.

"Grandpa. Look what I got!" He said, opening the pack and laying his kill out across an old, wooden table. "I did just like you told me to!"

"Good job," replied Buck. "Now, go ahead and skin 'em how I showed you. Throw the remains out back."

"Yes, sir," Roger answered, unloading his hunting rifle and setting it atop the cowboy style gun rack attached to the log wall.

He was an outdoorsy kid, skinny with short brown hair and long bony legs. He and his grandfather were all alone up there. But that was the way they liked it. Buck had the appearance of an old military man. He stood tall, at six-foot-three with a gray military buzz cut, the tales of his past seemingly etched into the wrinkles on his face. His slight limp was a permanent reminder of a war that ended long ago. An avid outdoorsman his entire life, Buck taught Roger to survive in the wilderness.

"All a man needs is a gun and his two hands," he would often say.

He likewise emphasized the importance of respecting nature—Never kill something you aren't going to eat. Unless, of course, it's shooting back at you.

The temperature that day was hovering around five degrees—the type of cold that can cut right through a person's skin. When Roger had gone out to fetch some firewood earlier in the day, his breath appeared to freeze in mid-air. That evening, grandpa cooked them up some squirrel stew, perfect for capping off a cold, winter day.

After the snow set in, Roger and Buck played chess and discussed the meaning of life. They were very close, closer than Roger was to his father. When he was with Buck, it was as if everything wrong, including his home life, had just faded. The man was his idol.

Roger stood for a minute to make them both some hot cocoa. He peeked through the window and saw that the breeze had picked up drastically. Trees were swaying in the wind as the snowfall swept in sideways.

"Grandpa, come here," Roger said.

As the man shuffled toward him, he switched on the battery-powered radio that had been lying on the counter.

"Guess we won't be going anywhere for a while," Buck said as they monitored reports of the incoming storm.

That was no concern—they had plenty of food and water and no other place that they needed to be. Roger didn't want to go home—the best thing about his disciplinarian of a father was how rarely he was ever around. Roger had long suspected that his father was jealous of his relationship with Buck.

The two loved to hunt and fish together and shared a love for the outdoors. His grandfather loved to tell old war stories about his stint as an infantryman during World War Two and fighting the NAZI's. The guy had undoubtedly lived an extraordinary life. While many children looked up to television stars or comic book superheroes, Roger adored his grandad. In his eyes, the man could do no wrong.

Buck, for the most part, was ashamed of the distance between himself and his son and wanted to do better with Roger. They'd had a blast over the past few weeks, building memories that would last for Roger's entire existence. That's why Buck didn't want the boy to know about his illness. He'd hidden it for some time, even from his children. But, he knew that it would destroy his grandson.

When the New Year began, Roger went back to school. He would run to his grandfather's house each day after completing his homework and doing his chores. But, those days ended on a sunny spring afternoon in April when he came home from school to see his dad waiting for him in the driveway, gazing down at the ground.

Realizing that something was wrong, he got off of the bus and approached him, nervous as to what he might say.

"Dad," Roger stated. "What is it?"

"I'm sorry to have to tell you this, son," his father said, a tear running down his cheek. "But, your grandfather has just been diagnosed with lung cancer."

"What?" He asked. "What does that mean?"

His father paused before answering him, not able to look his son in the eye.

"He has only weeks to live," he responded.

"No!" Roger cried hysterically, pounding his fist against his father's chest. "It can't be!"

But, there was absolutely no way he would be comforted. Roger ran to his bedroom, sobbing. For weeks afterward, he barely ate and only spoke when he had to. Superheroes aren't supposed to die. Three weeks later, on a Monday morning that seemed both sudden and lingering in the future for so much longer than it had to, Buck passed away in the Veterans Affairs hospice unit.

When memories are all a person has left, they tend to replay over and over in their head. His mother came over from Washington state to be with her son during that time. Roger, who was in school at the time of Buck's death, didn't even get the chance to say goodbye. He took it extremely hard. A few days later, after the funeral, his parents told him that his grandfather had left him a hefty sum of money, his old war pictures, and the cabin that they had spent so much time together in.

None of that would bring his grandfather and best friend back, so it didn't matter much to him at the time. Roger didn't want to be anywhere near that cabin without his grandpa. It was just too painful for him.

It was like a horrifying nightmare for the kid, and he didn't want to believe that Buck was actually gone. Everywhere he went, there appeared to be things that were a permanent reminder to Roger of what he had lost. But, as he began to reach maturity, he would soon come to recognize that the lessons that his grandfather had taught him would prove to be remarkably beneficial, not only in living life but, eventually, saving it as well.

CHAPTER 2

BAPTISM BY FIRE

Khost Province, Afghanistan

1100 HOURS, FORWARD OPERATING BASE SALERNO, close to the border of Pakistan. Elements of the Second Battalion, 75th Ranger Regiment, were awaiting transport on UH-60 Blackhawk Helicopters for insertion into the outskirts of a Taliban stronghold bordering the mountains near Tora Bora, Eastern Afghanistan.

Their mission—to assault and rid any remnants of Taliban fighters who were still left over after the last engagement in that area. Command had gotten word from local sources that they were attempting to reinforce and reestablish their presence in the region—something that they could not allow to happen after all of the blood and sweat the Rangers had put into clearing them out.

Waiting for his unit to move, Roger had found himself leaning against his rucksack and daydreaming about his late grandfather. Proud of the fact that he was only the second in his family to ever enlist, Roger wanted to live up to Buck's remarkable legacy. The young man joined the Army a year earlier as an infantry grunt. However, he had become a stellar athlete and dedicated Soldier, and wanted more of a test than merely being a ground pounder.

At the recommendation of his company commander, Roger went to Ranger School at Fort Benning, Georgia, and, was subsequently assigned to the second battalion at Fort Lewis, Washington. Now, here he was about to step into battle for the first time, hoping that his grandad was now watching over him.

As the whirling wind from the chopping rotors began to kick up dust surrounding the helipads, Roger positioned his NVG's (Night Vision Goggles) onto his kevlar helmet.

"Hey, O'Neil!" His buddy, Frank, yelled over the noise. "You ready for this?"

"As I'll ever be!" Replied Roger, sliding his tactical goggles onto his face.

"Hooaah!" Continued Frank.

It was Roger's very first mission as a Ranger. Although nervous, he wasn't about to show it in front of such a group of alpha men. As the platoon sergeant, Sergeant First Class Joe McGowan gave the order to proceed, and his platoon began filing one by one into the waiting choppers.

For the bulk of the roughly thirty-minute helicopter ride, Roger sat silently in his seat. His M-4, barrel down, held firmly between his thighs. He had trained hard and prepared both physically and mentally for that day. On the surface, he looked ready. Still, having yet to fire his weapon in combat, in the back of his mind, he questioned how he would react once the bullets started flying.

They say that all of the training in the world cannot predict how one will respond when that moment of truth finally arrives. Ninety percent of Roger's Ranger unit consisted of combat Veterans, those who deployed months after the 2001 terrorist attacks in the United States. And, as battle-hardened Veterans do, they were keeping a keen eye over all of the newbies, including Roger.

As the pair of Blackhawk's approached and hovered over the LZ, (landing zone) the black, metal doors were thrust open, and squad leaders flung the heavy ropes to the earth.

"Go, go, go!" McGowan shouted over the racket of rotating blades.

As the Rangers began fast-roping to the dirt, Roger was behind, biting his nails anxiously. Awaiting his turn to go, Frank patted him on the back from behind.

"After you!" he yelled.

M-4 strapped to his back, Roger clutched the rope tightly with his gloved hands, sliding to the ground and following the rest of the men to cover behind a nearby wall.

"Alright, men. Listen up, " said McGowan. "We have a little hike ahead. We'll make our way down this path in a staggered formation. Watch for IED'S (improvised explosive devices) and keep your head on a swivel. We don't know what we're walking into."

"Once there," he continued. "We split into teams and clear each house."

Roger took a sip from his canteen and clipped his rifle to the D-ring on his vest.

McGowan gave the order to continue, and the Rangers began pushing cautiously down the mountainside pathway. The entire area was rugged and steep, perfect for anyone who wanted to set up an ambush. All seemed quiet, so far. As Roger glanced at the hillside in front of them, he got a bad feeling in his gut.

"Do you see this?" he asked Frank, noticing men observing them from overhead.

"Yeah, I see them," he replied.

As they stretched along the path, Roger's friend, Shane, noticed one of the men holding a cell phone.

"He's got a phone!" Shane yelled out to Sergeant McGowan.

The men above had the perfect vantage to watch over the entire valley. McGowan held a fist up, and the platoon came to a halt, taking up positions along the side of the road and watching for anything that could contain an IED.

"I don't see a damn thing," Roger said to Frank.

"Me either," Frank replied. "Let's keep an eye on those guys, though. I have a bad feeling about this."

Sergeant McGowan was in the front of the formation, and he had the best view of the hillside from his position. He pointed to the Afghan villager who was standing above, cell phone in hand.

"Put the phone away, sir," he told the man. "Sir, please put your phone away."

But, he just nodded.

"I don't think he speaks English," Lieutenant Powers

said to McGowan. "Let's get the interpreter over here!"

Powers was the platoon leader. He'd only recently graduated from West Point and Ranger School. By all accounts, he was a greenhorn. McGowan, on the other hand, was an experienced combat Veteran. Powers stuck to him like white on rice.

As they remained, eyeing the gaggle of men watching over them, the interpreter, whom they called Mel, sped up from the middle of the formation. Mel was born in Islamabad, Pakistan and spoke English as well as any American. An out of work police officer, he jumped at the opportunity to become an interpreter for American forces.

"Yes, sergeant?" He said.

"Tell him to put his phone away," McGowan told him.

"Sir, he's asking you to put your phone away," the interpreter said in Pashto.

The man began motioning his arms erratically.

"I will not!" the villager shouted in Pashto. "I have done nothing wrong!"

"I don't like this, sergeant," Lieutenant Powers retorted. "Something's not right."

"You're telling me," answered McGowan. "Let's get out of here. I don't like having eyes on us."

As the Rangers hunched in the dirt, facing weapons

downward, Sergeant McGowan backed up and instructed his men to prepare to pass. They were going to leave the area and continue their patrol into the center of the village, ahead. But, before they could make it to the other side of the trail, Roger spotted a man flying to them in a sprint.

"Look out!" He shouted over the heavy wind.

Before the man could get twenty-meters from the Rangers, Frank raised his M-4 and sent a single bullet flying straight through the man's neck. As he fell to the sand, convulsing, they paused, waiting.

"Damn," he said. "That was a little too close."

Abruptly, there was a massive explosion that rocked the hillside and sent Sergeant McGowan flying off of his feet and landing flat on his back as the rest of the platoon hit the dirt.

"Holy shit!" Roger screamed as his ears began ringing. "That was fucking loud!"

"Shit. You ok?" Powers asked, clasping the McGowan's hands and pulling him to his feet.

"Yeah. I think so," McGowan replied, brushing the dust from his uniform. "Just busted my damn ass."

"Right call, guys," he said to Roger and Frank, as he straightened his tactical vest. "Damn, that rattled my eardrums!"

"You're telling me!" Answered Powers. "Let's get the hell out of here!"

They continued down the long, jagged, unstable pathway that led to the village half a click (kilometer) away. As the men rounded the corner, they could make out the remains of bombed-out earth-colored homes that seemed unlivable, even by Afghan standards.

"Damn. This place has seen better days," Roger said.

As he glimpsed around the area surrounding the village, though, there was nobody in sight. The placed seemed almost eerily quiet. McGowan gave the order to halt and pulled his binoculars from his vest.

"You see anyone?" Powers asked him.

"Nope. The place looks like a ghost town," he answered, scanning the surrounding homes.

But, before Sergeant McGowan could put his binoculars away, he overheard a blast echo against the steep slope and a long streak of smoke coming from the top of a crumbled structure a few hundred meters away.

"RPG!" He yelled.

The platoon of Rangers hit the dirt hard. As it sailed over their heads and exploded against a nearby boulder, Taliban members appeared from behind the village, and

AK-47 fire opened up from the outer perimeter.

"I knew that mother fucker with the phone was up to something!" McGowan said. "He was a freaking spotter!"

Crawling across the ground with bullets tearing over them, the group of men took cover behind nearby rocks. Roger understood the moment of truth had finally arrived. The ultimate test to determine if he deserved to be called a United States Army Ranger. With no more time to reflect, Roger pulled the charging handle and flicked the safety off of his weapon. After a second of delay, he looked out toward the buildings and began returning fire on the insurgents that were fast surrounding them.

"Shit!" Shane shouted over the loud sounds of combat. "There must be fifty of them!"

Roger, his ACOG (Advanced Combat Optical Gunsight) resting tight against his face, picked off three fighters who were speeding toward them, watching them slide across the dusty ground as they fell.

"Looks like O'Neil just popped his cherry!" Yelled Frank, firing through a haze of dust.

Sergeant McGowan, squatted, made his way to the center of the platoon.

"Keep pounding those bastards!" He told them. "I'm calling in air support!"

Shane, with his M-249, SAW, (squad automatic weapon) kept suppressing the enemy with a constant three-round burst of 5.56.

"It's the old west, boys!" Frank yelled. "They don't want this!"

As the scent of gun smoke filled the air surrounding the Rangers position, Roger continued to return fire with his M-4.

"They're still coming!" He said to his buds.

As Roger looked through his ACOG once more, he caught a flash of a group of men setting up a mortar tube on the horizon.

"Sergeant!" He screamed, running toward McGowan. "We need to reposition, sergeant! They're setting up mortars!"

Next, a hissing sound reverberated out over their heads. The shockwave from the massive blast rattled the men as they leaped for cover. Ears ringing, Roger was lying on his belly with his face in the dirt.

"Shit!" He said to himself, spitting sand from his mouth.

Raising his head and repositioning his helmet, he peered behind and spotted the silhouette of Sergeant McGowan through the smoke. Something wasn't right.

"Sergeant!" Roger yelled.

Dizzy and bewildered, he made his way toward Mc-Gowan, who was lying motionless in a pool of blood with a piece of shrapnel protruding from his body. As the thirty-strong Ranger platoon resumed holding back the Taliban with everything they had, Roger knelt beside his platoon sergeant, the man who taught him what it meant to be a Ranger. Grabbing him by his gloved hand, he said a silent prayer.

Lieutenant Powers, who was meters away when the mortar fell, stooped beside Roger.

"I'll call for evac," he said, pulling out his radio and taking cover behind the large rock formation. "Hang in there!"

But it was too late. Sergeant First Class Joe McGowan took his final breath with Roger leaning carefully over him.

"No!" Roger screamed, shooting his rifle in the direction of the insurgents.

"Come on, man. " Frank said, pulling him by his vest. "We have to get out of here!"

"We can't leave him here!" Roger maintained. "Give me a hand!"

Frank moved up from behind him, grabbing Mc-

Gowan by the limbs as he and Roger carried him down the rocky hill. No sooner than the Rangers made it to the bottom of the mountain, they could hear the roar of the Night Stalkers incoming MH-60L DAP (Direct Action Penetrator) helicopters hurling rockets and firing .50 caliber Gatling guns into the Taliban position.

With destructive force, the whole village went up in an incredible ball of flames. Next, the entire area fell silent. The attack choppers had decimated the enemy until there were none left to fight.

As they loaded Sergeant First Class McGowan's body onto the waiting BlackHawk Helicopter, a sense of darkness fell upon them. They had just lost their beloved leader. Roger stared through the window at the burning village as they rose into the air, bodies littering the ground below. He felt a sickness burning deep inside his stomach. If only air support had arrived ten minutes earlier.

CHAPTER 3

EPIPHANY

Bozeman, Montana.

IT WAS NOW the end of October, 2018. Roger reminisced about those earlier times often. Before his wife, his children, he had his Ranger brothers. He missed the camaraderie of being a part of something greater. They were a close group of guys. As he gazed at the picture frame on his office wall, Roger recalled the moment they pinned that Purple Heart to his chest. He would have gladly given it up if he could bring back the ones they lost.

He also thought of his grandfather and wondered if he would be proud of who he had become, or ashamed of what it took to get there.

Sitting in his law office all these years later, Roger

questioned where his life had gone. Everything occurred so fast, and time seemed to slip away from him. Thinking about his mishaps weren't going to improve them. Staring through his office window, recollecting of the past, it hit him in the gut like a hammer—what his grandpa had tried to teach him all of those years before.

Roger had aspired to be a lawyer for as long as he could remember. He took advantage of his Veteran's benefits to make that dream become a reality. But, with a great expense. He was slowly becoming a workaholic. And, as he had seen with his father, there remained a high price to be paid for a man who was never home.

Roger returned home early from work that day, which was something he hadn't done in quite a while. But, there was a good reason for it. He was drained and burned out and felt a deep-seated need to reconnect with his children, Patrick and Emily. He had been feeling it for some time. And it wasn't a great feeling.

Roger swung the front door open.

"Guys. I'm home."

Kate met him in the foyer.

"You're home early," she said.

Roger and Kate were high school sweethearts. They had broken up for a while, during Roger's stint in the

Army. But, they got back together shortly after his enlistment ended, while he was in law school.

"I decided to take the rest of the day off," said Roger.

Kate felt Roger's forehead.

"Are you feeling, ok?" She asked.

"Very funny," he responded. "I'm fine. Just work stuff. I need a break from that mayhem."

"Bad day at the office?" She asked.

"More like a bad year," he replied.

Kate was an attractive brunette, pretty brown eyes and long flowing hair, and a ball of fire in a five-foot-three frame. She was a registered nurse at the local hospital.

Roger continued to Patrick's bedroom to check up on him.

"Hey, son. What are you doing?"

Patrick rolled his eyes.

"Nothing, dad," he replied. "Just playing XBOX."

"You want to go throw the ball or something?"

"Nope. I'm good right here," said Patrick. "Besides. It's freezing out there."

He was right. But, Roger felt a sense of guilt. It appeared to him that he abandoned his principles and had slowly grown more like his father; something he swore that he would never do. But, he wanted to change that.

"Ok. Well, I'll be in the study if you change your mind," Roger continued, as he shut the bedroom door behind him.

He started to think about his grandfather's passing years before and how hard it was to lose his best friend. The only things he had to recall those precious memories were Buck's old war pictures and the cabin they had spent so much time together inside. But, it was looking more and more like Roger had skipped the most important lesson that he had acquired.

It was an easy trap to fall in. That rat race of our lives can get ahead of us if we aren't careful. Regrettably, that was certainly the case for Roger and Kate. They were both juggling careers and trying to raise two children.

Having the money to keep nannies at home sure didn't make up for not being there. It wasn't a matter of keeping up with the Jones's. No. For them, it was about losing track of what was truly important. Roger had been working so hard in his career that his personal life was beginning to suffer.

He approached Kate from behind, wrapping his arms around her.

"I feel like I can't relate to our kids anymore," he mentioned, as she gently caressed his hand in hers.

Roger had recognized that if they didn't fix their family situation, the children might end up resenting them as they got older. Ashamed, he was beginning to feel as if he had somehow let his grandfather down, having allowed the lessons that grandpa had taught him to fall by the wayside. He wondered if Buck was looking down on them, shaking his head in disbelief as he stood in Heaven.

That night, as they got ready for bed, Roger suddenly had an epiphany.

"I got it. I got it!" He said.

Kate placed the novel she was reading on the nightstand.

"You got what?" She asked.

"The Cabin. We can take the kids to the cabin!"

Kate gave Roger a bewildered look.

"I thought you didn't want to go back there," she stated.

"Well, I didn't before," he said. "But it's perfect. What better way than to be in the middle of nowhere?"

They planned the trip. Two weeks later, during the kid's winter break, they would be high up in the Montana mountains. Roger hadn't been there in years and felt a little eerie about it. But, the hope was that it would bring them closer together as a family. And hopefully help to strengthen the bond with their children, much like Roger had with his grandfather so many years before.

Roger had been thinking of those times a lot recently. Years after his world seemingly ended, he was about to return to the place he never thought he would. But, he had hoped the tranquility of it all would be enough to restore relationships and help them forget about the distractions that had plagued him and his family for so long.

A couple of weeks later

"You guys got everything?" Asked Roger, as Patrick came down the front steps dragging a heavy duffel bag.

He snatched the bag from his son and squeezed it tightly into the trunk.

"That should be about it," said Kate.

"Ok. Let's hit the road," continued Roger.

As they pulled out of the drive, Patrick took a video game from his pocket and began playing.

"Son. Could you please put that thing away?" Asked Roger.

"But dad!"

"But nothing, son," he said. "Just enjoy the ride, would

you? You'll have plenty of time to play later."

"Why do we have to go to the woods anyway, dad?" Patrick asked. "There's zero to do up there."

Kate chimed in.

"Do what your father tells you, Patrick, please."

"Fine!" He huffed, as he put the system onto the floor of the car.

Emily glanced over at Patrick, his arms folded as he looked through the fogged up window.

"You're such a baby," she said to him.

"Shut up!"

Observing them through the rearview mirror, Roger felt the sorrow of allowing his children to become so spoiled.

The cabin was a good three-hour drive from the house. They had left mid-morning, hoping to be there by noon. A thick coat of white capped the ground as far as the eye could see. An hour and a half into the trip, they decided to stop and grab a bite to eat. It was a nice little mom and pop joint, like so many of the other places around the mountains.

While eating breakfast, Roger had overheard a couple sitting behind them talking about a storm that was supposedly going to pass by the area that they were going to.

Not giving it much thought, they left and proceeded to their destination.

Big Sky, Montana

As they neared the cabin drive an hour later, Roger had noticed that the trail was utterly impassable and blocked with debris and collapsed limbs.

"Damn," he said. "Come on, son. Give me a hand."

"Do I have to?" Asked Patrick.

"Yes. You do."

Patrick's complaining was starting to get to Roger. But, he was trying to maintain composure. After all, this was his son, however annoying he may have been.

It took them both a half hour to clear enough space for the car to pinch through. As they drove down the long path, everything seemed somewhat more run down than Roger had remembered. It wasn't exactly falling apart. But, not pristine as it once was. He hadn't kept up the property as much as he probably should have. At first, he never expected to keep it. He just couldn't force himself to part with the memories.

Approaching the front porch, Roger noticed that the door was unlocked as if someone had been there.

"Honey, be careful," Kate stated.

As he cracked the door open and walked inside, Roger took a long look around the room. It wasn't in complete disorder, but things were strewn all over the place, almost as if someone had been searching for something.

"Well. Let's start by cleaning up this pigsty," Kate said.

They unloaded the bags, and she and Emily began picking up the loose trash and taking it outside to burn. The temperature outside was around ten degrees, and the inside of the cabin was freezing. They would need firewood if they wanted to stay warm.

"This sucks," said Patrick.

"Do you ever stop whining?" Roger asked him. "Come on. Let's get to work."

He brought Patrick and the ax sitting by the fireplace, and they went outside to chop some firewood. While cutting away, Patrick spotted something that looked like rising smoke a short distance from where they were standing.

"Dad. I think someone is back there," he stated.

Roger looked up toward the top of the trees.

"What the? There are no cabins back there."

Roger began walking toward the smoke, with Patrick following closely after.

Reaching the source of the smoke, Roger noticed a

scraggly looking fellow relaxing in front of a tiny camper in what looked like dirty overalls. This man could have easily doubled for Paul Bunyan. He was big enough to be a lumberjack and looked like he hadn't showered in a while.

His hair was long and unkempt, as well as his beard. He hadn't seen them hiding in the brush. The man seemed as if he was napping in his chair. Patrick and Roger quickly tiptoed back to the cabin, absentminded of what the future held for them.

They finally finished chopping enough wood for a few days, and later that afternoon the family sat in front of the fire making s'mores, something Roger dearly loved as a child. The children asked at least a couple of times why there was no internet.

"Guys, we are in the middle of nowhere, Not at Starbucks," Roger said. "This is how people lived back in the day."

"Well, this isn't back in the day, dad," Patrick replied.

Roger stretched over and put Patrick's iPad onto the floor.

"You guys are too dependent on technology," he said.

He and Kate were trying to stress the importance of simple, undistracted, family time. After all, they bore the burden for their children being brats. But, Roger assumed they would get used to it, eventually.

They planned for a trail hike the very next day. Roger figured if they got out and stayed active the kids wouldn't be bored enough to miss their electronics. The mountains were fantastic in the wintertime. The snowfall made the trees sparkle with white. That morning they awoke at 8 AM, ate some breakfast, packed a little food and drinks in their bags, and scrambled out the door.

The trail they were taking was about two miles long and led to a little pond. It cut straight into the side of the mountainside. On the one hand, there was a wooden fence and a bluff that went almost straight down for a hundred yards. On the other side, the mountain shot practically straight up.

About halfway down the trail, the terrain started to even out and became flat. There were deer tracks and what looked like paw prints from a big cat, probably a mountain lion. Roger made sure to bring the shotgun with him. Although the forest was breathtaking during winter, it could also be cruel. Owning firearms in that wild country was a necessity.

They made it almost to the end of the trail. Roger could see part of the pond off in the distance, although mostly frozen. As they advanced toward the bottom, Roger had a bad feeling. It was a deep awareness as if something or someone was watching them. They continued slowly wandering until he heard a snap. Roger glanced to his right, and one of his worst fears came true. It was a big, hungry-looking cougar, a couple of hundred feet from them, crouched in the snow. He was, most surely, searching for food.

Mountain lions are very stealthy, opportunistic creatures. You usually don't see them coming. But, on the white, icy ground, he stood out like gravy on rice.

"Damn. I hope it hasn't seen us yet," Roger remarked, trying to hide the fact that he was scared as hell.

"Everyone, just back up, calmly."

They began to step backward, trying to get out of sight.

But, as he stumbled over his own feet, Roger unwittingly stepped on a branch and made a snapping noise, hoping to God the animal hadn't heard him. But, he had. The big cat glared in Roger's direction. Staring him down, he looked as if he was getting ready to pounce at any moment. Abruptly, out of nowhere, a loud crack of a sound. The beast dropped right where he stood like a heavy sack of rocks, blood spilling from his forehead.

Kate and the kids were trembling with fear as Roger tried to catch his breath.

"Who the hell was that?"

Roger began shuffling toward the cat, now lying lifeless on the ground. As he got a little closer, a man approached from the tree line, sporting a high-powered hunting rifle, and startling him.

"Hi neighbor," he said to Roger, who jumped slightly backward.

"Damn. You scared the shit out of me, mister," Roger admitted. "I thought I was cougar dinner for a minute."

"You almost were," the old man continued. "These cats up here are ruthless, man."

It was the same guy that Patrick and Roger had seen behind the cabin.

"I was just taking my family for a walk," Roger replied, still shaking with fear. "Thanks for that by the way. I don't know what I would have done if you weren't there."

"It is dangerous out here, friend," the man continued.

Was it just a coincidence, or was he following them? "I'm Walter," he said to Roger, reaching his hand out.

"Roger," he replied.

"You should be more careful, Roger," Walter told him. "There are things out there that can kill you.

That was quite an uncanny response. Roger thanked him, and he and his family continued downwards toward the pond, trying to gain as much distance as possible from the strange fellow.

Who is that guy? What was he doing out here? His family was pretty shaken up at that point and just wanted to go back. That mountain lion scared the shit out of his children. Walter seemed to pop up out of nowhere and kills it? Was he a hunter? Or something else? No matter. Roger preferred to put it in the back of his mind, for the time being.

They sat in front of the fire for a little while, trying to thaw their hands and feet, then made the trek back toward the cabin to make it before dusk. That night they sat around playing board games. Roger told the children stories of their great grandfather.

They never knew the man. But, they knew a lot about him, thanks to Roger. That cabin held a lot of emotional value to him as he got older, and he hoped to leave it to his children someday too. Maybe one day it would prove to hold the same meaning to them as well.

Roger had decided to take Patrick hunting the next morning. He taught Patrick to shoot many years before. But, he had never killed anything more significant than a squirrel. Roger was hoping they could bring a deer or something back to the cabin to cook. It was a frosty, crisp morning. All decked out in camouflage and hunting boots, he and Patrick began following some deer tracks in the snow.

Roger didn't care if they killed anything or not. They had enough food. He was just appreciative of the opportunity to be with his son in nature, only the two of them, without hearing him moan about not being able to play video games. It appeared to be working.

Technology drove most of what they did daily. But it could also be a distraction. Most of the time, people forgot about the simple things. It did make their lives easier. But, Roger knew that too much reliance on technology made certain aspects of their lives lose purpose.

They hadn't brought any food back that day. But father and son bonded in a way that they hadn't in quite some time. And it was a very refreshing change of pace for them. Sitting on the edge of their bed that night, Kate by his side, Roger couldn't help but wonder about the gentleman behind the cabin.

What was he doing up there alone? It was as if he was hiding away from society. And showing up out of nowhere, like he was stalking them, didn't sit right with

Roger. Something seemed off. And, Roger didn't instantly understand how right he was about that.

CHAPTER 4

ESCAPE

Montana State Prison

IT WAS LATE at night and snowing at the penitentiary. The quiet demeanor of the indoors wasn't a testament to what was about to happen on the outside. Most of the inmates were sleeping in their cells, except for one.

James was getting ready to do something that he had meticulously planned for six months. After being locked away for just over ten years, the man was prepared to feel freedom again.

Prison had not been kind to him. He'd been battered, stabbed, and thrown in the hole more times than he cared to count. He was almost left for dead on one occasion if the warden hadn't found him motionless and bleeding in the shower.

Joining the Aryan Brotherhood seemed like his only way of protection from the other gangs. It's difficult to defend yourself in prison when you're all alone. The Aryans ran that place. James's background certainly wouldn't serve him well in there. After all, he couldn't sleep with one eye open.

To everyone's astonishment, James had the perfect escape plan, thanks to a pretty, blonde, prison employee that he had befriended a year earlier. He promised her a relationship on the outside, in return. Of course, the man had only one concern, busting out of that dreadful place. That night the snowfall was heavy, and he had hoped that it would mask his movements and make him hard to track. That was the plan, anyway.

He was an old, Vietnam Veteran. With long hair, scars all over his body, and tattoos up and down both arms, he was unquestionably a rough site to behold. Most of the wounds he got from Vietnam, some from prison. James had prepared himself mentally for that day. He was ready.

It wasn't his first time escaping captivity, however. Starving and sick, he had broken out of a North Vietnamese labor camp in 69. Those correctional officers had nothing on the NVA. His main obstacles, getting past the guard towers and over the razor wire fence. He left a balled up pillowcase and bundled up blankets on his bunk in place of his body, hoping that the patrolling guards were none the wiser.

It was the middle of the night. James squeezed his way through a gap in the wall of his cell, which he had worked on for what seemed like forever. It remained hidden behind a poster on his cell wall. Prison noise covered up the sound of cutting and sawing.

Days earlier, he had finally widened the hole enough to allow his slim body to slide through. James' next move, making his way through a maze of wiring and piping to get to the vent that led to the yard, outside. If anything, the man was resourceful.

With a tool that his new friend smuggled in for him, he jerked the vent from the wall and climbed through. Sliding down the roof of the prison, James shimmied down some piping that led to the ground and shot over to the fence directly in the middle of two guard towers. Launching a blanket over the razor wire fence and climbing over, he sliced part of his right arm in the process.

"Son of a bitch, that fucking hurts," he mumbled to himself, as he rolled over and fell to the ground on the other side, applying pressure on his bleeding wound.

Left behind was a bloody piece of his orange, prison jumpsuit. He slipped into the darkness between the searchlights, never looking behind him. His plan seemed to be working, so far. James knew that he had at least a couple of hours before anyone would realize he was gone. So, he wanted to be a long way from that place by the time the alert sounded.

As promised, his so-called girlfriend left him a new set of civilian clothes in a suitcase that she had set in the woods, hidden underneath a tall evergreen tree and blanketed with snow. But, he had no plans to meet up with her. James was a free man now. And he didn't want to associate with anyone from that prison, ever again. Desiring to get the hell away from there, he immediately changed into his new clothes, tearing a sleeve off of his prison clothes, tying it around his arm, and burying the rest.

A storm was brewing in the distance. James needed to make it as far as he could before dawn. The snow began to fall remarkably hard. He wouldn't be able to make it very much further in the impending blizzard. So, he found an abandoned building to take shelter in until the storm passed. It was an old, run down, rickety shack in the middle of the woods, barely a roof over it. But, at least it was something.

Wake up would be in approximately one hour. But, for the time being, James was stuck. As soon as the storm passed him by, however, he would be ready to continue his trek. Hiding out in the mountains might have been possible, but park rangers patrol that area pretty routinely.

James could hardly keep his tired eyes open. Slipping in and out of consciousness, six AM came fast, and the sound of the high-pitched alarm system reverberated throughout the surrounding hills. Heard for miles around, it served as a warning system to residents. They knew what it meant. It was only a matter of time before everyone around would be alert and on the lookout for him.

Road signs scattered a full perimeter around that place, warning the public not to pick up hitchhikers, and for a good reason. The place was bustling with guards searching every inch of the grounds. One of them found the torn, bright orange bloodied piece of a prison suit whisking in the wind.

"This is where he got out," the guard confirmed to the others. "Must have torn him up pretty good."

The sound of chatter and dogs barking seemed to carry with the breeze. James knew he was in a race for time. Pretty soon, roadblocks would be up, and a search party organized to hunt him down. Every vehicle and person would be looked over, and the only way that he would have a chance to remain undetected is by moving through the dense forest, relying only on his wit, and hoping to be long gone by the time the hound dogs picked up his trail.

It was over a decade old now, but James had periodic flashbacks of the event that led him to prison. As he paused for a time to rest, his memory took him back to that moment when he became a criminal in their eyes. It was just another in a series of daydreams that haunted him.

He was defending her, he proclaimed. It was during the spring of 2007. His sister, Jessica, had lousy taste in men. She was a decent looking blonde. But, their rough upbringing didn't exactly breed self-confidence. With low self-esteem, she would always choose abusive over good-natured.

Jessica's old man, Terry, was beating her again, as he had done so many times before. James tried desperately to stay calm, pleading for the belligerent man to leave her alone. But, he wouldn't listen, a fatal mistake. The drunken fool began shoving and striking her. James, furious to the point of boiling over, leaped out of his chair.

"Leave her alone!" He shouted.

Terry, holding Jessica by the hair, released her for a

moment, and rushed for James.

"Yeah? What are you going to do about it, punk?" Terry asked him.

"Punk? I'm not the one who can't hit someone my size, asshole!" James replied as he grabbed Terry by the shirt and slammed him against the wall.

James' anger got the best of him, and he just snapped. All he could remember was glaring at the man in anger. He must have blacked out shortly after. Bystanders reported that he punched the guy so hard that he must have cracked his skull because Terry went limp and fell, never to get up again.

When James awoke, he was lying on the floor in a jail cell. He had no recollection of the event, but witnesses and the bar owner claimed that James just went crazy and killed the man. Not trusting cops, he took the matter into his own hands.

"He never had a chance," they said.

Once the trial was over, James had been convicted of second-degree murder and sentenced to twenty-five years to life in prison. Everyone called him a lunatic, even his own family. According to them, he was a crazed madman who didn't deserve ever to see daylight again. It didn't seem to matter to them that his sister was black from

Terry's fist. An unusual family dynamic, indeed.

All of a sudden, James snapped back to his reality.

"Damn it. I can't fucking shake it," he grumbled to himself. "Got to keep going."

He rose to his feet to get his bearings. Tired and fuzzy, the man planned to continue. Making his way through the forest, James located a tiny cottage up ahead of him in a clearing, with a dirt bike stationed out front. Slowly progressing toward it, he noticed that there was a light on inside. James noiselessly edged toward the front door and carefully began turning the doorknob.

To his astonishment, the cabin had been left unlocked. He shoved the door open slightly and peered inside. A man was sitting on the couch, and his legs propped, eyes glued to the television. He hadn't noticed the unsightly figure standing behind him.

James opened the door the rest of the way and stepped casually toward the man.

"Don't move," he said in a low, determined tone.

The man glanced back at James, hysterically.

"What the hell?" He questioned. "Who are you? What are you doing in my house?"

Taking another look, the stranger could hardly believe his eyes.

"Wait a minute," he continued, bouncing out of his chair. "I know who you are. You're the man who broke out of the prison, aren't you?"

"Never mind that, friend," James replied. "I need your bike. I don't want to hurt you. I need a way out of here."

The agitated stranger pointed to a set of keys lying on the coffee table.

"Right there," he said. "Take it and get the hell out of here, please."

James marched over to the table and took the keys. "Much obliged," he said to the man, before shifting to leave.

As he approached the door, James glanced back at the stranger one last time.

"Keep your mouth shut mister. I wouldn't want to have to come back here," he continued, closing the door behind him.

With one kick of his foot, the bike cranked up, and James rode out like a man on a mission, disappearing into the whiteout.

CHAPTER 5

DILEMMA

THE FOLLOWING MORNING, Roger and family re-laxed around in the cabin, playing checkers and drinking hot cocoa. He was thinking about Walter. Roger couldn't manage to escape the notion that maybe he was a danger to them. And, he was worried, for their children's sake. As he sat, contemplating, something loomed over him. Kate could tell that Roger was preoccupied.

"Honey. You ok?" She asked.

"I'm ok, babe. Just thinking about something." Roger answered.

Surprisingly, even though the place had been in the family for ages, he had no idea how much land he had out there. And he was beginning to question if Walter, being so close, had unknowingly set up camp on their property.

"Kate. Come here for a minute," Roger said, grabbing

her by the hand and drawing her into the next room.

"What's the matter?" She asked, confused.

"I want to confirm a suspicion," replied Roger.

He explained his intention, and she was less than thrilled about finding out.

"Roger. Don't obsess over that. It's not a big deal," she said.

"It is to me," he stated. "I have to worry about you guys. It's my job to worry."

Kate wasn't keen on the idea or confronting Walter if Roger's doubt had proven to be true. But, reluctantly, she agreed.

"Fine then," she said, letting out a sigh. "Let's get it over with so we can go about our day."

The only room they hadn't ventured to since arriving was the small attic above their heads. Roger never thought to check it out before. He hadn't been there in so long that he didn't believe it would hold anything significant. The loft had been used as storage previously, with only a few old boxes lying in the corner.

They both started going through them, one at a time and found old documents, a bunch of old pictures, and even some old military records that were left over by his grandfather. They combed through every bit and every piece of paper they held, stacking them in a neat little pile.

As Roger reached the third and final box, he unloaded it onto the floor, and there it was. The old property map, an old paper that had since turned to an off colored, antique brown. While inspecting the old piece of paper, Roger reached a startling conclusion. According to the map, Walter was camping slightly on the property.

"Oh Jesus," he thought to himself. "I freaking knew it."

Roger sat for a moment, considering how he was going to handle things. He didn't know the man. But, he had seemed a little off the reservation. Roger would go over there and confront him. But, as he rose from his chair, Patrick stood in his way.

"Dad. What if he is a psychotic killer or something?" He asked.

Roger just laughed and shrugged it off.

"No worries, son," he answered. "I'll only be a minute."

As a precaution, he took his shotgun and slung it on his back. As Roger approached the campsite, Walter was sitting by the fire, beer in hand, and mumbling to himself. Roger stood there for a moment, silently, observing him.

Could this man have possibly escaped from a mental institution? He seemed a little unbalanced. As Roger got closer, Walter caught him out of the corner of his eye.

"Hi fella," he said. "Want a beer?"

"No, thanks," replied Roger.

"So. What can I do for you, mister?" Walter asked.

Roger took a deep breath.

"Well, sir. I just noticed that you might be camping slightly on our property," he answered.

Walter glared up at him for a second.

"Oh, I see," said Walter.

He rose from his chair and began pacing toward Roger.

"Would you like me to move?" Asked Walter.

"Well. Yes. Please. If you moved back just a little bit it would be greatly appreciated," Roger replied.

"Sure. No problem buddy" replied Walter.

He was hopeful that Walter would comply and move, and that would be the end of it. Roger still had an uneasy feeling about him, though. The last thing he needed was some crazy, deranged individual wandering around the woods while his children were out there. Still, not wanting to be quick to judge, he left the gentleman, confident that it was just a misunderstanding. However, the mystery surrounding Walter was a source of confusion and apprehension, and Roger had yet to come close to realizing his real intent.

The following day was the day that Roger would take his family to chop down a real Christmas Tree. Roger didn't like fake trees. There was something about the smell of an evergreen tree coupled with a wood burning fireplace that set the Christmas spirit. There was a place deep in the forest that his grandpa would take him. He and Buck used to go hunting back there.

Upon leaving, Roger noticed that his ax and chainsaw were not where they had been sitting. Where in the hell did they go? They searched everywhere; in the shed, behind the cabin, in the car. But they were nowhere to be found. He began to wonder if Walter had stolen them. But, Roger was one to give the benefit of the doubt.

"Well. I guess we'll be making a trip to the hardware store," Roger said.

While browsing the store a short time later, a breaking news report came across the television screen behind the counter.

"An escaped convict is on the loose," it said in big, bold letters.

"Excuse me, mister. Could you turn that up please?"

Roger asked the clerk.

As he placed his items on the counter, a police sketch of the fugitive flashed onscreen. Roger's jaw quickly dropped to the floor.

"Oh, my God. It can't be," he said under his breath.

"He looks just like Walter."

His heart skipped a beat, thinking of the trouble this might bring. What were the chances that there was a convicted felon hiding behind them? As Roger paid the clerk, Kate approached from behind him, putting her hand on his shoulder.

"Honey. You Ok?" She asked.

Snatching the items from the counter, he knew that she hadn't seen it yet.

"Yep. Let's get out of here," Roger said, speeding toward the front door.

"What's the hurry all of a sudden, Roger?" Asked Kate, giving him a peculiar look.

"I'm just excited. That's all. Let's go."

As they got ready to leave, she had a sense that Roger was concealing something, although she wasn't sure what.

The family drove out to his favorite spot to choose a tree, leaving the car on the side of the snow-covered roadway. Patrick and Emily quickly exited and dashed toward the forest. They were thrilled. It seemed that they were beginning to enjoy themselves. Roger wanted very much to keep everything as usual as possible, trying not to jump to conclusions. But, deep down, he was worried. Roger was doing his best job, not to show it in front of his kids. He didn't want to scare them, needlessly.

As they rambled along, eyeballing every tree for perfection, Emily called out to them.

"Mom. Dad. What about this one?" She asked.

Kate stood by, glancing up at the tall tree.

"Good job, honey," Kate said. "That one is excellent!"

"Nice!" Roger stated. "That's the one you want?"

"Yes, daddy," Emily replied.

"Ok. Good enough for me," Roger answered.

He cranked the chain saw and began cutting it down.

The tree was huge, approaching almost seven feet. Its limbs were long and even, with bright green pine needles. Patrick and his father took opposite ends, hauled it to the car and tied it to the luggage rack on top. They would spend the rest of that night decorating and spending time together, drinking hot chocolate, with Roger telling stories of his earliest times at the cabin. Christmas' time had always been very special to Roger.

But, as a child, he would instead, rather have been with

his grandfather than home. His parent's divorce was tough on Roger. Decorating the Christmas tree helped him forget about being bounced around between two worlds. His mother's coddling and his father's strict rules were a source of confusion for him.

They came together during the holidays, trying to keep things as healthy as possible. But, Roger could always sense the tension between them and did his best to ignore it. Thinking about that time in his life made him want to be better even more. He couldn't allow the shadow of his father to dictate how he was to raise his children.

As he and Kate laid in bed that night, the cabin was quiet, and Roger thought about what he had seen earlier in the day. Could that have been Walter? He wasn't sure. And he didn't know if he wanted to be. But, as he gazed up at the ceiling, she could tell that something was weighing on his mind.

"Roger. What's the matter?" Asked Kate. "Is there something you need to say?"

Exhaling deeply, he peered over at her, knowing that he couldn't keep it from her any longer.

"Ok. fine," he said. "I saw something on the news today."

"What? Tell me."

Roger delayed for a split-second before answering her.

"It was about a man who escaped from prison a couple of hours from here," he told her.

"And? What about him?" Asked Kate.

Roger took in a big gulp of air.

"And, he looked like Walter," he said.

"What?! Are you sure?" She asked.

"Yes. No. I don't know. I don't know anything for sure," said Roger.

Kate veered toward the other side of the room. For the next few minutes, the bedroom was utterly silent. Then, she broke that silence.

"We have to go to the police," Kate urged him.

She was probably right. But, Roger didn't want to go there just yet. The last thing he wanted to do was incriminate an innocent man. But could it be? Or was he just some crazy old coot hiding away from society. Sometimes, the truth is stranger than fiction.

CHAPTER 6

ON THE TRAIL

Somewhere in the forest

JAMES AWOKE ABRUPTLY. His head shot up instantly as if someone had just rocked him violently. But, nobody was there, only the winter gale howling through the trees and blasting against his face.

"Shit!" He shouted, his heart racing as if he had just escaped from someone.

Faded and weary, the man's old body couldn't take the constant running anymore. He was no longer young. Although James still had some fight left in him. He didn't remember falling asleep, let alone venturing into the woods. But, there he was on the ground, leaning against that tree, eyes gaping through the icy limbs at the dark sky above him.

"What? Where the hell am I?" He asked himself, wiping his distressed eyes with his sleeve.

James had been experiencing periodic blackouts since his head injury from the whipping he took in prison. All he remembered was getting off of the bike for a minute to urinate. He sure didn't remember sitting down. Still, James was fatigued. He hadn't slept a full night for as long as he could remember. It seemed every time he did doze off he had that same dream. It took him right back to that instant, groaning and bleeding on the wet shower floor of that dreadful place.

James needed to force that memory away, for a while, at least. He had to get out of there. There was no way the man could spend the night on the frozen ground. He began to struggle, forcing himself to his feet against the frosty, forest floor.

It was a dull and dreary Montana night, and James desperately needed to find a spot to lie low for a little while, if that was even possible. He pointed himself back toward the deserted road, seizing the dirt bike from the ground, not positive of where he was going. Still, anywhere was better than there.

As he zipped down the roadway, the harsh, stiff draft

was like a whip hitting the side of his neck. It woke him up, surely. But it was far too cold outside to be riding a bike. He couldn't manage it for too much longer. Continuing around a sharp curve, he noticed a house straight ahead of him with the lights on.

James smashed on the brakes, skidding sideways as he came to a halt beside the sleek, gravel driveway. He quickly glanced behind to make sure nobody was trailing him. Staring at the large, timber-framed house, he let out a deep sigh.

"James. What the hell are you doing?" He thought to himself.

But, all he could seem to think about was getting warm. Setting the bike down, and anxiously advancing down the long drive, he was well-informed that if anyone recognized him, it was all over. James reached for his beanie cap, pulling it tightly over his long, gray hair. And, as he approached the front door, he began to thump loudly.

As he heard footsteps coming near him, the door slowly creaked open. Suddenly, there was a large, heavy-weight of a man standing before him.

"May I help you?" The man asked.

"I am so sorry to bother you, sir," James replied. "But

may I use your telephone?"

The man balked for a moment, as he studied James up and down.

"Strange for an old fellow like yourself to be out here at this time of night, don't you think?" He asked.

"My truck broke down, sir. and now I'm lost," James claimed.

The burly man shook his head as he cracked the door a little more.

"Come on in then," said the stranger. "But, only for a minute."

James felt a sigh of relief throughout his body. He hadn't recognized him so far.

"Oh, thank you very much," he responded.

The man grabbed the phone from the kitchen counter and gave it to James.

"Go ahead and make your call," he said. "I'll just wait right here."

He didn't actually plan to call anybody. James was trying to buy himself enough time to figure out what he was going to do. He was very aware that at any moment, they could realize who he was. James felt like kicking himself for even trying. But, he was desperate.

James stood by anxiously, pretending to make a phone

call. He could feel the man's eyes glaring him down. James covered the phone to hide the dial tone, pretending he was talking to someone. But, before he could hang the phone up, the stranger interrupted.

"Can I take you somewhere, mister?" He asked.

James casually put the phone on the receiver. Before he could answer him, the nightly news came on television, and once again, the police drawing of James.

"Oh my God," the wife uttered from the living room, as she twirled around to confront him.

"Is that you?" She asked in a screeching voice.

"I knew there was something off about you!" Her husband added.

James noticed a set of car keys lying on the kitchen counter from the corner of his eye. Sooner than they could say another word, he jerked them up in a hurry and darted through the front door.

James dashed toward the man's car, sliding across the hood with the stranger steadfastly closing in behind him. Slamming the door and locking it, he fumbled through the car keys as the enraged man pounded on the driver's side window.

"Get the hell out of my car before I call the cops on you!" The man yelled as he pulled out a .45 pistol and pointed it right for his head.

James cranked the car and hit the gas as hard as he could, rolling over the man's foot and hightailing it toward the highway.

Traveling down the dark, twisting road, it looked like he was in the clear. He knew they would call the police. But, James was hoping to well away by then. That is until he saw police lights swirling in the distance.

"Damn it!" He yelled aloud.

It was pretty apparent that it was a checkpoint. The man thought to turn around, but cop cars were nearing from behind him. If he bolted, he would risk giving himself away. He must remain calm.

As the car edged to the front of the line, a State Trooper advanced toward the driver's side window.

"Must be Montana's finest," he thought to himself, as the officer got closer.

"License and registration please," he ordered.

"I forgot them at home," added James, glancing up at the officer with a smirk.

The trooper gave James the once-over.

"Step out of the car, please sir," he said.

"What have I done, officer?" James asked, glancing up and noticing the name 'TILLMAN' written across his nameplate.

"Is that really necessary, sir?" Asked James. "I'm kind of in a rush."

"Get out of the damn car!" Tillman said intently.

"Fine, I'm going," replied James, as Tillman forced his hands onto the hood.

As the officer commenced patting James down, he snatched the black beanie from his head.

"Why do you look familiar to me?" Asked Tillman.

"I guess I just have one of those faces," James replied.

"Stay right where you are. Do not move," Tillman told him. "I will be right back."

The officer strolled back toward his patrol car as James felt a sharp sense of reprieve that he hadn't found the handgun strapped to his ankle. Before the officer could make it back, James took off in a scurry straight for the tree line.

"We have a runner!" Tillman shouted to his fellow officers. "I think it's him!"

Trooper Tillman quickly grabbed his radio to call for back up as the gaggle of state patrolmen started their pursuit. Though, James, as old as he was, was just too quick for them. He was as elusive as they come. Besides, he barely remembered a time when he wasn't wanted for one reason or another.

He maintained his scamper until he could no longer hear anyone behind him. Deep in the Montana thicket, James didn't think anyone would be able to find him, especially during the darkness of night. He kept wading through the almost impenetrable forest, feeling his way along with his hands and feet. It slowed him down, but still, as long as he continued moving, he could put some distance between himself and the search party.

The police were preparing to mount their search for him, armed with service pistols and flashlights. Superintendent Jameson Weber, who arrived in his unmarked patrol car, was getting prepared to assemble his men. Weber was a no-nonsense kind of guy. He was short, at five-foot -seven, and commanded more respect from his troopers than his tiny frame would have a person believe.

He'd been a football star in his youthful days. But, an injury caused him to fall back on his second career choice, law enforcement. A third-generation cop, he was a by-the-book type of guy. Weber stood by his car, bull horn in hand.

"We believe this to be the same man who escaped from the prison a couple of weeks ago," he echoed. "Please assume he is armed and extremely dangerous.

And let's go get this jackass."

"10-4," the trooper's replied, almost in unison.

The search was set in motion, as Weber's posse formed up and made their way into the thick backwoods, knocking away limbs and brush with their arms and flashlights. A group of K-9 officers headed the search, as everyone else followed closely after.

James flat out ran for as long as he could. He needed to pause and rest for a few. His old bones and arthritis made sure James wouldn't be able to sustain as well as he once could. Still, that didn't mean that he was going to give in. No. Not James.

While he wasn't as agile as he once was, he made up for it with his intelligence and his will not to get captured. Crouching on one knee on the white ground, he listened for any sound that would carry with the crisp breeze.

As the search unit drew closer, James could vaguely overhear them spouting to one another in the distance. The sound of snarling canines began to echo throughout the landscape. He positioned himself upward promptly and bounded oppositely. Knowing he needed to get the hounds off his scent, James discarded his socks, exposing his feet to the cold climate, and hung them from a nearby tree.

K-9 Officer Grant, a muscle-bound African American, and twelve-year state police veteran was in charge of the local K-9 Unit. Having been a sergeant and dog handler in the Marine Corps, he was well versed in the abilities of police working dogs.

As they zigzagged in and around the thick brush, Grant's bloodhound picked up a strong smell.

"I think I have something here," he told the rest.

"Alright. Let's go," advised Tillman. The troopers began following closely behind Grant. As they circled the place where James had just been, the hound surged forward, growling and yapping at one particular tree.

"What the hell?" Trooper Tillman said, dismayed as he glanced to his right and noticed the pair of socks tied to the hanging branch.

"Damn it!" He said. "That slick bastard."

Tillman picked the pair of socks with his light and tossed them to the ground.

"Listen up, everyone. That jackass was here," he continued. "Let's finish this. But, be extremely cautious. We don't know what he is capable of."

One of the younger troopers, whose nerves were getting the better of him, glimpsed at Tillman for a moment.

"You think he'll do anything?" The young guy asked,

trembling in fear.

"I don't know," Answered Tillman. "But, I sure as hell don't want to find out."

At the same time, James carried forth, gaining a swath of separation from the searching unit. Eventually, he reached a road on the other side of the wooded grove. Spotting headlights in the distance, he held ready. As the car moved closer, James marched into the middle of the road and began flapping his hands high in the air. The bright glow lit him up like a deer in the headlights. The car halted abruptly, skidding tires to keep from hitting him as he ran to the driver's side.

"Are you alright, sir?" The driver asked, visibly shaken.

James paused for a bit, hunched over, trying to catch his breath.

"I just need a ride out of here, mister," he answered, panting.

"Uh, ok. Sure, mister. Hop in," the driver spouted, unknowing that he had just allowed a fugitive into his car. James glared through the back windshield to ensure nobody was chasing them.

"What's the matter?" The stranger asked reluctantly. "Are you in some trouble, mister?"

"Just keep driving," James replied.

Behind, sniffing at the iced ground, the K-9's had picked up his scent again and quickly pulled their handlers right to the edge of a two-lane road.

"This is where the trail ends," Grant declared to the other officers.

"He must have hitched a ride from here. Damn it," Added Tillman.

"What do you want to do, boss?" Asked Grant.

"We'll have to set up roadblocks and a wider perimeter," He responded. "Quickly. We can't allow him to escape us again."

CHAPTER 7

REGRET

Frozen lake

ROGER HAD TAKEN his family ice fishing. It was
something of a past time that was taught to him by his
grandad. Having hooked a few, they were getting all gathered up and ready to go back. But, making their way up
the main trail toward the cabin, the breeze started to pick
up significantly.

Roger zipped his coat and pulled his cap tight over his
head.

"That's not good," he mumbled under his breath
as he viewed the clouds above shifting colors fast.
"What dad?" Asked Patrick. "What is it?".
Roger thought back to that couple in the diner.

"Nothing, son," replied Roger. "Let's keep going."

As they extended up to the snow-white pathway, trees started to swing fast, and the roaring blast made it hard for them to push much farther. They tried walking against it, but the flurry was steadily driving them backward.

"Follow me," said Roger. "Let's get into the woods!"

"What is it?" Kate asked him.

"It's a snowstorm," answered Roger. "Come on. Get under here."

"We aren't that far, dad," said Emily.

"There's no time. Come. Hurry up," Roger urged them.

He stooped on the ground under a large fir tree and opened his long winter coat so his family could huddle beneath.

"Guys," he continued. "Hold the ends, so it doesn't blow away!"

The roaring storm howled and wailed around them, hurling snow sideways as if mother nature was pissed off about something. The mighty wind was a testament to what could happen up there for the unprepared. Roger was beginning to wish he had listened to that couple in the restaurant.

They remained, shivering, for what seemed like an

hour or two. By the time the weather had let up, the family could barely feel their hands. Roger couldn't believe that he had led his family into a situation like that. But, they didn't seem to be bitter at all; only relieved that it was finally over with and nobody was seriously hurt.

"Is everyone ok?" Roger asked them.

"Yeah, dad." Said, Patrick.

"I think so," Emily answered.

"We're ok. I think," Kate affirmed. "Holy crap that was fierce."

"I'm sorry guys. I should have checked the weather report before coming down here," said Roger.

Everyone brushed the remnants of the storm from their clothes and resumed the uphill hike, stepping over downed tree limbs. As the cabin began to come into view, Roger spotted someone in the distance. It could have been Walter. He wasn't sure. But, he was carrying something over his shoulder in a large plastic bag.

"I'll meet you guys in a minute," he told them, knowing they hadn't seen him yet. "I need to check on something."

"Ok, hun," Kate said.

As they made their way back home, Roger followed the suspicious character into the woods, trailing casually so as not to be seen. Moving closer, he noticed the long hair protruding from the man's coat hood. It was definitely him.

"What are you doing, Walter?" Roger thought to himself.

Then, something strange. Walter dropped the object into a shallow hole.

"Oh, no. What is that?" Roger asked himself.

He couldn't quite believe what he was seeing.

"Jesus Christ," thought Roger. "Did he just freaking kill somebody?"

Roger observed as Walter began throwing snow covered dirt into the hole. He couldn't quite believe what he was seeing. But, Roger wanted to get out of there in a hurry, before he was spotted. Creeping away quietly, he returned to his family in shock for what he had just witnessed.

Upon his return, Kate could tell that something was amiss. But, Roger didn't know exactly how to say it. And, he surely didn't want to address it in front of their children.

"So. What were you doing?" She asked.

Not knowing quite how to put it, there was distress written all over his face.

"Roger. What is it?" Kate persisted, pulling him into the next room. She knew her husband. And it wasn't very often that he became bothered to the point of being speechless.

"Talk to me!" She continued.

Roger stood by, and his head hung low. He was trying to grasp what he had just witnessed.

"Honey. You are worrying me," said Kate.

He glanced up at her with dread in his eyes.

"We have to go to the cops," he said in a soft tone.

"What? Why?" Kate asked. "What's wrong?"

"What's wrong? I just saw Walter bury a damn body back there!" Roger answered. "That's what's wrong."

It was as if a bomb had just gone off. Kate's mouth hung open. She couldn't perceive what he was telling her.

"No way!" She said. "Are you sure?"

Roger sat at the foot of the bed, his head shaking apprehensively.

"I'm pretty sure," Roger said.

Kate gasped as she took a seat right beside, wrapping her arms tightly around him.

"Walter? I knew the man was strange," she said. "But, a murderer?"

For a few minutes, they both sat still, trying to make

sense of it all.

"Why?" He thought to himself. "Of all the places in the world. Why did this need to happen there?"

It was enough to make Roger sick to his stomach. He had to protect his family. How could a pure family retreat turn into this? And, who, or what was that in the ground? Neither of them knew what else to say. But, Roger could tell that his wife was startled. And for that, he was utterly angry.

Their children peeked in at them from the corner of the doorway. They knew something wasn't right. Roger and Kate never hid anything from them. It's the only reason their parents would ever speak in private. And, neither had noticed them yet.

Patrick was the first to walk into the bedroom.

"Mom, dad, what is it?" He asked them. "What's wrong?"

Kate glanced back at her son with fear in her eyes, not breathing a word. How do you tell a child something like that?

"Dad?" Patrick continued, as Emily approached from behind.

Roger just sat in awkward silence, questioning to himself if this was real, or if he would wake from this wretched dream at any minute.

"You guys are scaring us," Emily added, a teardrop rolling down her cheek.

Even though they had no idea what the problem was, they knew it must have been bad for their parents to refuse to tell them.

"Honey, listen," Kate said to Emily, clutching her by the arm. "It's nothing your daddy and I can't handle, ok?"

Kate wiped a tear from Emily's face.

"Are you sure, mom?" Asked Patrick.

"Yes. We are sure." She answered. "You two go to bed and don't worry about anything, ok? Tomorrow will be a new day."

For the rest of that night, Roger and Kate laid speechless in the bed, until, what seemed to them like hours later, they finally fell asleep.

The next morning, Roger awoke with one goal in mind. He was going to report to the police what he had seen the evening prior. Not even bothering to eat anything before leaving, he just wanted to get it over with and behind them, fast.

"Be careful, Hun," Kate told him.

"Don't you worry about me," said Roger, kissing her on the cheek and pointing himself toward the front door and out to the car. But, before he could reach it, a shock.

Walter, as if from out of nowhere, appeared before Roger, causing him to flinch.

"Hi neighbor," He said. "That was some rough weather we had yesterday."

"What the hell, Walter?" You scared the shit out of me!"

Had Walter been spying on him? It all seemed like too much to be a coincidence. Did he know what Roger was about to do? All he knew was that he didn't trust him one bit.

"Oh, I'm sorry," said Walter. "I sure wouldn't want to do that."

Roger was taken back by this man. He had no idea what he was capable of doing. But, he was beginning to believe that a killer was living behind them. Roger thought he knew what he had seen. And, there didn't seem to be any other explanation. And he feared that if he didn't report him soon, he would get in trouble and put his family in jeopardy. He would do anything to keep that from occurring.

"I want to show you something," Walter declared. "Follow me."

It gave Roger a bad feeling in his gut. But, however reluctantly, he agreed.

Walter led him straight to his campsite.

"Have a seat," he said, as he withdrew into his camper.

He returned seconds later, a lever action rifle in hand. Roger couldn't help but wonder what he was planning to do with it. But, as Walter took his seat, he gave the rifle over to Roger. It was an old 30-30 Winchester model, the type used in the old west.

"That is a nice rifle," Roger told him, cocking it to ensure it wasn't loaded.

"Thanks," Walter replied. "I am a shooter of sorts."

Was that his way of saying he'll use it? Roger was beginning to get a little agitated, figuring that Walter knew what he was up to. But, he sure as hell wasn't going to ask him. As Walter took his prized rifle back inside, Roger quickly got the hell out of there. That man gave him the chills. So much so that he had completely forgotten about going to the cops.

As he and Kate were lying in bed later that evening, Roger felt numb inside. Kate had her reservations. It wasn't that she didn't trust Roger. She was always the one to see the good in people. It's one of the qualities he loved about her. But, being an attorney, cynicism came naturally to him.

Roger couldn't manage to fall asleep for more than

thirty minutes at a time. The thought of a man breaking in and murdering them was foremost in his mind. As he laid there, restless, the wind whisked and blustered all night long, almost as if it were a sign of things to come. Before he knew it, the rising sun was shining through the window drapes, and another day was fast upon them.

CHAPTER 8
VISITOR

Emigrant, Montana

JAMES MANAGED TO AVOID all roadblocks by hiding out in the forest. He was well aware that sticking to the major roads was a mistake that he couldn't afford. They were looking for him. And, they wouldn't stop looking for him until he was back in that cage, or dead. But, he was running low on what little he had on him.

The man was starving. Light on his feet, he had barely eaten anything in two days. He knew that he would need to venture into town to get supplies. James had been feeling sorry for himself. He was far too old to be running around the woods like an animal.

He remembered when he used to get visitors at the

prison. It seemed like so long ago. To him, those were the days when people, at least, pretended to care. His sister, Jessica, would come almost weekly. But, she stopped talking to him a few years back, after a big blowout of a fight. He hadn't seen his estranged, twin brother since they were in their forties. James had no idea if he was around, or even if he was still alive. He did remember his sister mentioning something about a trailer that she had that was somewhere close by. But that was years ago.

Somehow, he needed to get out of the brutal, Montana weather. But first, he had to get a bite to eat. Getting weak from hunger, James wouldn't be able to go for much longer. He made his way through the dense woodlands toward the nearest convenience store, pulling his hood over his head to keep from being easily recognized.

Taking a look around, it was an eery feeling. The gloomy overcast, snow-covered ground and few shops lining a single road were a testament to small town, USA. It was like the setting for a low budget horror film. James grew up a small-town guy. But not here. Not now. The place was the kind with only one stop light. And everybody knows everybody. People talk. News travels fast in a situation like that. It's not the right place to be when you're wanted. He would need to hurry.

He entered the town's only general store, and the woman behind the counter followed his every move like she was up to something. As James approached the table to pay the clerk for the items, his eyes locked onto hers. For a moment, it was as if she knew him.

"Have I seen you before?" She asked, with a certain curious, small-town charm.

His body suddenly went tense. Did the lady make him? Would she call the cops? Damn it. Why did he have to take that chance? He felt like his head was about to explode. But, he hid it. Well. James remained silent for a moment as the lady looked him up and down.

"Have you heard?" The lady continued.

"What's that?" He asked under his breath.

"The escaped prisoner, silly," she added.

James felt the immediate need to get the hell out of there as fast as possible.

"Nope, sorry. Just passing through," James answered as he grabbed his stuff and darted through the double doors.

"Wait, mister. You forgot your change!" The woman said, watching James disappear behind the building.

He had learned to look over his shoulder everywhere he went. Even in prison, he never trusted people. His so-called brother Aryans said they were family. But, James knew better. He figured that ultimately, he would become their enemy. And, he did. Survival was the name of the game in there. It was the only way to keep from getting beaten or worse. That is until they turn on you.

Survival was also the name of the game out in the wild. James would do anything to keep from going back. Anything. His whole life had seemed to be one big game of survival of the fittest, especially while he was in the Army and afterward.

There was nobody in this world that he could trust since his wife, Tricia, died years ago. She passed away believing that James had lost his mind, and now he was all alone. After a stint in Vietnam, and being recruited into a particular CIA program in the eighties, he pulled away from society altogether. James had turned into a recluse and became paranoid that people were coming after him. His primary coping mechanism was alcohol. He would down a gallon of Vodka a day back then.

Using the information in his head from years before, James continued walking toward where he thought his sister's trailer was supposed to be, hoping to find it still sitting there and unoccupied. But, as he approached the place just on the edge of town, his mood changed to disappointment. The only thing sitting there was an empty lot.

"Fuck!" He shouted aloud, not knowing where else he would go.

Upset, he whipped around to leave and noticed a stranger walking toward him.

"Hey, buddy. You looking for something?" The man asked.

"Yes. I was looking for my sister, Jessica's place," said James. "It used to sit right here."

"Short blonde. Fiery temper?"

"Yep. That sounds like my sis," James answered.

"Oh, yes. I knew that one," the guy confessed. "She hasn't lived here in a couple of years, though. Last I heard she moved to Livingston."

James, finicky from roaming all over the place, was thinking of how he was going to get there. And, if she would shoot him or turn him in once, she saw him. But, before worrying about that, he needed to figure out exactly where she was living.

"Can I use your phone partner?" He asked the stranger.

"Sure," the man retorted, as he handed over his cell phone.

James dialed the operator and asked for an address under his sister's name.

"Perfect," he said to the operator, as he wrote it on his hand with a magic marker.

James gave the fellow his phone back and departed for the highway to hitch a ride. He was finally able to flag down a logging truck, and the driver pulled over to the side of the road.

"Where are you trying to get to?" The man asked.

"Livingston," James responded.

"Well. I don't normally pick up hitchhikers," the stranger continued. "But, I am headed just past there. Go ahead and hop in."

As he climbed up, James' eyes focused on the floorboard as he noticed a big double barrel shotgun lying between the torn cloth seats of the old semi. He sure as hell wasn't going to cross this guy. However, he seemed friendly enough.

The stranger introduced himself.

"I'm Daryl, by the way."

"James," he answered, munching on pork skins.

They carried on a lengthy conversation during the roughly two-hour ride. To his unnerving surprise, Daryl had recognized James from TV. He wasn't scared of him, though. Also a convicted felon, he hated the police as much as James did.

"As long as you don't mess with me, we won't have any problems, man," Daryl remarked.

He breathed a sigh of relief that, momentarily, he didn't need to worry about running away. They continued riding until the trailer park came into view. It looked like Jessica's type of place. She could never afford a whole lot. But, she was no doubt happy to have him out of her life. And, James had no idea how she would react to seeing him again.

"This is the place," James said to Daryl.

He halted the truck, and James hopped out.

"Thanks for the ride," he said, slamming the door shut.

Feeling uncertain about being there, he just knew that his sister hated him, especially after what happened. But, he was hopeful that she would have a change of heart. Although, not likely. Their upbringing had ruined Jessica. She was molested by their uncle as a child and didn't trust men. Which probably explained why she was always with the ones who treated her like garbage.

He walked up to the front porch steps and knocked on the door loudly. But, there was no answer. James waited for a minute and then tapped one more time. Still no response. So, he sat on the porch, made himself comfortable, and waited. Would she turn him in? Even though James believed he had a good reason for his actions, the jury didn't see it that way. Jessica, as well as the rest of the family, had turned against him shortly after being sent to prison.

Nobody, including the police, knew his background. The media portrayed him as a vicious killer. If he had it to do all over again, he would have left the country. Immediately, James began having a rough time in prison. He got attacked pretty regularly. That's why he turned to the Aryan Brotherhood. James never was a racist.

But, in prison, you have to go along to get along. Loners didn't last very long in there. But, the catch was that the gang wanted something in return. They asked him to take out a rival gang leader. He'd already been serving a life sentence, and certainly didn't want to die in a death chamber.

When he refused, they turned against him. Not only was James now wanted by the police, but the Aryan Brotherhood as well. They want him dead. It is hard to say which would be worse, being killed or sent back to prison. If the Aryan Brotherhood were responsible, it would no doubt be a slow, cruel death.

CHAPTER 9

REALIZATION

ROGER TOSSED AND TURNED all night long. Although he had done well at burying it up to that point, the stress of the unknown was starting to get to him. Early that morning, he rolled out of bed quickly, gasping for air while trying to remain steady on his feet. He could feel the room spinning as his eyes struggled to gain focus in the pitch black darkness.

"What the hell?" He said, startled as he began to inspect the place for intruders.

Was the noise there? Or was it all in his head? Roger peeked behind every corner, in the bathroom, and down the hall. There was nothing to be found. So he made his way back toward his bedroom. But suddenly, frozen in place, he glanced down and noticed his right hand gripping a loaded 9mm handgun. He couldn't remember grabbing it. But, there it was. Did he have it in his sleep?

"I am losing my damn mind!" Roger said in anguish.

It was just a bad dream. Something of a nightmare that Roger wished he could forget. A strange faceless figure was trying to murder his family. It was a shadow of a man who lurked in the dark while they were sleeping. And, he couldn't protect them.

He was powerless. Hopeless. But, a nightmare wasn't real. He had hoped. Was his conscience trying to tell him something? God, it was all too real. Roger unloaded the gun and placed it back in the drawer.

"Damn," he said aloud, leaning against the cold window to cool his overheated body.

Kate, hearing the commotion, rolled over in bed and squinted at his silhouette with sleepy eyes.

"Honey. What are you doing?" She asked him. "It's five o' clock in the morning."

Roger shrugged his shoulders, trying to maintain his composure. But, deep down, he was terrified. It wasn't very often that he had nightmares. And, this one made him break out in sweats.

"Couldn't sleep," he remarked.

"What was that noise?" Asked Kate.

"I don't know. Maybe the wind," Roger continued.

He didn't want to admit how he was feeling, or what he was thinking. And, he didn't want to scare his family. It was his job to protect. If not for anything else, for them.

Catching a glimpse of Roger shaking in the corner, Kate sat up in bed and pulled the chain on her nightstand lamp.

"Babe. You don't look too good," she stated. "Are you sick? Do you need to go to the hospital?"

"No," Roger persisted, jolting his head back and forth. "I'll be fine. I need some coffee."

"You don't look fine to me," Kate observed.

"I said, I'm ok!" Stated Roger, raising his voice.

She backed away from him, hands in the air.

"Fine. Jesus. I was just concerned," She pleaded.

Roger folded his hands over his face, ashamed for speaking to her in that way. He needed to get a grip on things. Kate would understand if Roger just admitted it. She gazed at him, flustered, as he stepped toward her, wrapping his arms around her tightly.

"I'm so sorry, hun. Just had a bad dream," said Roger. "I'll go take a hot shower. I should be ok after that."

But before he could make it to the bathroom, Emily appeared in the doorway holding her fuzzy little teddy bear.

"Mommy, what was that? I heard something." She said.

Kate rushed to her side, grabbing her by the hand.

"It was nothing sweetheart," she answered softly. "Daddy and I were talking. You can go back to sleep, ok?"

"Ok, mommy," Emily said in her quiet voice.

She dragged her teddy down the hall as Roger slipped off his clothes and stepped into the steamy shower. As he soaked his head underneath the broad cascade of water, he was attempting to wash away any fragments of anxiety from his body. He felt tense. Apprehensive. But, determined not to allow it to ruin their time together, he would press on as usual.

Later that morning, Roger decided he was going to take the family for a ride on snowmobiles. He needed something to occupy him. After all, it was supposed to be a fun-filled family outing. He wasn't going to allow anything to get in the way of that.

In front of the cabin, Roger and son were hooking the trailer up to the back of their all-wheel-drive-vehicle.

"You got it, son?" He asked Patrick.

"Yes, sir. All setup," Patrick replied, as he hooked the chains onto the back of the car.

"Alright, let's hit the road," Roger said, climbing into the driver's seat.

Kate peered at him from the passenger side.

"Are you sure you're alright, hun?"

"I am fine, Kate. No big deal," he answered. "Don't worry about me."

But, she was concerned about him, having never seen Roger as flipped out as he was that morning. Quite frankly, it scared her. But, if he said he was ok, she would be inclined to believe him.

Roger was a Veteran. He used to have nightmares of combat that would wake him from a deep sleep. Though, that was a long time ago. And, it was something that he thought he had gotten past with the help of his doctors.

But, Roger had hoped it was just a fluke. He wasn't going to stress about it until he needed to. Roger was adamant not to allow that paranoia into his life again, no matter what it took.

They made it to the rental place in no time. After paying the rental fee for two days, they began loading the snowmobiles onto the trailer. The family was excited to have a little fun finally. As Roger prepared to exit the parking lot, they observed two police cars, sirens blaring, traveling at a high rate of speed toward their way home.

"Oh no," said Kate, as they watched the cops fly past them in a blur. "I hope nobody is hurt."

"In this weather, it wouldn't surprise me," Roger responded, pulling out of the drive.

"Somebody probably forgot to put the snow chains on," he continued, as they watched the police cars speed out of view.

They kept driving, slowly making their way home. They were in no hurry, after all. But as they continued around the last curve leading to the driveway, they noticed sirens up ahead of them. And they were blocking the road from both sides. That's when Roger realized it was a checkpoint.

"Shit. What the hell is going on up there?" Roger questioned.

"Dad. Are they after us?" Patrick asked.

"Of course not honey. Why would you say that? Kate asked him.

"Everybody, just remain calm," said Roger, as the officer held his arm out to slow the vehicle. "Let me do the talking."

Roger had an idea of why they were there. But, not wanting to get his family involved, playing dumb seemed like the better option.

The officer approached the driver's side window, holding what looked like a photo in his hand. He was a big guy, tall and muscular. And he looked like he commanded authority.

"Afternoon officer," Roger said with a half-smile. "Is there a problem?"

"Hi, folks. Officer Regan," he said, as he showed the photo to them. "We're just asking everyone coming through here. Have you guys seen this man around?"

Roger felt uneasy about lying to the police. But, in this case, he didn't think that he had much choice. Glancing at the photo, it looked just like Walter. But, the hair was slightly longer. Could it have been an older picture? Roger hid the tension that was going on in his head as he gave the photo back to Officer Regan.

"No, sir. Sure haven't," he answered, handing the photo back to him.

The officer took a peek at everyone in the car as if he was trying to detect a lie. But, Roger told them to remain calm. And, that's what they did.

"His name is James Flanagan," continued Officer Regan. "He is a fugitive and is to be considered possibly armed and dangerous. If you do see him, do not approach and call 911."

"What the hell?" Roger thought to himself.

Now he was perplexed. Did the police have the wrong name? Or the wrong man? That information threw Roger for a loop. He was fully expecting to hear Walter's name. Who was this other guy?

"Yes, sir. Will do," he responded.

"Alright. Have a good day then," the officer told them before heading back to his patrol car.

Roger paused for a moment, attempting to make sense of the information he had given him. But, it didn't make any sense at all. How could they be in the right place, searching for somebody else? Now he was happy he hadn't said anything. He wasn't sure that he wanted to know.

If they were looking for Walter, how did they even know to look there in the first place? He didn't tell anyone, and nobody else was out there. As Officer Regan waved them through, they sat, silent. Roger felt chills down his body as he drove down the long drive back to his cabin.

"Mom, dad. Are we still going to ride the snowmobiles?" Emily asked as the car came to a stop beside the front porch.

Roger glanced at his children in the back seat.

"Yeah, guys. We'll go for a ride," he replied. "Just give me a few to think."

CHAPTER 10

THE RECKONING

AN HOUR LATER, having pulled the snowmobiles off of the trailer, Roger was looking forward to forgetting about recent events. There was nothing he could do about it, anyhow. He reasoned that if he kept them out of it, they wouldn't be affected by it. What would anyone have against an innocent family on vacation together, anyhow?

As they exited the property, Roger felt the adrenaline spread over his body. Feeling like a child again, the roar of the engine fired him up. He was glad to be able to spend that time with his kids. It was the reason they were there in the first place. And, he wasn't going to let anything get in the way of that.

Gliding and cruising across the smooth road, one hand held against the breeze, Roger was leading the others down the hillside to the frozen pond a couple of miles from home. The bitter cold was slapping them across the face. They were all bundled up in heavy coats, winter gloves, and racing helmets. None of them could feel a thing.

"Dad, you want to race?" Patrick asked as he raced up alongside his father.

They were having the time of their lives. And, Roger felt like he could relate to them for the first time in a long time.

"You're on!" Roger answered as he high-tailed it past his son.

"Hey, I didn't say go yet!" Patrick shouted.

They whipped and flew down the winding road as Kate and Emily remained at a constant speed behind them.

"Crazy boys," she said to Emily.

Their surroundings went by in a daze as they accelerated, hauling over the winter landscape with breathtaking quickness. But, they didn't care. Both were having a blast together.

Roger made it first to the bottom of the hill, skidding across the ice and coming to a stop in the middle of the pond. Patrick lingered closely behind, pulling up right beside his father. Both were smiling and bonding in a way that had escaped them for the longest time. And it was a great feeling, like a natural high that neither wanted to come down.

"That was awesome!" Patrick said, taking his helmet off.

"Sure was," replied Roger. "I can't believe we didn't do this before."

He glanced down the pathway they took coming down.

"I wonder what's keeping the girls," Roger stated.

"They are slowpokes, as usual," answered Patrick.

But, before either could say another word, they appeared, moving at a gradual pace around the curve. Approaching the pond, Kate saw Roger's thousand-yard stare, as if something in the distance had caught his eye.

"What is it?" She asked as she came to a standstill, engine idling next to him. "What's wrong?"

"Nothing hun," he told her. "Just give me a minute."

Kate watched as Roger pointed his snowmobile directly for the tree line. Then, she saw it. It was smoke, probably from a campfire, rising high above the forest cover. As he moved in closer, that's when he observed Walter. He was sitting on a tree stump, noticeably shaking, fingers held over a fire.

"Walter?" Roger said calmly.

But he didn't answer. He just kept his eyes glued to the flames as if staring right through them. Roger snapped his fingers in front of Walter.

"Hey," he continued. You ok?"

While Walter's head slowly turned to face Roger, his eyes seemed hollow, lost.

"They are after me," he stuttered.

"Who?" Asked Roger. "Who is after you, Walter?"

There was a short silence as Roger paused for him to answer the question.

"Have to keep moving," he mumbled. "People are after me. Can't stay still."

Walter wasn't making a whole lot of sense. He seemed troubled like he was on the verge of a mental breakdown or something. Roger didn't know if he should have to push him any further. However, he needed to figure out what was going on, one way or the other. The security of his family was paramount. He couldn't have them stuck in the middle of some type of criminality.

Before Roger could say anything else, his family gathered behind him.

"Honey. Everything ok?" Asked Kate.

"Yes. Everything is fine," Roger said. "You guys head back, alright? I'll meet you there in a few."

"Ok, hun. Just be careful," she said.

Eyeing Walter with confusion, she flipped the snowmobile around, and they took off toward home. Roger took a seat next to Walter on the stump, determined to get to the bottom of it.

"Walter. Talk to me," he insisted. "What the hell is going on?"

Then, silence.

Walter sat for a while, seemingly staring into space. He wasn't ready to talk. As Roger glimpsed over at Walter, the man looked afraid and nervous, and not at all like the hardened criminal that Roger thought he was. He was behaving more like a victim. But, if that was true, then who in the hell were the police after?

The sun was beginning to fade behind the mountain, and Roger didn't want to be out there all night long. But, strangely, he was starting to feel some pity for Walter. Although Roger wasn't sure why. He couldn't envision what in the hell would drive a man to hole up in the harshness of the Montana backcountry. Still, whatever it was, it must have been severe.

Suddenly, he spoke.—

"Can't do this anymore," Walter mumbled. "I'm tired."

Roger sat, listening, and pondering what Walter was rambling about.

"You can't do what, Walter?" He asked. "Come on, man. Talk to me."

Walter had the look of a man weathered. He looked like he hadn't slept in days, and was filthy from head to toe. His scraggly, long hair hung over his face as if to hide the shame and fear in his eyes. Against his better judgment, Roger was trying to see through the man's rugged exterior to what was beneath. He was willing to give him the benefit of the doubt, for now.

"Hey, Walter. Look at me," he said. "Tell me what is happening. Right now."

He slowly turned his weary eyes toward Roger, as if looking straight through him.

"Who is coming after you?" Roger asked, once again. "Damn it, Walter. Talk to me!"

"Bad men. Evil men." Walter said trembling. "The white supremacists. The Aryans."

Was he talking about the Aryan Brotherhood? Why in the world would they be after this man? It was not making any sense to him. Something was missing. And, Roger was going to find out what it was, somehow.

"What were the police doing here, Walter?" Asked Roger. "Were they looking for you?"

Walter reached into his pocket, pulling an old Polaroid photo from his billfold. It was discolored, wrinkly, and not in perfect condition. The picture must have been from decades ago. Walter placed his wallet on the log and handed the photo to Roger.

"What's this?" Roger asked him.

It was hard to tell from the grainy image. Nevertheless, glancing at the picture, Roger noticed a striking resemblance to Walter.

"Is this you?" Roger continued.

Walter shook his head back and forth.

"No. My brother," he mentioned. "Taken the last time I saw him. November 3rd, 1986."

Roger looked astonished. How is his brother related to any of this?

"So, you have a twin brother?" Roger affirmed. "Walter. What does your brother have to do with it?"

His head lifted as he scowled at Roger with fear.

"He was in prison. Now, he is not," Walter said. "They think I am him."

Roger's jaw quickly dropped. At that moment he wished he had just stayed out of it. But, his ability to do that was slowly decreasing every day. Considering what to do, he returned home very confused. Was Walter the victim? Could his story be correct?

As they settled in for the night and Roger rested his head next to Kate's, fire sparkling in the background, he couldn't get Walter out of his head. If only he could have predicted what was to come. They had absolutely no clue.

CHAPTER 11

DEAR SISTER

Livingston, Montana

JAMES GOT TIRED of waiting for his sis to return home and had broken into her place, eating her food and snoozing on the couch. If anything, he was persistent. He could no longer remain on that porch and chance anyone recognizing him. He needed a place to lie low for a while and recuperate for a while. He had no idea where Jessica was, or when she'd return back. However, he was reasonably sure that she would not be pleased to see him in her house, or at all.

Stepping out of the blazing shower, James wrapped a towel around his worn body, combed his long, gray hair, and made himself a cup of coffee. For the first time in a long while, he was in no rush to move.

As he sat in the dining room, James took a sip from his coffee mug and opened the Sunday newspaper that he had found lying on the front porch swing. While browsing from back to front, as he usually did, he received a shocker in the form of his mugshot above an article on the cover page.

Livingston, Montana. Sunday, December 15th, 2018. Escaped convict, James Flanagan remains at large. He is presumed armed and dangerous. Multiple sightings were reported, but all were proven to be invalid. He is believed to be hiding somewhere in the mountains between Livingston and Bozeman. A tip-line has been set up for your convenience. If you think you've spotted this man, do not approach him. Dial 911 or 1-800-555-6594 immediately. The authorities are offering a $10000 reward for any information leading to his capture and arrest.

Balling up the newspaper in a burst of rage and tossing it into the garbage can behind him, James lowered his head into his folded hands. He knew right then that things were about to change from bad to worse.

"Shit," he thought. "Now everyone and their mother

will be looking for me."

As he sat, reflecting on the many questions he had in his head, he heard something. It was the distinctive noise of a vehicle driving over snow and gravel. James stood erect and made his way to the living room window. Glancing through the curtains, he spotted a red, faded Jeep Cherokee, and it was coming his way.

"Ok, dear sister," he said to himself. "Let's see what you have to say."

As the vehicle came to a halt, James opened the screen door that led to the porch and parked himself on the front steps. Glaring at him through her windshield, Jessica could not believe who she was looking at. Seeing red, she bounced out of the Jeep and hurried toward her brother.

"What the hell are you doing here, asshole?" She asked him.

As James tried to stand, she shoved him back down in a frenzy.

"Jessica, I..." James said before she interrupted him.

"You what?" She asked. "You broke into my house? Answer the damn question! What are you doing here?"

Jessica was a bit feisty and had a fierce temper when she was angry, something that happened to run in the family. James would expect nothing less from his little sister. She had been that way since they were small, playing in the backyard as their mom and dad got drunk and did hard drugs. It was a lousy childhood they had. But, to her, it was no excuse. He was the last person she ever expected or wanted to see.

James thought about his response for a moment before peering back up at her.

"I have nowhere else to go," he claimed.

"Yes, you do. Back to jail!" She answered. "My life is hard enough without you in it!"

"I don't deserve prison," he said. "If I go back they will kill me!"

She had a bewildered look on her face.

"What do you mean? Who?" Asked Jessica.

"Your ex was one of them," said James. "Now they are plotting against me. That's why I escaped."

"One of who?" She asked.

"The Aryans," James continued.

Jessica got into James' face, her eyes staring into his.

"I don't care. You killed the man, you moron!" She shouted. "Why should I give a damn if they slaughter you?"

James was no cold-blooded murderer. At least, he didn't think so. He only meant to defend his sister. But, it no longer mattered. He was facing a dilemma with no idea how to proceed.

"Why do you need to come to fuck up my life again?" Jessica asked him. "What did I ever do to you?"

James rose to his feet, looking down at his sister.

"He hit you. I hit him back," he asserted. 'He deserved what he got."

"You still had no right," she vowed. "It was my problem. I don't care what your intentions were."

Jessica used to get hit by that man daily. One day, James was at her place, having some beers when he heard the slap from the other room. Before the fellow could raise his hand again, James had him by the throat.

He put him down with a fist to the nose, not meaning to kill him. Jessica didn't believe that. Nor did anyone else. But, he knew that his sister had always been insecure. She seemed to always choose the men who liked roughing up women. That didn't fly with him.

The Aryan Brotherhood was a different story. At first, he was on good terms with them. But, one day he got into a fight with one of their guys in prison. The man was making fun of James, thinking it was just a game. James snapped after that. He jumped the guy in the showers, banging his head on the tile wall, and leaving a trail of blood running into the damp, shower drain.

Prison became much harder for James after that. The gang had put a hit out on him. Now, he was on the run. Honestly, he didn't know which was worse, being caught by the police or the Aryan Brotherhood.

"What the hell do you want from me?" Asked Jessica.

James lit a smoke to calm his nerves and lowered himself onto the porch swing.

"Just let me stay here a few days," he insisted. "I'll sleep in the shed. That's all I ask."

"You want me to let you put my kids in danger?" She asked him. "You are out of your mind."

James let out a sigh as he flicked the ash from his cigarette.

"Your kids aren't even here," he said. "Besides, nobody will ever know I am here. I swear."

Jessica deliberated for a moment as she glanced back at the road.

"I swear to God, James. If you put us in danger, I will shoot you myself!" she asserted.

"Thank you, sis," he said, extending his arms to hug her.

"Don't thank me!" She yelled, shoving him away from her. "Just stay out of my way."

Jessica had informed her brother that he was only permitted to stay for a couple of days. He knew that eventually, the police would catch on and visit her. James was hoping to be long gone by then, however. But, as far as he knew, the Aryan Brotherhood had no idea where she lived. He just wanted to bide his time so he could figure out his next move.

James moved his duffel bag to the tool shed, setting up a cot in the back corner. He didn't even bother to remove what little he had in his sack. James understood that the time might come when he would need to flee in a hurry, not wanting to take the risk of leaving anything behind. James planted himself firmly on the cot and began wiping the pistol he had hidden on the inside of his pants, just in case. After packing it back into his waistband, he laid back, head resting on his green Army duffel, and drifted off to sleep.

The very next morning.—

The sun rose to a golden orange over the Montana mountain range. With the birds chirping and squirrels frolicking, it was a new day. But, not a regular day, as they were about to find out. Sitting silent in the kitchen, Jessica was reluctant to open dialogue with her wanted brother. She didn't want to be close to him. Helping James went against every emotion she had buried inside of her. Despite, he was there for the time being.

As Jessica continued to struggle with the thought of his presence, she removed herself to the living room, switching on the tube and flopping down on the sofa. Flipping through the channels, every news broadcast she came across was talking about her brother. She could not believe she was related to this man.

"Jesus," she thought. "He certainly fucked up this time."

Watching the report, Jessica heard a racket coming from behind her. As she shifted her body on the couch, it appeared through the window as plain as day: To protect and serve.

She flew off of the sofa and grabbed James by the arm, pushing him down the long hallway.

"Hide!" She shouted at him. "It's the cops!"

James suddenly darted through the back door and slipped into the storage shed, ducking behind the toolbox in the back. Hearing the car door slam, Jessica swung the front door open and stepped onto the porch. The trooper proceeded toward her, removing his aviator shades. It was Trooper Tillman. Jessica had no reservation as to what he was looking for.

"Hello, miss," he said. "Are you Jessica? Jessica Flanagan?"

The last thing she wanted to do was seem nervous or as if she was hiding something. Swallowing the tension inside, she answered.

"Yep. That's me," Jessica calmly replied. "What can I do for you, officer?"

"Has he contacted you at all, Ms. Flanagan?" He asked her. "Your brother?" Keep in mind, there are consequences for lying to the police."

"No, he has not," she answered. "We haven't been on good terms for a long time. And if you do see him, feel free to beat his sorry ass for me."

"So you don't mind if I look around a bit, do you?" The trooper continued.

"I don't give a shit," she said. "Knock yourself out."

However, She was extremely apprehensive underneath, knowing that she could go to prison for harboring a fugitive. Tillman and his partner began searching the area. They entered the house, skimming every room, one by one.

They resumed down the long hall and through the back door, glancing around her back yard. Jessica was standing by, following them, and hoping they didn't venture into her woodshed. Just when she started to get ahold of her breathing, the two troopers went straight for it.

They opened the door and stared into the dark building, flashing lights. But, luckily. James was well hidden in the back. Jessica was praying to herself that the officers didn't walk in. Just as she exhaled, they turned around and strolled toward her.

One of them reached into his pocket, pulling out a card.

"Ms. Flanagan," he said. "If you see or hear from him, give me a call at this number. The name is Tillman."

"Ok. Yeah, sure," Jessica responded.

"Thanks for your assistance," Tillman said, as the two spun around to leave. "You have yourself a good day now."

Not twenty seconds after they pulled out of her drive, Jessica flung the shed door open.

"You are damn lucky they didn't find you!" She said. "You could have gotten us both in a load of trouble."

James rose to his feet and wiggled his way through the maze and out the door.

"Listen, sis. I need you to trust me," he told her. My life depends on it."

Jessica pulled back and punched James in his left arm.

"Your life?" She asked. "What about my life, huh? You know, the one you ruined?"

"It was an accident," replied James. "I swear to you. I didn't mean to kill him. But, if I would have stayed in prison, I would be dead right now."

Jessica took a rest on a folding chair and tipped back a bottle of beer.

"Who would have killed you?" She asked him, placing the bottle back on the table.

"The Aryan Brotherhood," he continued. "I thought I told you this."

"And if they find you here?"

"They won't." He replied.

"They better not," answered Jessica. "Because if they do, I will give you to them and wash my hands of it."

The police were already skeptical of Jessica. They knew by then that she was the closest family that he had around there. But, they had yet to connect the dots with Walter. The police discerned that it was natural for a fugitive to go to a place that he was familiar with. And, if they understood, the gang could catch on too.

She wouldn't allow James to stay for much longer. He was already placing their safety at risk. Luckily, she had sent them to their grandmother's house a few days prior. She couldn't afford to get locked up. Jessica could hardly take care of her children as it was. If she went away, they would inevitably end up in foster care.

James and Jessica always seemed to forget that they had another sibling. Walter had been separated from them for years by then. He never really got along with his family, anyhow. Their father would get drunk and hit them pretty regularly. They lived in an abusive household. One fateful Saturday night, the man came home from the bar, drunk, and began striking their mother. When young Walter tried to intervene, his father began beating on him and ended up fracturing his skull. He was never the same after that.

That day was the last day, either of their parents saw or spoke to him. They died in a mysterious car crash a few years later. Jessica was the only one of the siblings to attend the funeral. James was drafted into the Army shortly after that and went to Vietnam. When he returned, he was a changed person, a hermit.

Ever since he has had a problem with people, James was the type of person a black ops outfit could take advantage. His weaknesses became strengths when adequately exploited. He used to have a high sense of duty.

But, eventually, the government ruined that, and him. He killed for patriotism, not for love of killing. And he never executed anyone who didn't deserve it.

When the government tried to contract him to kill a man that he presumed innocent, he refused. After that, James went underground; until years later, when he contacted his sister. His brother had crossed his mind from time to time. He didn't even know where he was, or if he was still living. As far as James was concerned, he no longer had a brother. But, the problem was, he did have a brother. And Walter meant more to him now than he would ever understand.

CHAPTER 12

WOUNDED

THE TREE WAS STUNNING. And, it was just the distraction that he wanted. Roger and his family had just added the finishing touches to make the place a winter wonderland. The shining angel resting on top seemed to be watching over them. Flashing Christmas lights mirrored off of the cabin windows, and, for a while, sinking back in his recliner, Roger had forgotten about recent events that troubled them.

That Holiday reminded Roger of an old novel he read. Assembling by the crackling fire, snowflakes falling, stockings dangling from the mantle. Everything was as peaceful as could be. Grandpa would have been pleased. But, not everything was as it appeared.

They sat there in each other's company for most of that evening. Roger told the children tales he had never told anyone before; stories of his childhood that remained untold for a long time, for some reason. Maybe as he got older, he was ashamed to admit it. But what is there to be embarrassed by? Sure, he had money and was successful. But, he didn't raise himself. Somewhere along the way, he lost that part of his life. Maybe he was trying to live it over again through his children's eyes; a way of remembering when life was less stressful.

It could be hard for some people to understand for a person who seemingly had it all. Still, Roger discovered over the years that money couldn't buy happiness. A lonely, wealthy man is just as miserable as a lonely, poor one. The family had sat there all night long, drinking eggnog and playing board games. He felt like a child again. Even his children were enjoying the simplicity; something they never did before.

Roger stood for a second and stepped into the kitchen for a refill. Leaning against the window, he took a sip from his cup. Watching the snowfall through the crystallized glass, he was grateful to be in a warm cabin. Roger wondered what Walter was doing out there, and if the poor guy was freezing his ass off.

He did feel a little sorry for the man. Not everyone could be so fortunate. He thought about how thankful he was to have a family to stand by him. Seeing his children playing with their mother on the sofa, Roger couldn't help but grin back at them. He began marching back to the living room when, all of a sudden, there was a booming sound off in the distance that seemed to reverberate against the mountainside.

"Honey. What was that?" Kate asked from the next room.

"Sounds like shooting," he replied. "It could be hunters."

Roger cleared the fog from the window, trying to figure out where the noise originated. Glancing through the glass, a silhouette emerged out of the shadow of the forest. It was the profile of a man, looking very disoriented and staggering from side to side. And, he was coming right for the cabin. Roger could vaguely make out what the fellow was wearing. It had to be Walter. As his image became more apparent, he saw blood oozing down his arm onto the white ground.

Not a hundred yards from the front door, faltering through two feet of snow, his body gave out and collapsed head first onto the cold turf.

"Stay here!" Roger said to his family, tearing through the front door.

Racing toward Walter, he came to a sudden halt and slid on his knees next to him.

"Jesus, Walter! You ok?" He asked as he rolled his body over.

"What happened?" Roger continued. "Who did this to you?"

Walter tried to speak, but he couldn't stop quivering and puffing. Roger removed his coat and placed it over the man's cold body, trying to warm him up. Walter, heaving for air, managed to force the words out, one by one.

"They-are-hunting-me," he said between each agonizing breath.

"Who, Walter?" Roger asked. "Who is hunting you?"

"Those Aryan bastards," he mumbled, out of breath.

Walter was barely intelligible and going in and out of consciousness. Following the trace of blood down his body, It looked like he had a gunshot wound to his left arm. Roger instantly clutched Walter, raising him on his back and hurried him inside, blood spilling down the end of his shirt.

"Kate!" Roger called out, as he thrust the door open with his foot. "I need help!"

"Oh my God," she uttered, taking Walter's legs and helping Roger carry him into the spare bedroom. "What happened to him?"

"I'm pretty sure somebody shot him," Roger answered, as they placed Walter onto the bed.

"Ok. We need to elevate his body," said Kate, placing two pillows under his head. "Hurry."

Tearing an old t-shirt to use as a tourniquet, Kate bound it tightly above his gaping wound. As she applied enormous pressure to his arm, the bleeding slowly subsided. Pulling the first aid bag from their gear, she began wiping the blood away.

Roger, enraged as he was, snatched his shotgun from the gun rack and headed toward the front door.

"Roger. Where are you going?" Asked Kate.

"I'm going to get to the bottom of this," he said.

"No, Roger. Please don't!" Kate hollered. "You don't know who's out there!"

But, it was no use. Roger was determined not to back down. With his gun at the ready, he began to follow Walter's tracks in the snow. Crouching, Roger made his way through the bush, studying for any sign. As Roger moved toward the area, he believed the shot had come from, he found a blood stain on the side of a tree.

"This must be where he was," he thought to himself.

Walking for a half a mile into the forest, he explored

for any sign of someone being there. Finally, he came across some boot prints in the slush. He followed for a little while, and the trail led to a clearing at the edge of the woods; one that was used by hunters in the area. He began to hear a sound coming from the other side of the plot. Roger bent on the ground and waited to see if whatever or whoever it was would come out. But, suddenly, the noise stopped.

He moved forward, clutching the shotgun from his back and holding it to his face. Roger examined the edge of the tree line. A flock of birds flew up as if something had scared them away. Then, without warning, another blast rang out.

Surprised, he looked around the area in total shock, but couldn't tell where the shot came from. Feeling an intense burning coming from his lower body, he glimpsed down to see his pants tainted a sharp, blood-red. The light began to fade as Roger's weak body fell behind with a thump. Silence.

Thirty minutes later—

A mammoth of a man, rifle hung on his shoulder and dressed in white camouflage, snagged a 20 gauge shotgun shell from the ground. As he moved toward him, Roger was slowly starting to regain consciousness. He could somewhat make out the shape of the stranger's cumbersome frame. However, everything was hazy. A few minutes later, lying on his back, he realized that someone was dragging him by his arms across the freezing ground.

"What?" Roger asked. "What's happening?"

"I'm getting you out of here, sir," the man said.

Roger peered up at the stranger.

"Who in the hell are you and where are you taking me?" He asked.

"Don't worry mister. I am no threat," the stranger replied. "I was out deer hunting when I heard the blast. I came to investigate, but by the time I got here, you were lying face up in the snow."

"I was shot?" Roger asked him, glancing down at the belt that was cutting the circulation to his leg. "I can't feel a damn thing."

"Yeah, mister," the man answered. "We need to hurry and get you out of here."

"Where are they?" Continued Roger. "Did you see anybody?"

"No, man," he continued. "Whoever it was is gone now, or I would have shot them."

"Where are we going?" Roger inquired.

"To the hospital," he replied. "My truck is parked near

the road."

"No, no, no. I have a cabin nearby," Roger explained, pointing the stranger in the right direction. "Take me there, please. My wife is a nurse."

"Whatever you say, brother," he answered.

He changed direction and resumed pulling Roger until they reached the porch. Kate, spotting them through the living room window, raced out to see what was going on.

"Oh, my God!" She yelled. "What happened? Is he ok?"

"He'll be fine," confirmed the stranger. "Just a little bird shot. It isn't that bad, except he has a huge knot on his head from slamming into that tree."

"I am fine," Roger insisted, attempting to rise to his feet. "I can walk from here."

"You stubborn man," continued Kate. "I told you not to go out there!"

Struggling to rise, his head was throbbing with each heartbeat. Roger's legs gave away, and he dropped back into the stranger's arms.

"I got you, buddy. I got you," he said, wrapping his arms around Roger's and carefully pulling him to his feet as he gripped his hand tightly around the front porch rail.

"Come here, babe. It'll be alright," Kate told him,

wrapping her arms tight around his waist.

"And who are you?" Kate asked the man, guiding Roger up to the front steps.

"Oh, sorry, Miss," he answered. "I'm Manny. I was hunting a trophy buck when I found your man here lying in the snow."

"Well, thank you, Manny," Kate replied, pulling out a hundred dollar bill to give to him. "I'm thankful you were out there. My husband is a little hard-headed."

"Oh, no. Please. It was my pleasure," said Manny. "I'm just glad I found him when I did. He could've frozen to death out there."

"You want to come in for some coffee or something, Manny?" Kate asked.

"No thanks, mam. I must get going," Manny replied. "Just make sure he takes it easy for a while."

"I will do my best," she answered. "My husband isn't known for taking it easy."

"Well, have a good evening, mam."

As Manny faded into the cold, bitter night, a glint of full moonlight parted through the trees and into the cabin window. Kate carefully escorted Roger to their room and prepared to remove the shotgun fragments from his injured leg, thankful that he wasn't seriously injured, or worse.

CHAPTER 13

REUNION

ROGER DIDN'T GET MUCH sleep that night. The feeling in his body had come racing back hours earlier. With his head pounding and aching limbs, he tried to sit in bed. However, he couldn't manage to force himself upright. Peeking down at his wrapped leg, Roger called out to Kate from the master bedroom.

"Kate? Honey," he said. "Can you give me a boost?"

Roger gripped a wooden cane and pushed himself up as she held her arms under his.

"How are you feeling this morning?" She asked. "You were tossing and turning all night."

"Awful. This damn thing stings," Roger replied. "Plus, I have a piercing headache. But, other than that, I'm ok. I guess."

Shifting the weight off of his injured leg, Roger

limped to the kitchen to dabble a little rum into his coffee mug. Liquor seemed to help dull the pain, temporarily. Taking a sip from his cup, he winced, feeling an immediate jolt shooting down the lower right half of his body.

"Honey. Are you sure you're alright?" Asked Kate, wrapping her arms around his waist. "You gave us quite a scare."

"I just need to get some fresh air," he said, shuffling out to the porch and propping his leg on the wooden bench.

As Roger set his mug next to him on the deck, he gazed out at the snow-white forest, noticing how pretty the winter is up in mountain country. Yet, in the back of his mind, he was wondering if anyone was out there. Would they be back? What did they want? He didn't have much time to think about it before. Then, without warning, it hit him like a hammer to the gut and caused him to sit right up in his seat.

What about his family?

"Shit," he said under his breath.

Roger wasn't concerned about himself. His family, that was another matter, entirely. Do they know where to find them? What if they returned to finish the job? These were all questions that were now engulfing Roger's mind.

And, with Walter resting inside, would they come after him?

Having a stranger in their cabin wasn't exactly ideal. They didn't know him. But, Roger couldn't think of anything else to do. He didn't want to leave the man bleeding in the snow. However, he had yet to figure out why they were so intent on getting to Walter. Is the Aryan Brotherhood responsible? How could they have mistaken him for his brother? All mysteries that Roger must get to the bottom of, in time.

For now, his family must come first. He knew that he needed to get them out of there for their safety. Only would they understand? He couldn't forgive himself if anything ever happened to them. Roger also knew that Kate would not be keen on the idea of allowing him to remain behind, alone. Helping a strange man who is being pursued by deranged psychopaths wasn't part of the plan.

As he watched the dark clouds forming through the forest trees, Roger knew it was the safest option. It's not that he wanted to. Roger didn't feel he had any other choice. Besides, if this fight ended up at his doorstep, he wanted them to be as far away as possible.

As he staggered through the front door, Kate recognized the somber expression on Roger's face. She understood her husband. She knew it wasn't the pain. No. It was something else. But, she hesitated to ask him what it was. Kate squeezed Roger from behind, resting her hands on his shoulder.

"Babe. What is it?" She asked into his ear.

He held her arm and guided her into the next room.

"You need to pack the kids up and leave here," he told her. "Just for a little while."

"What? No!" She replied, shutting the door so the kids wouldn't overhear them. "No!"

Roger stood speechless for a bit, trying to imagine a way to make Kate understand. She was stronger than she seemed. There was no way that Kate wanted to leave him alone with Walter or anyone else. She knew that he could take care of himself. Although, that wasn't precisely the point.

"Listen," he responded. "It'll just be long enough for me to figure out what's going on here."

"It's not your fight to figure out!" She said, tugging him by the shirt. "I'm not leaving you alone out here."

Roger clutched her hands gently and brought them down to her side.

"I will be fine, Kate," he said. "You're going to have to trust me on this one."

"It's not you that I don't trust, Roger," She replied.

Unsettled, Kate squatted silently for a moment, stationary on the bed. She didn't know why he felt the need to put himself in the middle of some madness. Then again, he did have a few holes in his leg to remind her of just who her husband was. He has never been one to start a fight. But, he wasn't the type to back down, either.

Kate would never pretend to understand what was going through Roger's mind entirely. However, if he said he knew what he was doing, even if she had her reservations, which she did, she would be inclined to believe him. But, this time was different. She was starting to ask herself if he saw something that she didn't. She wasn't sure what to make of any of it.

Roger calmly sat next to Kate on their bed.

"Look, hun, don't worry," he told her. "Everything will be ok. I'll see what I can do, and then we can finish our trip as planned. I promise."

"You sure?" She asked. "Promise you'll be careful and come back to us?"

Roger gently grabbed Kate's hand and peered into her brown eyes.

"I promise," he continued. "It'll be ok. I'll call when it's ok to come back."

"if you say so, Roger," she said, snatching her suitcase from the corner and spreading it out on the bed.

As she began packing, Roger went to the next room over to check on Walter, who'd remained quiet pretty much the whole time he'd been there. He seemed like he was in a state of hysteria, and for a good reason. Roger still needed to question Walter about those who were after him. But, he was in no shape to talk, as of yet. There was something about that man that he just couldn't put his finger on.

Cracking the door open slightly, Roger peeked into the spare bedroom. Walter was bundled up in the blankets, snoring like a freight train, and sleeping as if he hadn't slept in weeks. Roger couldn't help but think of how damn fortunate that man was to be alive. Then again, Roger could have also met the same fate, especially if it weren't for that mysterious hunter who miraculously discovered him. Still, nobody has nine lives. He couldn't let that happen again.

As Roger softly pushed the door shut, Kate met him in the hallway.

"What's he doing in there?" She asked.

"Sleeping like a rock," replied Roger.

Kate coiled her arms around him one last time.

"I don't have a good feeling about this," she conveyed in a hushed tone.

"Kate. We've been through this already," he replied.

"I just worry," she continued.

"Well. You're just going to have to trust me," said Roger. "Now go. I'll call you later."

Roger followed her and the kids out to the front drive and helped pack bags into the vehicle. Just as they were reversing to leave, Kate blew him a worried kiss. Her gaze met his, and Roger spotted the sight of pure panic in her eyes. It was a look that he had never seen coming from her. Roger knew she was scared. Nevertheless, Roger was doing what he thought was right. He guessed that, in time, she would understand what he was about to do.

He parked himself on the front steps for a few, listening and enjoying the sounds of the isolated forest scenery. It was exemplary. It wouldn't last, however. Roger began reflecting back to his time in Afghanistan when he and his team came under an ambush while riding back to base.

He had a bullet wound to the leg. His buddy, Frank, pulled him out of the line of fire so the medics could load him up. Roger received a Purple Heart for that, but he always thought that Frank deserved a medal for saving his life. He recalled those times often. If it weren't for his team, he'd probably have died on a few occasions.

Staring out at an infinite sea of white, Roger recognized what he needed to do. Holding his cane and pushing his body upwards, he made his way to the kitchen to pour himself a shot of Wild Turkey. Dropping it back with one gulp, he snagged the telephone from the receiver and began dialing.

Hitting the last number, Roger placed the phone to his ear and waited.

"Hello?" Said the voice on the other end.

"Hey, Frank. It's me, Roger." He said.

"Roger? Hey, brother! Haven't talked to you in a while," Frank replied. "What's going on?"

"Not much, bro," answered Roger. "Up here in the mountains."

"Taking a break, are you?" Asked Frank.

"Well, sort of," Roger said. "That's kind of the reason I called."

"Something wrong?" Frank continued.

"Well. You could say that," answered Roger. "Listen, can you meet me up here? I'll explain when I see you."

"Worries me when you talk like that, man," replied Frank.

"Trust me. I'll explain things then." Roger answered.

"You at the old cabin?" Frank asked.

"Yep." Roger retorted, hearing the concern in Frank's voice.

"Alright, man," Frank mentioned. "Give me a few, and I'll be on my way."

"Thanks, buddy," said Roger. "I'll explain it all to you then.

"Roger that, bro," Frank replied, speaking in military jargon. "Williams, out."

After hanging the phone up, Roger went back outside to await his buddy's arrival. Resting his injured leg on a rocking chair, he closed his eyes and slowly drifted off to the sound of the winter breeze stirring against the forest trees. All of a sudden, Roger was right back in KANDA-HAR PROVINCE, AFGHANISTAN.

IT WAS MORNING, 0800 hours on a bright, eventful Saturday in 2005. His team and the rest of the platoon had just met with local tribal elders who were trying to get rid of Taliban influence in their tiny village.

As they were entering their vehicles to return back to base, a familiar noise sounded throughout the surrounding valley.

"Sniper!" Roger yelled as a shot pinged off of a nearby wall. "Get down!"

As they were racing for cover, another blast rang out shortly afterward. Roger glanced to his right and spotted their platoon leader, Lieutenant Gary Powers, lying in the dirt with a gunshot wound to his neck. He scuttled toward him, keeping his head low to evade incoming bullets. Removing the lieutenant's battle dressing from his vest, Roger applied pressure and called for his team to assist.

"Guys. We need to get him out of here!" He yelled. "He's bleeding out!"

The villagers were all dashing for their homes as Roger, and his team pulled Lieutenant Powers to cover in the back of the nearest vehicle. Fearing the worst would happen, they knew they had no time to drive him back to base.

"I'll call for chopper evac," said Frank.

"Roger that," replied Roger.

The lieutenant was bleeding badly in the back of the vehicle. As Frank picked up the radio receiver, one of the team members noticed a burst of smoke coming from a nearby hill.

"RPG!" He shouted, as it sailed over their heads and exploded with devastating force twenty meters behind them.

The Taliban had surely been spying on their meeting with the villagers, as they regularly did. But this was more than that. It had ambush written all over it. They were not thrilled that the Rangers were affecting their control over the region. That much was painfully clear.

Hearing Blackhawk helicopters buzzing in the distance, Roger and the rest were hopeful that Lieutenant Powers would make it through. However, in a split-second, machine-gun fire came raining down from the foothills.

"The LZ is too hot," the Night Stalker Pilot said over the radio. "I repeat. The LZ is too hot. We cannot land until you deal with them, over."

"Damn it!" Said Frank. "I guess we're in for a fight."

"I guess so!" Shouted Roger, sprinting for cover at the side of the entrance.

As the platoon took positions behind the large village wall, dozens of Taliban members descended upon them. All four sides were hit with overwhelming AK-47 and PK Machine-Gun fire. Worrying that they would soon become overrun, Frank, as brazen and brave as he was, climbed into the gunner's hatch and began firing his .50 caliber machine gun in all directions, continuously rotating his turret as enemy bullets bounced off of the gunner's shield in front of him. As Frank continued suppressing the Taliban, he gave his platoon mates enough time to reposition and begin holding the enemy back.

When it was all said and done, they hightailed it back to the hills as if their lives depended on it. And, they did. Thanks to Frank, the Rangers were barely able to evacuate the wounded Lieutenant, who was in critical condition and had lost more than half of his blood. You see, Frank had saved Roger's life more than once, too. He was the type of guy who would go to war with his buddies. And, right now, Roger needed him more than he knew.

As the memory of combat began to fade, the sound of a powerful, diesel engine snapped Roger back to reality. Squinting his eyes, he noticed the outline of a massive, silver F-350 pickup truck, Army Ranger tag mounted to the front, fast approaching. The vehicle came to a grinding halt, and three occupants jumped out, all decked out in woodland camouflage and baseball caps.

"There he is," Frank said to Roger. "I brought some friends."

Like Roger, Frank had also been a team leader in the platoon. With a bit of a crazy side, as most of them had, he was a tobacco spitting, deer hunting, jeans-wearing country boy in every sense of the word. But, with all of the craziness, Roger had never known a more dependable guy.

"I see that!" Roger replied as he flung himself off of the bench. "I hope I didn't interrupt anything."

"Oh, bullshit," Lamar said. "I was just out shooting my .338."

Lamar was a sniper from their old unit, and a hell of a shot at eight hundred meters. He was a giant African American, at six foot three, and an avid bodybuilder. Not the type of guy you want to piss off.

"What the hell happened to the leg?" Asked Shane, as Roger stepped toward them with a slight limp. "The old lady finally get tired of you?"

Shane, Roger's assistant team leader in the Rangers, was a great guy to have around when the shit hit the fan. Short, at five-foot-eight, he was a hell fighter at close quarters combat.

"Very funny," Roger answered. "It's a long story. How about I fill you boys in over some drinks?"

"Sounds good to me," Frank said, spitting a stream of Skoal next to the front porch. "Lead the way."

The guys continued into the cabin for a long evening of drinking and conversation. Having not seen his brother's in arms for such a lengthy period, Roger had much to catch them up on. As far as the Aryan Brotherhood went, they would get what was coming to them, soon enough.

CHAPTER 14

RESPITE

Livingston, Montana

AS SNOW CLOUDS ROSE to replace the morning sun, James was resting on the back porch of his sister's double-wide trailer, bouncing his leg apprehensively. He'd been chain-smoking Marlboro Red's and sipping a bottle of Kentucky Bourbon to warm his old body up. It was a cloudy day and bitterly cold out.

In deep thought, he was attempting to plot his next move in his head. The man was worn and tired of going. Neurotic, he knew that he couldn't stand to relax for very much longer. Though, it seemed that reality would prove right earlier than he anticipated.

James stood momentarily to stretch his legs. Suddenly, he heard the sound of a vehicle pulling into the gravel driveway. Making his way toward the side yard and glancing around the corner, he noticed the tail end of a police car sticking out just past the side of the trailer.

James quickly grabbed his cigarettes and his woolen cap from the table and dashed for the tree line as Trooper Tillman and his partner beat loudly on Jessica's door.

"Ms. Flanagan. We know you're in there," Said Tillman. "Open up!"

Jessica cracked the door with the chain still attached.

"What's this about, officer?" She asked.

"You know damn well what it's about," replied Tillman. "Now, open the door, please!"

She parted the door just wide enough for them to enter.

"So. I am guessing you haven't seen your brother," Tillman uttered, looking around the place.

"No, I haven't," she answered.

"And, you have no idea where he is. Correct?"

"That's right," she replied.

"So, you don't mind if we look around, do you?" He continued.

"Be my guest," she said sarcastically. "But you won't find anything."

She had hoped they wouldn't find anything, at least.

She didn't have time to warn James and had hoped that he made it away, for her sake. The two troopers began searching through the house, room by room. They opened the spare bedroom and noticed a pair of men's jeans and a t-shirt lying on a stool next to the bed. Tillman snatched the clothes and moved to the living room to confront Jessica.

"So, whose are these then?" He asked.

"My boyfriend's," she replied nervously.

"Right. Like I believe that," said Tillman.

He and his partner headed through the back door and onto the porch, Jessica following behind them. As they glanced around and out to the yard, his partner noticed a cigarette still smoking in the ashtray.

"Are you going to tell me this isn't his, either?" Tillman asked.

Flustered, she had no idea what to say.

"That's what I thought," he continued.

"Hey, partner. I got something here," he stated, pointing to a set of boot prints in the snow.

"Looks like he went straight toward that tree line," he continued, pointing to a gap in the trees. Tillman glanced back as Jessica was watching them, anxious.

"Boyfriend, huh?"

The troopers continued toward the forest, stepping directly over the set of prints. It certainly seemed that they were closing in on James. They made their way through the thick bush, moving slowly and cautiously, listening for any sign of movement while pointing weapons at the slightest sound. All of a sudden, the partner heard something snap.

"What was that?" He asked alarmed.

"I think it was just a squirrel or something," said Tillman. "Let's keep moving,"

They advanced through the shrubbery, weapons drawn, but there were no more tracks to follow. At that point, it seemed as if they were chasing a ghost.

Tillman barely made out another sound in the distance.

"You hear that, partner?" He asked, pointing to his left. "Sounds like it came from that way."

As they drove through the backwoods, the vegetation got increasingly thicker. Tillman's partner stepped through a pile of leaves on his way up the hill. Swiftly, his foot became stuck in some device. Instantly, Tillman heard his partner scream in pain as a loud snap, like a whip, sounded throughout the forest.

"Shit! He got me!" His partner yelled.

"What the hell?" Said Tillman, loudly. "I'm coming, partner!"

As he reached his position, he knelt to see blood splatter on the tree as a wooden booby trap jammed into his partner's leg.

"Holy shit!" Yelled Tillman. "We need to get you out of here, quick!"

"It's stuck in your leg. I'll radio the air ambulance," continued Tillman, as his partner's loud cries of pain reverberated through the trees. "Just hold on, man!"

James had learned about booby traps in Vietnam while fighting the Viet Cong. There was no better way to slow down pursuers. He was lying on the ground some ways away, viewing them through his binoculars.

"That should slow those bastards down," he said to himself, as he began running up the slope and toward a dirt road, not looking back.

He needed to find his cellmate's bunker soon. James pulled a compass out of his breast pocket. He remembered the guy informing him that it was near that road about ten miles outside of town. James had some hiking ahead of him. The sun had begun to set, which should have made him hard to spot if he stayed off the road a bit.

"I need to hurry before I fucking freeze to death out here," he uttered to himself, pulling the collar up on his coat. At that time, he had almost wished he was still in his warm cell. Of course, he just might have been lying there, dead.

Hoppers, Montana

Two freezing hours went by, and James was tired of walking through the heavy snow. He finally arrived at the spot his cell-mate marked on the map. The man had mentioned that there was an old white house just off of the road, with a chicken coop in the back. The plan said to go behind that property about five hundred paces, and there would be a large pile of branches lying over the top of a steel door.

James slowly slithered behind the property, counting paces to himself. Reaching five hundred, he halted, taking a long survey around. Not able to see much in the night mist, he removed a tiny light out of his pocket and flashed it around, looking for any sign of debris.

Not noticing anything out of the usual, James began moving around in circles, looking and hoping to be somewhere near the mark. Turning around to backtrack his steps, he tripped over a large limb and fell forward, breaking the fall with his hands.

"What the hell?"

As he rose back onto his feet, James looked behind him, shining the light across the ground and noticing a pile of limbs straight in front of him.

"This has to be it," said James.

He immediately began tossing the tree branches to the side. As he removed the final one, James laid across the ground, moving his hands around to feel for a hatch.

"There it is," he said.

He gripped the metal latch with both paws and tugged with all of his strength. But, the door wouldn't budge. James shined his flashlight once more and found a big lock attached to the door. Picking up a rock, he began hitting it as hard as he could, hoping not to alert anyone to his presence.

After twenty whacks, the lock finally broke off. James opened the hatch and gradually made his way down the metal ladder inside.

"Now we're getting somewhere."

As he made his way through the deep bunker, his head grazed up against something dangling from the ceiling.

"What's this?" He mumbled to himself, pulling the hanging piece of rope and watching the entire place filled with light.

"We have power!"

James held a feeling of relief that he had finally made it. He closed the hatch above his head, securing it from the inside. Taking a glimpse around the room, he could not believe what he was seeing; canned food stocked on the shelves, handguns and ammunition, and enough survival equipment to make it through the apocalypse.

His cell-mate must have been planning for some standoff before being sent to prison. As luck would have it, they ended up in the same cell. For a guy who'd been having such a long string of bad luck, James was feeling exceptionally lucky right about then. Finally, time to re-gather his wits and plan his great chess move.

CHAPTER 15

THE MEETING

LIGHT SNOWFALL ON THE ridge made that spot seem like a peaceful, winter refuge. However, its tranquil surroundings were a facade. Walter had been fidgeting, restlessly the night before. And, for a good reason. He was frightened to death that those people would return to finish him off.

They failed the last time. Roger and his buddies were there to assure they didn't get another opportunity. Plus, he wanted to make them hurt for what they did to his leg. Though, he didn't get the worst of it. Walter's wound could have easily been fatal. The shot penetrated the artery in his left arm, and he would've bled out if Kate hadn't stopped the bleeding.

As the boys sat around the cabin playing cards, Roger's mind was deep in thought. He remembered what his wife had told him. She was worried that he was going to get himself killed over what seemed to her like absolute madness. It was conflicting to him. Does he listen to her? Or, follow his instincts? But, he also knew that if he left Walter out there, he was as good as dead. There was no other way around that. They seemed to want him badly.

As Roger sat quiet, seemingly staring into space, and not weighing on the card game, Frank noticed the puzzled look on his face.

"You ok, man?" He asked.

Roger's head lifted up.

"What?"

"Are you alright?" Continued Frank.

"Yeah," Roger replied. "Just thinking about something."

"You don't look ok, man," Shane said. "What's going on?"

"Ok. Hear me out for a second," said Roger. "What if we give them an out?"

"What do you mean by that?" Lamar asked.

"We go talk to them. Threaten the bastards to leave Walter alone," Roger said. "Then, if they don't, we bring the heat."

"Ok, let me get this straight," said Frank. "You want to

go into the house of some deranged skinheads and ask them to leave him alone?"

"Well, it sounds terrible when you put it that way," Roger continued. "But, yeah, that's what I'm thinking."

"And, if they don't want to let you out alive?"

"Well, that's what I have you guys for," Roger stated.

It sounded crazy. But, that was Roger's way of validating what they were planning to do. If he could say that, at least, he tried to reason with them, then Kate would be more understanding of what was to come. That was very significant to Roger.

He knew their leader. Or, at least, he knew of him. He'd seen him in court. His name was Paul, and he was as relentless as they come. But, he never did any of the killing himself. He always ordered his cronies to do it.

Paul had a solid grip on his power, and his subordinates would have done absolutely anything he told them to do. Law enforcement had never been able to connect him with any murders. If they could have, he would have most likely been in prison for life.

While Roger helped Walter down the steps, handgun tucked under his shirt, the man had a look of despair burned onto his face. He knew where they were going. But, they weren't about to leave him there by himself. As frail as Walter was, he needed protection. They wouldn't let him out of their sight until they could figure out why the Aryan's were after him.

"How's the leg?" Asked Shane.

"It's ok," Roger stated. "It seems to be healing fast."

"Are you positive about this?" Frank asked, climbing into the driver's seat of his pickup.

"No, I'm not," replied Roger. "I'm not positive of anything right now."

"How do you even know where this guy lives?" Continued Frank.

"I've had run-ins with him in the past," Roger answered. "I'll just leave it at that."

"What if they decide not to let you out?" Lamar asked.

"Well. That's what I have you guys for."

As they continued down the glossy road in Frank's four-wheel drive, Walter was utterly silent in the back seat, staring through the window at the passing trees.

"Walter, you ok?" Asked Roger.

"I'm fine," he answered. "It just burns."

Kate had bandaged the upper part of his arm. She'd managed to remove a bullet fragment. But, the hole itself would take some time to heal. Walter lost a lot of blood, which left him feeling very unsteady and shaky. If Roger hadn't seen him, he would have certainly either died of blood loss or froze to death on the ground.

"By the way," Frank said. "I brought some goodies."

"What?" Roger questioned, as Frank pulled the truck to the side of the road.

"Check that container in the back," Frank continued as they hopped out of the vehicle.

Roger walked over to the side and noticed a large case sitting in the bed of the truck. As he opened it, he could not believe his eyes.

"Hell yeah!" He said to Frank, removing three AR-15's and a .338 Lapua long gun from the box.

"Just in case they decide to fuck with us," said Frank.

"That long gun is mine!" Lamar stated, removing the camouflage cover and gazing through the scope.

"Well, of course, it is!" Frank said to him. "You're the sniper of the group. The rest of us are just plain ole door kickers."

"Don't you forget it when I'm covering your ass from six hundred meters, either!" Lamar continued as they bounced back into the cab and sped away, spinning tires in the snow.

Springdale, Montana

Turning into Paul's drive a while later, they began to sense that they were in the presence of a white supremacist. Confederate flags and NAZI symbols littered the driveway that led up to the old house.

"This place gives me the creeps," Lamar said as they came to a stop in front of a rickety, wooden porch. "Looks like the headquarters for the inbred, racist hillbilly association."

"Don't worry, man," replied Shane. "Just another one of those flag waving, skinhead pussies."

"You're not black!" Lamar continued.

"Very true," Shane said.

"Stay in the truck," Roger told Walter as he slipped under a blanket in the back seat. "Get down low. I don't want them to see you."

As they got out of the vehicle, Roger spotted Paul and three of his friends watching them through the screen door. Paul was the poster boy for the NAZI movement. With an uncanny resemblance to Charles Manson, he had tattoos from head to toe, and a swastika imprinted in the center of his forehead. What he represented was undeniable.

"Hello Paul," Roger said in a firm voice.

Paul looked them up and down as he slowly pushed the door open.

"You have a lot of guts showing up at my house," Paul replied. "What the hell are you doing here?"

"Just like your man had a lot of guts shooting me in the fucking leg?"

"That was you?"

"Yeah, asshole," Roger answered, sliding his pant leg up and exposing the wound. "That was me."

"Shit," said Paul, laughing. "What are the odds?"

But the fellows didn't think he was very amusing. As Roger stood by, his hand resting on the gun in the back of his pants, he stared Paul down.

"Maybe you shouldn't have gotten in the way of our business then, should you?" Paul continued. "But, if we wanted you dead, you'd be dead."

"Tough talk coming from a moron," Frank said. "I'd like to see you try it."

As one of Paul's associates rushed toward Frank, Paul pressed his arm in front to stop him.

"I could very easily send some of my buddies here to visit your wife and kids at home," Paul continued.

"You NAZI jackass!" Roger yelled. "You will leave my family out of this! Understand?"

Just as Roger began to charge at him, Frank and Shane came up from behind, holding him back.

"You know what we want, Roger," Paul demanded. "We want your new neighbor. He has been causing some problems for us, and we need to deal with him. If not, we'll just deal with you."

"That a threat?"

"It is whatever you want it to be," said Paul.

Roger stood there, fists balled up, full of anger, feeling as if he'd erupt any second.

"What you say, partner? You know where we can find him?"

"No, I do not," Roger replied. "And, I'm not your fucking partner!"

"That's too bad," replied Paul. "Guess we'll just have to settle this the old-fashioned way, huh?"

Roger stepped back and took a deep breath.

"Look, I came here to try to resolve this peacefully," Roger told him. "I don't give a damn about your drugs. I don't give a damn what you do. But you'd better stay far away!"

"Hand him over," Paul balked. "I don't want you. I

want him. I know you know where he is."

"Sorry, pal," Roger answered. "I wouldn't do that even if I did know where he was."

"If you don't, then trouble is surely coming your way," continued Paul. "Starting with that muscle-bound negro you got standing behind you!"

"Come on then, you inbred mother fucker!" Lamar shouted. "This Army Ranger will make you swallow your teeth!"

As he pressed toward Paul, Roger stopped him mid-stride.

"It's ok, Lamar," Roger said as Paul gave a grim smirk. "You'll get your chance."

"That's right," Paul continued. "Keep that monkey on a leash!"

"I'm going to enjoy putting a bullet between your eyes, asshole!" Added Lamar.

As Paul and his friends stood on the porch, Roger and the rest started backing away to the truck.

"We'll see you soon, buddy," stated Paul.

"Look forward to it," Roger replied, leaning against the open door.

As Frank put the vehicle into gear, Roger had an angry look on his face as he lifted the blanket to check on Walter.

"You ok, Walter?" He asked.

"Yeah," he answered. "Just want to get the hell away from this place."

"That prick makes my fucking skin crawl," Said Frank, spinning out of the driveway. "Negotiate? We should've just came in blasting."

"Yep," Shane added. "Should've put a hole straight through that NAZI symbol on his forehead."

"I agree," Lamar replied. "Those racist idiots don't deserve to breathe."

"They'll get what they deserve," Roger assured them, eyes on Paul as they gained some distance from the house. "It's only a matter of time."

CHAPTER 16

CLOSE CALL

THE SUN WAS SLOWLY retreating below the rolling horizon, and dusk was giving way to heavy snowfall and blistering gusts. James had been hunkered down in that concrete bunker all evening, listening to police chatter on the radio scanner. All he could do was try to wait them out. With the Aryan's and the police looking for him, he couldn't take the gamble of wandering around aimlessly any longer.

His goal was to flee to a non-extradition treaty country. It was the only way he could see coming out of this alive. However, with an ever-growing number of people wanting him dead, that would be easier said than done. They were close, far closer than James was comfortable with. He just prayed that they didn't just happen to stumble upon the bunker entrance by accident.

AS TROOPER TILLMAN and the rest of the men combed through the thick woods outside of town, he pulled the collar up on his jacket to protect him from the bitter gust. The snowdrift began to blow forcefully across the roadways and mountain paths, covering up any remains of footprints that James had left behind. As the police neared a field at the edge of the woods, Tillman shined his light against the frost-covered ground.

"Damn it! I lost it," he said to the others. "Can't see a damn thing!"

"We can't possibly find him in this, anyway," his partner replied. "Weather's getting rough. Besides, we are running out of daylight."

"Let's go question some of the surrounding neighbors," continued Tillman. "I'm not ready to give up just yet. I want this guy."

The two partners went back to their patrol car, and Tillman tossed his flashlight into the back seat, slamming the car door.

"Damn it!" He shouted in disappointment.

They both lit a cigarette, shivering as Superintendent Weber approached them, looking less than happy.

"So, any luck?" Asked Weber.

"Not yet, sir," Tillman answered. "We lost him in the

storm."

"You mean to tell me this whole God damned department cannot find a single man?"

"We believe we are close, sir," replied Tillman.

"That's not good enough," Weber retorted. "Nobody ever won anything by being close."

The superintendent leaned against the car, lighting a cigar and taking a long drag. Blowing cigar smoke, he glanced over at his men with concern in his eyes.

"As much as I don't want to do this,' he said. "I think I'm going to have to call the Marshals."

"Sir. No. We don't need them," Tillman urged him.

"You don't think so?" Asked Weber. "When was the last time you chased a fugitive?"

"Well, never, sir."

"Exactly my point," the superintendent replied.

Tillman glanced over at his partner, rolling his eyes.

"That's just perfect," he mumbled under his breath as Weber went back to his unmarked car to make the radio call.

AT THE SAME TIME, James had eavesdropped on the search party's radio traffic on the police scanner. He was troubled that, once the feds arrived, they would eventually close in on him. If they discovered him in there, he would have no way to escape.

"Damn it," James said to himself. "I have to get away from here."

James knew that things were about to change for the worse. He could deal with the police. The feds were a different matter, altogether. They were capable of chasing him to the ends of the earth if they had to. James discerned that he couldn't stay in that shelter forever. But, at least he got some stocks out of it. He jerked the duffel bag from the floor and started filling it with equipment and canned food, enough to feed a team of people.

If he was going to evade the clutches of the U.S. Marshals, it was crucial that he move under cover of darkness. James lifted the metal hatch and peeked through the opening, duffel strapped to his back, looking and listening to ensure nobody was about. Climbing out and quietly securing the latch, he faded back into the mountain grove, gaining as much distance from his pursuers as he possibly could.

An hour later

As the wind continued pounding the mountainside, two dark colored SUV's pulled up to the police checkpoint. Coming to a screeching halt, four men in dark trench coats got out and approached the troopers. The senior man, US. Deputy Supervisor, Marshal Kyle Jones, forty-five, was a fifteen-year veteran of the Marshal Service. Lean and athletic, he was certainly capable of chasing down most. Having never lost a target, Jones commanded respect from his men. They knew he was all business. But, nobody was more suited for the job. There was a thin line that they would never dare to cross with him.

"Who's in charge here?" Jones asked.

Weber walked over from the other side of his car.

"I am," he replied.

"Not anymore," said Jones. "So, somebody please brief me. What have we got?"

"One man escaped from the local prison," answered Tillman. "Name's James Flanagan."

"Got any leads?"

"Not really," Weber answered. "We have been chasing him throughout the area, but we lost his tracks in the snow. This damn blizzard is making this son of a bitch hard to follow."

"Don't worry," replied Jones. "We'll find him."

"Yes, sir."

"Somebody, please get me a damn map," Jones continued.

"Yes, sir," said Tillman, scurrying to his patrol car and removing a folded up map from the glove box.

Tillman spread the map out onto the hood of his car, clearing the snow away with his jacket sleeve.

"Where did you lose him?" Asked Jones.

"Right here sir," Tillman said, pointing to a place on the map.

The Marshal pulled a pen from his jacket pocket.

"Ok, we need to set up roadblocks out to about fifty miles," he ordered them, drawing a red circle on the map. "Every vehicle in sight gets checked. In the meantime, we need to visit that prison and interrogate his cell-mate or anyone else who may know him well. If there are any clues left behind, we'll find them."

"Yes, sir," Weber agreed. "Will do."

"Then, get to it!" Jones ordered. "If there are any updates, call me on my cell phone."

"10-4," said Weber.

The superintendent and his troopers got into their vehicles and left the scene, preparing to execute as the Marshals sped up the highway in the opposite direction toward the prison.

Montana State Prison

The Marshals pulled into the parking lot of the enormous penitentiary. They headed into the intake area, flashing badges to the clerk.

"U.S. Marshals, madam," Jones said to her. "We are here about the escapee. We need to speak with his cellmate."

"Yes, sir," replied the clerk. "Right this way."

She accompanied them down a long corridor, through a locked door to an empty room with two chairs and a metal table in the center.

"Please wait here," she continued. "I'll send some officers to get him."

Jones sat down with two other Marshals standing behind him, pulling a notepad and pen from his pocket and setting them in the center of the table. A couple of minutes went by, and the officers arrived with the inmate, handcuffed, and legs shackled.

He was an older gentleman, something of a survivalist, with glasses, long silver hair, and scars down the left side of his face. The man sat down in front of Jones, glaring as if staring straight through him. Jones glanced up at the officers.

"That's not necessary," he said. "Can we un-cuff him

please?"

"Yes, sir," one officer replied.

He unlocked the handcuffs, and the two officers stood guard by the door.

"United States Marshals, sir. I am Marshal Jones," he conveyed to the man. "We just need to ask you a few questions if you don't mind."

"Name's Fred," the inmate replied.

"Nice to meet you, Fred," answered Jones. "Now, I'm going to get right to the point. We know that you know James Flanagan."

"Well. We weren't exactly friends," Fred said. "But, yes. I do know him, sort of."

"So, were you aware of his intentions to escape?"

"I was. But, I didn't participate," Fred asserted.

"Why didn't you report it, then?" Asked Jones.

"Because he threatened to kill me if I did," he added. "That's why. I'm already doing two life sentences, buddy. I want to die of natural causes."

"Fred. If you assist us and give us what you know, I can make sure that your time here is a little easier," added Jones. "You can't possibly want to stay in solitary indefinitely."

"Look," Fred admitted. "All I know is that he went

through my stuff and found the map to my bunker. I didn't give it to him. A few days later, he was gone. That's all I know. I swear."

Marshal Jones nudged his pad and pen toward Fred.

"Can you draw a map to the bunker for us?" He asked.

Fred took the pen from the table and began drawing. A couple of minutes later, he tore a sheet out of the notebook and placed it onto the table in front of Jones. His eyes got big as he glanced at the other Marshals standing behind him.

"Shit!" He said, pointing to the road in the drawing. "This is less than a freaking mile from where we just were."

The Marshal stood abruptly, pushing the chair in as they got prepared to leave.

"Damn it," he continued. "We have to get back right now. Thank you for your cooperation, Fred."

Marshal Jones called for the guards to get their inmate. But, before they reached the door, Fred stood up, pounding on the table.

"Hey," he said. "Don't forget our deal."

Jones turned around to face him. "

"You fulfilled your part, Fred," he replied. "So will I.

I'm a man of my word."

Fred nodded as the officers put the cuffs back on him. The Marshals rushed to the parking lot to get back to Weber and the rest of the search party.

"We better hurry," said Jones, putting the vehicle in drive and barreling through the parking lot and out to the roadway. "If he's in there we can corner his ass!"

CHAPTER 17

CONTACT

BACK AT THE CABIN, Walter had finally fallen asleep after being up for almost two days straight. He just knew that somebody was going to kill him as he slept. Before, the man was all alone. He refused to remain in one place for too long. Now, he had people watching over him for the first time in a long time. But, he couldn't really rest easy.

The Aryan Brotherhood set their eyes on Roger and his boys. They seemed determined to get to Walter at all costs. It didn't matter why. There was no rationalizing with them, as they had recently come to understand. Now, it was just a matter of time before they did something extreme. This time, he had friends. And they would be ready.

As everyone else drifted off, Roger took the first watch,

leaning back into the sofa as he listened to the sounds of a crackling fire. With his AR-15 Rifle located next to him on the floor, and his .40 caliber Glock 23 handgun resting firmly in his hip holster, Roger's eyes became fixed to the orange glow rising in front of him. As he took a sip from the bottle of Jack Daniel's lying next to him on the end table, Roger's mind began to wander. Once again, his thoughts diverted right BACK TO AFGHANISTAN.

1600 HOURS, JULY 1ST. *THE HINDU KUSH MOUNTAIN RANGE*. Roger and Frank were part of a six-man RRD (Regimental Reconnaissance Detachment) from the 75th Ranger Regiment who were attached to a JSOC (Joint Special Operations Command) task force. Intelligence sources had indicated that a high-ranking al-Qaeda commander would be entering the area from Pakistan. At an elevation of 4000 meters, the team sat in their OP (observation post) and waited.

"You think this fucker will show up?" Asked Frank, leaning against the sandbags as he finished wiping down his M-4.

"He better," Roger replied. "I hope it's not another wild goose chase."

"I don't know man," Frank answered. "He was due to arrive hours ago."

"I'll be sure to tell him that when we capture him," said Roger, chuckling.

The mighty wind cut right through the Afghan mountains as the task force continued observing the dusty pathway below.

"I got something over here!" Staff Sergeant Gillan, a Special Forces Intelligence Sergeant, shouted as he glanced through his binoculars. "I have a company-sized group of tangos with AK's and RPG's moving along the route."

"Do you see the target?" The task force commander, Captain Graham, asked.

"Negative. No visual."

"Fuck," Roger said. "I knew it was too good to be true."

As Gillan peeked through his binoculars once more, he located a group of insurgents pointing in their direction.

"We got a problem over here," he said. "I think they just spotted us!"

Gillan tossed the binoculars to the ground and clutched his weapon as small arms fire came bursting into the task force's position.

"Shit!" Said Graham, ducking behind a pile of sandbags, bullets flying past him. "Return fire!"

Everything seemed to move in slow motion as the men sent rounds flying into the hillside trail beneath them. The men spent their magazines quickly as they fired a constant barrage of bullets down below. Dropping his empty magazine to the ground to reload, Roger glanced to his right just in time to see a shot enter the commander's head just below his headgear. He collapsed back to the ground with a loud thud as medics ran in to assess him.

"Man down!" Yelled Roger. "Captain Graham's been hit!"

Both Roger and Frank hurried toward him, grabbing his legs and preparing to move him.

"Captain!" Roger yelled as they hauled his body out of the line of fire while the rest of the men countered the attack.

But it was too late. The commander was KIA. There was nothing anyone could do to save him. As the smell of gun smoke filled the air surrounding their position, the task force called in a B-1B Strategic Bomber to decimate the advancing insurgents. When it was all said and done, over fifty enemy fighters were killed. However, their original target was not among them. It was a grave intelligence failure.

Captain Graham was an unknown number in a long line of good men that Roger had seen drop right before his eyes. And, for what? He wasn't entirely sure. At that instant, he swore never to let that happen again if he ever had the choice. Which, surely had something to do with his decision to help Walter. Now, he does have that choice. This time, he'd be ready to make it count.

AS ROGER'S MIND snapped back to the present, he had a notion in his gut that something wasn't right.

"Shit," he said to himself, sweat dripping from his forehead. "Get a grip, Roger."

Snatching his rifle from the floor and yanking back on the charging handle, he quietly made his way onto the front porch. Peering out into the dark forest, Roger bowed on the wooden deck, glancing through his night vision optic as he rested the bipod on the porch railing.

Moving the weapon from side to side, he slowly scanned the perimeter of the cabin property, watching for any sign of movement in the pitch blackness. Everything seemed calm as he listened, wondering if he was just paranoid. Then, instantly, Roger saw a flash of something through the green-tinted scope. Something or someone was advancing behind the dense scrub. But, not being able to make out precisely what, or who it was, he waited.

Frank, awakening from light sleep, peeked over at Roger, alert as to what he was doing.

"Guys. Wake up," he whispered, patting his buddies on the feet. "Come on. Put your game face on."

Grabbing his weapon, Frank stepped out onto the porch and crouched beside Roger.

"What you got?" He asked.

"I'm not sure yet," replied Roger. "Could be an animal. Maybe not. Probably not."

Frank steadied his elbows on the rail and glanced through his night vision binoculars.

"Yeah, well," he said, as he followed a strange figure dashing from cover to cover. "Animals don't wear camouflage jackets, do they?"

"They sure don't," said Roger. "Get prepared to pound these assholes."

"Roger that," Frank answered.

As Shane and Lamar proceeded through the front door, Roger glimpsed back at them.

"We have contact," he told them. "Get down and get ready."

"Shit. Go watch Walter, Shane," continued Roger. "Don't let him out of that room and watch the windows.

We'll take care of this."

"Roger that, boss," Shane replied, as he headed for the back of the cabin.

"Lamar, you go up to the attic," Roger added. "Take your long gun and position yourself directly above us, by that window. Make sure you put in your earpiece."

"On the way," Lamar replied, going right for the pull-down ladder in the corner of the living room.

Climbing into the attic area, Lamar opened the window facing the front of the cabin yard and stacked boxes to rest his sniper rifle. Picking his night vision scope from the black case, he attached it to the top of the weapon.

"In position and ready," he confirmed over the radio.

"Roger," whispered Frank.

Roger and Frank piled wood in front of the porch rail to use as cover and waited for them to move in a little closer.

"You see anything up there?" Roger asked Lamar.

"Roger," Lamar said as he peeked through his 50mm night vision sniper scope. "I got four tangos. Two moving up the left, two more on the right."

Lamar paused for a second, glancing through his scope once again.

"Wait," he said. "Shit. Four more coming up the middle."

"Ok," Roger said. "Wait for my word. Then we'll exterminate these fuckers."

The men stood by, allowing the Aryan Brotherhood members to believe they had the element of surprise. But then, one of them spoke.

"Mister O'Neil!" He said. "We are here for your friend!"

"Shit," said Roger. "That's Paul."

"We know you are up there. Hand Walter over or die!"

Outnumbered and outgunned, Roger and his buddies knew they had to rely on their training and their superior equipment.

"You should not have come here, Paul!" Roger shouted. "We have every one of you in our crosshairs!"

"All I wanted was him," said Paul. "You just had to get involved. Playing the hero, right?"

"I'm protecting an innocent man, jackass!" Added Roger. "Your men come any closer, they're dead."

"Finish them," Paul said to his men before retreating into the wood line. "Light 'em up!"

Paul's men began shooting, tearing splinters into the log cabin as Roger and Frank took cover and commenced firing from the side of the porch.

"Got one!" Shouted Frank. "Who else wants it? Come on, fuckers!"

Roger, staring through his ACOG, began picking off one, two, three men rushing for the porch.

"These guys must have a death wish!" He said.

Lamar, following them carefully with his long gun, sent high-powered rounds straight through two of the four remaining men, as they fell straight back against the snow-covered ground.

"Got you, you racist bastards."

"I think maybe your boss should've brought more of you for us to kill!" Screamed Frank.

"Still a couple more left," Roger said. "Where are they?"

"I don't have a visual," Frank added.

"You see anything up there?" He asked Lamar.

"Negative," Lamar answered. "Just bodies."

As Roger began to reload a new magazine into his rifle, they heard a crashing sound coming from the back of the cabin.

"What the hell was that?" Asked Frank.

"Shit!" Replied Roger. "Sounded like breaking glass! Come on!"

"Lamar. You keep watching the front!" He added.

"Got it," said Lamar.

As Roger and Frank made it to the bedroom, they spotted two of Paul's men holding Shane and Walter at gunpoint.

"I tried to stop them," said Shane, visibly upset with himself. "I… tried."

"It's ok, buddy," Roger replied. "We can resolve this without more bloodshed."

"Isn't that right, guys?" He asked the two men.

"You let us take Walter," one of them added. "And we'll forget the whole thing. You can go on living your life and forget about all your heroics."

"Sorry, Mister asshole," Frank mentioned. "Can't do that."

"You want to die for this little weakling?"

"Seems like the only ones dying are your men," said Roger.

As he and Frank stared the two men down, they saw Lamar approach softly from the shadows on the outer side of the window, holding a .45 caliber pistol. Shane began to pull a small knife from the back of his pants as Roger tried to get their attention.

"Hey, jackass," he said. "You guys think we are going to let you take him?"

"I don't see how you have any other option," the man added. "But, it's pretty ballsy for you to think so. I'll give you that."

Roger noticed Shane bringing the small knife down to his side, concealed in the palm of his hand.

"Hey, asshole!" Roger shouted to get his attention.

As the man stepped toward Roger and Frank, holding Shane with a gun to his side, he drew the knife up and inserted it straight into the man's abdomen, and he slid down to the floor, screaming in pain.

"You... mother.. fucker." The man moaned, falling forward with blood pouring out of his mouth. "You... fucking... stabbed... me."

Then, the talking ceased as he exhaled his last breath in a pool of blood on the cabin floor.

"You jackass!" Said the other man, with a firm grip on Walter. "He was my pal!"

"We'll kill the rest of you, too!" Yelled Frank.

As he threw Walter down and darted for Shane, Lamar, with his bulging arms, reached into the window, dragging him through by the throat.

"Remember me?" Lamar asked sharply. "I'm the muscle-bound negro who is about to kill you. You fucking bigot!"

"You won't do it," he replied. "You God damned monkey!"

"Oh, no?" Lamar added, bringing the pistol up to the man's temple. "You don't think so?"

"Come on then, Soldier," said the man. "What are you waiting for?"

Lamar squeezed the trigger point-blank, and the bullet went straight through his head, leaving a large exit wound and splattering blood all over Lamar's face and the wall, dropping him like a sack of concrete.

"Fuck you," Lamar said, spitting on the man's body.

"Good call," Roger said to Lamar.

"Don't mention it. I can't stand those guys."

"Me either."

"You two, alright?" Roger asked Walter and Shane.

"I thought those guys were going to kill me this time," Walter said,

"Don't worry," added Roger. "You're safe now. That won't happen again."

"I'm sorry, guys," Said Shane. "I don't know what happened.

"It's over. For now, anyway," Roger continued." Lamar, go wash that blood off your face."

"Yep," Lamar replied.

"Let's clean this shit up," Frank said. "What a damn mess."

As they started removing the bodies from the cabin, Walter could breathe a temporary sigh of relief that they were able to stop them from taking him. Still, Roger understood it wouldn't be the last they would see of the Aryan Brotherhood. Not by a long shot. Such a gang of degenerates was not known for being level-headed. Paul would surely retaliate for the slaughter of so many of his men. This battle was far from over.

CHAPTER 18
RESOLVE

AFTER MUCH THOUGHT and consideration, Roger decided the next morning that it might be smart to call on the police. But, he wasn't going to waste his time with the local, small-town cops.

He guessed that since that big noise of a fight, they would come snooping around, eventually. Roger wasn't a vigilante, just protecting those who couldn't defend themselves. Besides, he'd rather be on the right side of the law, whether he trusted it or not. It does not exactly fit when an attorney doesn't trust law enforcement.

Still, they had shown up to pick a fight. There was no time to get the law involved in such a remote corner of Montana. He would testify to that in any court of law. Though, he would do it all over again in a heartbeat if it meant saving lives.

"Are you sure about this?" Asked Frank, planting himself on the edge of the sofa.

"Am I sure? No. Not really," Roger replied. "But, they might have information about Walter's brother that we don't."

"I don't like cops," Lamar added. "Too many racist police out in the sticks."

"I agree. I'm not crazy about them, either," Roger continued. "And I'm a lawyer."

"Haha. Good point."

"Before we do anything, though, I need a drink," Roger said to his buddies, walking over to the bar to pour everyone a shot of Patron.

As they all sat down in front of the wooden bar counter, Frank lifted his shot glass in a celebratory toast.

"To the Aryan Brotherhood," he said. "May they spend eternity in a fiery hell-hole."

"Ha! I'll drink to that!" Lamar replied.

The men dropped their glasses back with a single gulp and slammed them back down on the counter.

"Man, that's some strong stuff," Shane said, drying his mouth with his long-sleeve button shirt.

"Well. Shall we get this over with?" Roger asked them.

"After you," replied Frank, as they grabbed their stuff

and made their way to his lifted truck, stacking weapons in the toolbox in the back.

"Come on, Walter," Roger called out. "We can't leave you here!"

"I'm coming," he answered.

Walter in tow, they climbed into the vehicle and prepared for the hour-long drive. With a turn of his key, Frank hit the gas, and they took off toward the road, it's massive tires leaving their imprint in the snow behind them as the powerful engine hummed.

Highway Patrol Office, Belgrade, Montana

Wandering into the station, they noticed numerous officers and civilians typing away on their computers and talking on their phones. The place was bustling with people walking in and out. They could hear the loud commotion of a man being interrogated in one of the locked rooms as he plainly protested his innocence.

"Wait here, guys," Roger told them. "Let me do the talking."

It seemed like a pretty busy place for a small corner of Montana. Nonetheless, Roger approached the counter as the desk sergeant was hanging up his phone.

"Excuse me, sir," said Roger.

"Yep. Can I help you?" The officer asked him.

"I hope so," he continued. "I need to speak to a detective."

"What's the problem, sir?"

"May I please just speak with a detective?" He insisted, glancing down at the man's name tag. "Officer Butler."

"One minute," Butler replied, holding a finger up as he made his way to the back of the building.

He returned a few moments later, walking with a middle-aged gentleman all decked out in a black suit and tie, and shiny, black Oxford shoes. He seemed professional and not at all like the small-town cops that Roger knew so well. As the man neared, he held his hand out to shake Roger's and make the introduction.

"Detective Sergeant Miles," he said.

"Roger O'Neil," he replied, shaking the detective's hand. "Attorney from Bozeman."

"This a legal matter, Mister O'Neil?"

"Well, In a manner of speaking."

"I see," Miles answered. "So, how are you, sir?"

"I'm good, considering."

"Good, good. So, what can I do for you?"

"Well, I have a little problem," Roger stated.

"Ok, I'm listening."

"It's about the guy who escaped from Montana State Penitentiary," he added. "I'm not easy talking about it out here, though."

"Oh, I see. Well, let's go back to my office, shall we?" He continued. "More comfortable back there, anyway."

Detective Miles escorted Roger to his office, located in the very back of the station while the rest of the guys, including Walter, waited for him in the lobby. As they entered the office, he pointed to a leather chair sitting directly in front of a shiny, wooden office desk.

"Have a seat, Roger," said the detective.

"Thanks," Roger answered as he pulled the chair in closer.

"So, Mr. O'Neil," Miles said. "You have information about our fugitive?"

"Sort of," said Roger.

Detective Miles reached into his office drawer and pulled out what looked like a large photograph, possibly a mug shot.

"Do you know or recognize this man?" Miles asked as he showed the photo to Roger.

Roger stared at the picture for a second, noticing the striking resemblance to Walter. The only distinguishing mark that separated him from his brother was a small scar located underneath his left eye.

"I know his brother," Roger replied.

"He has a brother?" Asked Miles.

"Yep. Estranged brother. They're twins," he said. "His name is Walter. I met him a couple of weeks ago up in the mountains. The Aryan Brotherhood is after him because of his brother. They attempted to kill him, but they failed."

"You serious?" Miles asked.

"Yeah, I'm serious," Roger affirmed. "And I need to confess something. We killed a bunch of them up at my cabin."

"Did you now?" He asked. "You didn't call the police?"

"No time. Those men came after Walter and attacked us at my place," said Roger. "We had no choice."

"I see. Unbelievable," Miles replied. "I'd lock up all those Aryan bastards if I could."

The detective seemed as if he was considering what to say as he placed the mug shot back into his desk drawer. Closing the drawer, he folded his arms on the desk and looked Roger in the eyes.

"Between you and me, mister," he continued. "Those gang members are a real problem around here. You probably did everyone a favor. But you understand we'll still have to send some folks that way to corroborate your story, right?"

"Sure."

Not really knowing how else to respond, Roger just gave the detective a half-grin.

"You military, Roger?"

"Why?" He asked. "Would it matter?"

"You just have that look is all."

"I was a Ranger," Roger continued. "The second battalion, 75th. We all were. Eight tours in Afghanistan."

"Excellent. I was a Marine myself," said Miles. "Back during Desert Storm."

"Am I in trouble here?" Asked Roger, believing the detective may be sizing him up.

"Should you be in trouble, Mister O'Neil?"

"Nope. I don't think so. Not when it's eight to four."

"Attacking a bunch of special ops guys isn't very smart on their part, anyway," The detective said. "Right?"

"Apparently not."

"Listen," Miles continued. "This man is a dangerous fugitive. Finding him is our number one priority."

"I understand," replied Roger, relieved that the detective didn't seem concerned about the prior day's effects.

"So, they have no doubt mistaken him for his brother," he said. "The way I see it, you guys could help us find both."

"How would we do that?" Roger asked.

"We'll link you up with the Marshals and some of our guys who are already on it," Miles stated. "That is if you are up for it."

"What about my family? They need protection."

"We can post some officers at your place twenty-four hours a day until the matter is resolved."

"Ok, good," said Roger. "And, what about that other thing I mentioned?"

"Well," said Miles, grinning back at him. "It was self-defense, right?"

"Right."

"Follow me, Roger," said Detective Miles, as he escorted him back to the front of the station.

"These your buddies?" He asked as Frank, Shane, Lamar, and Walter stood from their seats.

"Come on, guys," he continued. "Mister O'Neil will explain everything on the way, I'm sure."

Roger was sure that Walter would like to find his brother alive. He couldn't help but wonder to himself how the hell they ended up in the situation they were in.

Roger knew Walter was going to have a hard time buying it. He didn't trust cops. Roger was an attorney, and he didn't fully trust the police, either. But, it was the best deal they had. Still, Walter seemed extremely nervous about what they were getting ready to do. He had a criminal past that had remained buried for some time.

"I do my best to avoid the police," Walter said as they pulled out of the parking lot.

"He's your brother," replied Roger. "I know you guys aren't close. But, I don't think you want him dead. Plus, maybe we can kill two birds with one stone."

"Close? I haven't seen him in over thirty years. Knowing James, I assumed he would've been dead by now."

Livingston, Montana

The Marshals and State Police Officers were all waiting beside the road as Detective Miles, and the rest of the men came into view. Walter wasn't at all happy to see so many law enforcement officer's in one spot. But, he was keen to locate his brother if it meant that he could stop hiding and finally live his life in peace. As they exited the vehicles, Marshal Jones gave Walter a strange look.

"Hey Miles," Jones said, shaking his hand. "Who's this?"

"This man happens to be the subject's twin brother," he replied.

"You are shitting me!" Marshal Jones remarked.

"Nope. I couldn't make that up if I tried!"

"Who are the rest of you?" He asked.

"These guys are here to assist you. All former Army Rangers," Miles answered. "They recently had an unfortunate run-in with the Aryan Brotherhood."

"They are some nasty sons of bitches," added Roger.

"And, yet you somehow lived to tell us about it," Jones commented.

"Lived?" Frank boasted. "They didn't have a fucking chance."

"They tried to kill us and kidnap our friend here. We killed a bunch of them, but their leader got away," said Roger.

"Paul? Shit, you'd be doing us a favor."

"You know him?" Roger asked.

Marshal Jones leaned against the door of his car as he lit up a cigar.

"He's been on our radar for some time now," he said. "Gun-running and dope-selling. We've served federal search warrants on his house many times. Haven't been able to connect him to any of it. He has a solid network."

"That's one way of putting it."

There isn't a shortage of 'em around here," Jones continued. "Get rid of a few, and they'll find more to replace them. It's

unfortunate."

"Unfortunate, indeed."

The Marshal paused, momentarily glancing over at Walter, standing behind Roger and his friends.

"So, you're the brother, huh?"

"Yes, sir," Walter replied. "That's right."

"You think you might have any relevant information to help us catch him?"

"Sir," Walter added. "I will do anything for this to end. I'm tired of hiding because of him."

"I understand."

"So, look," the Marshal continued. "We don't normally enlist the help of civilians. However, you guys seem uniquely qualified to assist us. We do have the power to deputize. Is that something you'd be interested in?"

"Anything to finally resolve this so I can go back to my wife and kids," Roger answered. Believe me, after getting shot, I want them all as bad as you do."

"Are you all in agreement?" Jones asked.

"Yeah."

"Yep."

"Hell yeah," they said, almost simultaneously.

"Alright, then. I'll make it happen."

Walter may have had the one piece of information they needed to finally catch up to James, who'd remained a step ahead of them ever since he escaped from prison. However, it was old information. But, at present was the only thing he could recall, having not seen or spoken to his brother in three decades.

They had distant relatives over the border in Canada. James had always told Walter that if he ever were in trouble, that would be the one place he could hide. They were more or less delinquents, as far as he could remember. All he knew was that they lived somewhere in Saskatchewan, close to Grasslands National Park. Walter didn't know them. He didn't want to know them.

If James managed to sneak across the Canadian border, he would be much more tricky to find in that vast wilderness. Their best option, indeed, would be to capture him before he made it that far. They knew they needed to act fast before the weather made a shift for the worse.

CHAPTER 19
GETAWAY

Somewhere along the interstate

JAMES WAS LESS than ten miles from the search unit's location, trying to thumb a ride north. Hiding in the bushes at the side of the highway, he had seen the cars whistling by him with the sirens going as they raced toward where they believed him to be. He was good at deceiving law enforcement. But, the longer he remained exposed out there, the higher his risk of capture.

He knew he needed to get out of there as quickly as possible. Holding his thumb high in the air, James walked along the path at the side of the busy road as many vehicles passed him over. If he couldn't hitch out of there, he'd have to resort to stealing a car again. Even so, he would be ready to do whatever he had to to survive.

ANYTHING. It was in his nature. If the Aryan Brotherhood couldn't have him, neither could the cops, in his mind. Survival was his only concern.

After strolling along for what felt like an hour, at last, someone began to pull his truck over in front of James. It was an old, beat up looking semi-truck hauling an empty container. The driver hadn't been listening to news reports, because he acted as though James was just another random encounter on his travels. He had no idea that he just picked up a wanted man.

"Hey there," fella, the driver said as James climbed into the dirty cab.

"Hey mister," James replied. "Thanks for stopping."

"No problem, amigo," he retorted.

"Nobody would give me the time of day," continued James. "Like I'm a scary looking guy or something."

"Well, to be honest, mister, you are kind of scary looking," said the man, his fat belly rising as he chuckled. "I'm just playing, man. I'm Bill, by the way."

"James."

"Nice to meet you, James," said Bill.

"You too, partner," he replied with a half-smirk.

Privately, James was praying that Bill wouldn't find him out. If he did, things could go south very fast. If he could fake his way out of danger, that was what he was planning to do.

"So, where you headed, buddy?"

"North," James told him.

"Hmm, ok. Anything more specific?"

"Nope," he continued. "

"You must be running from an ex-wife or something, huh?" Asked Bill.

"Something like that."

"Alright, friend," Bill said. "Well, just lean back and enjoy the ride then."

James was hesitant to talk much or share any information with anyone. He would have to lie, regardless. The fewer people knew about him, the better off they, and James would be. As they made their way northbound, he spent the majority of that time staring through the side mirror and hoping he wouldn't notice anyone following closely behind them.

Miles and miles from the ones who were hunting for him, It seemed as though he was finally in the clear. But, then, Bill broke the silence by switching on his radio. As the sound of country music faded away, a news bulletin flashed across the speakers.

Fugitive, James Flanagan remains on the loose. He is seventy years old, long hair, with a scar down his cheek. He is presumed to be armed and dangerous. Citizens are advised to keep their doors and windows locked, and not to pick up hitchhikers. If you spot a man fitting this description, do not approach him. Dial 911 immediately. This is a message from your local law enforcement agency.

With his mouth wide open and a confused look across his face, Bill glanced back over at James and he knew the gig was up.

"Don't say a word, partner," James said, smoothly. "Just pretend you never heard that."

Bill, suddenly frozen in fear, locked his eyes onto the road.

"ok... sure," he said anxiously. "Whatever you say, mister."

They rode for a few more miles in complete quietness. Bill, in fear for his safety at that point, wasn't about to open any more dialogue with this man. It was his worst nightmare coming true. To him, the less he said, the better off he'd be. Until they noticed vehicles blocking the roadway up ahead.

"Shit," said James.

"Is that for you?" Bill asked.

"What do you think?"

James climbed into the sleeper and pulled the blanket up over his body.

"Just act natural, Bill, and it'll all work out for you," he said, peeking his head out from under the blanket. "You never saw me, understand? I know it's not the first time you've lied to the cops."

"Whatever you say, mister."

As the state patrolman waved the truck down, Bill began rolling down his window.

"How are you doing sir?" the officer asked.

"Doing alright, officer," replied Bill. "Just heading home."

"Where's home?"

"North," Bill answered, not knowing what else to say.

"North, huh?"

"Yes, sir."

"Well. We're stopping everyone coming through here," The trooper told Bill, holding up a mugshot of James. "Have you seen this man?"

"Um, no, officer," replied Bill. "I haven't seen anyone like that."

"You sure?"

"Yeah, I'm fairly sure," he answered. "I wouldn't forget a face like that."

"Well, if you do, please call this number," the trooper said as he handed Bill a card. "He's a bad man."

"Will do, sir."

"Alright. You have yourself a good day, now," the trooper said just before Bill rolled his window back up.

The troopers allowed Bill to proceed through the roadblock, and James slowly removed the blanket from over the top of him as they passed.

"Good boy, Bill," he said. "If I didn't know better, I would've thought you were an actor."

While they were heading toward the border, the search party was busy coming up with a plan. As they got ready to head out, police dispatch received a call that could completely change the course of the search. A Hispanic woman spotted a man fitting the police description of James getting into the semi.

The woman barely spoke English. But she was able to muster out the words "prison" and "police." The dispatcher on the other line had to run and get another employee who was fluent in Spanish and eventually deciphered what the woman was trying to tell her.

"They go north in an old, red semi-truck," the lady said in Spanish.

The dispatcher quickly notified her boss, who contacted state police, who then relayed the information to the Marshals. After numerous close calls, this could have been the one break they had been looking for if they could corner James before he was able to slip away again.

"I think I know exactly where they are going," Marshal Jones said as he hurried to his car. "Follow me."

Walter had no idea what he was going to do or say if and when they ever caught up to his brother. Their relationship was always complicated. They hadn't spoken in so long. James became the drunk, violent type after returning home from Vietnam, still picking fights in bars.

Walter, on the other hand, was trying to survive and wanted no part of it. They fought every time they were together. Eventually, he had left the family and went his own way. Walter had always preferred the isolated lifestyle, away from people.

He loved his brother, weirdly. But, he couldn't handle being around him anymore. Walter didn't want to get caught up in James' bullshit. Of course, he ended up being in the middle of it anyway. Having a twin brother wasn't easy, especially for a hot-headed guy like James.

Now, it was all coming back to haunt Walter in a big way. He was so pissed off at his brother for his predicament that he began to think that life would be more comfortable if he were dead. That was a harsh realization for anyone to come to terms with, especially a man like Walter.

As the convoy of vehicles sped up the interstate, Jones keyed his radio and called for a police helicopter to give them eyes in the sky. They desperately needed to find that vehicle before James found out that they were onto him and disappeared again. They may not get another shot.

Bill and James were now riding down the highway at seventy-five miles per hour. All seemed well and good until he heard a distinctive sound that he never wished to hear. It was the police chopper, and it was approaching fast from high above them.

"Shit!," He said. That ain't good!"

"What?" Bill asked, frantic. "What is it?"

James peered through the passenger side window at the helicopter following directly above them.

"Damn it!" He yelled, furiously. "They're right on us!"

The sun was beginning to go down as the chopper shined a bright spotlight right on top of the semi.

"What the hell did you do, mister?" Asked Bill.

"Nothing that concerns you," James replied. "Now just shut up and let me think!"

Pausing for a second to regain his senses, he grabbed bill by the arm.

"Get back there!" He shouted.

"What?"

James snatched the wheel from Bill's hands and began shoving him toward the sleeper.

"I said, get back there!" He continued, hopping into the driver's seat, swerving left and barely missing a passing car. "I'm driving!"

"Fine!" Bill said. "I'm going!"

"Come on. Focus, James," he said to himself as he took a deep breath.

The spotlight was following the vehicle precisely as he weaved around traffic, trying not to crash. James' eyes were becoming very distressed as he rubbed them with his sleeve. The law was closing in, and sooner or later he would run out of places to hide. But James was a capable guy. He wouldn't go down without a fight.

At that point in his life, he either ran, or he died. There frankly wasn't another alternative. If the Aryan Brotherhood were to catch him, it would be much worse than the police could ever do. That gang didn't just kill people.

They were barbaric and made them suffer. James didn't feel like dying a slow, agonizing death, which is what would have happened if he went back to prison.

He began to speed up, trying to lose the chopper. But there was no losing them in that thing. He needed to ditch that big target of a truck. James abruptly swerved into a cabin rental, slamming on the brakes and skidding to a halt underneath a tall overhang.

"See you, Bill!" He said as he hastily jumped from the cab and darted for the trees.

The helicopter light shined on him and followed him out of sight.

"I lost him in the woods," the pilot said over the radio. "I repeat, I have no visual."

The convoy of Marshals and state police pulled in minutes later, spotting the dirty red truck sitting idle next to the cabin office. As Marshal Jones approached the vehicle, pistol at the ready, he saw a frantic man come out with his hands up, shaking like a leaf. As Roger and the rest stood ready next to the Marshal's car, Walter couldn't help but stare at Bill, trying to understand what his brother made him do.

"That can't be good," he told Roger.

"Sir," Jones said to Bill, lowering his weapon. "Are

you alright?"

"I almost pissed my pants," stated Bill. "That man is crazy."

"Which way did he go?" Asked Jones.

"That way," Bill answered, pointing to the nearby wood-line.

"Ok, sir," said the Marshal. We'll need you to write a statement for us of what happened. Ok?"

"Yeah. Ok."

The Marshal escorted Bill to a waiting state patrol car sitting behind the truck and handed him off to Trooper Barry.

"Take his statement for me," Jones said.

"It's alright, sir," said Barry. "You're safe now. Just have a seat in my car, relax and write what you know."

"Ok, sure," replied Bill.

"And, call for reinforcements," the Marshal continued. "We need all the help we can get!"

"Yes sir," Barry replied, grabbing the radio receiver to call for reinforcements.

"Alright, men," Jones continued. "We have work to do. He's got a decent head start."

As he and the rest of the search party made their way toward the forest, Jones glanced back at Roger and his buddies.

"You guys coming?" He asked.

"Right behind you," Roger answered as they took their weapons from the back of Frank's truck.

"Let's go, boys," he said. "Let's find this bastard and finish this."

They followed the Marshal into the dark woodlands, Walter trailing close behind them.

"I don't like this one bit," Walter said to Roger.

"Just stay behind us," Roger replied. "You'll be ok."

"I don't think you understand," he continued. "My brother can be very unpredictable when he is cornered. These men have no idea how dangerous he is. I am worried they are going to get themselves killed."

Roger and his friends were the only guys in the group who had any military experience. The rest of the men had no clue of the danger they faced. James was willing to do whatever he had to do to make sure that he didn't go back to prison. ANYTHING.

He also knew that as long as the cops were trailing after him, Paul and his Aryan buddies would stay well away. For him, it was the lesser of two evils. All he cared about, at that point was survival. Nothing else mattered. James was oblivious that he was endangering his brother in the process.

They knew the Aryan's still wanted Walter. He would stick to Roger and his buddies like glue. They would soon realize, as if they hadn't already, how much farther they would be prepared to go to get to him.

CHAPTER 20

BROTHERS

Green Mountain, Montana

JAMES HAD BEEN SITTING in the bushes, doing what he did best. He wasn't trying to kill anyone, slow them down. It was an old, ambush tactic. He knew that if he injured one, it would stop them dead in their tracks. Hopefully, it would also buy him a little time to slip away, unseen. James had set up it up and moved away to a safe distance to wait for his plan to work. Under cover of night, he remained in cover and steadily anticipated their approach.

A half an hour later. Flashlights and low chatter in the background. They were moving straight up the trail, just as James had intended. As he listened and traced the movement of the bright lights, he overheard a woman's voice.

Female State Trooper Susan Anderson, by all accounts, was a rookie to the force. Short in stature, with blonde hair she had put up into a bun, had never pulled her service weapon on the job. She was slightly skittish, having never been involved in anything so dangerous before.

"Damn," James said to himself, not expecting a woman to be there.

No matter, his design was already in motion. Not willing to back out now, James anxiously waited as they moved in closer to his trap. Suddenly, James detected the unmistakable noise of someone tumbling over the rope. Anderson had fallen forward with incredible force, and the sharpened wooden spike thrust right into her right calf.

"Shit!" She screamed in pain as she doubled forward, blood dribbling down her leg and into her shoes, painting her socks a bright red.

"Help!"

"What the hell just happened?" Roger asked as he raced to her side.

"Damn it! Call EMS!" He continued, bending to assess the damage. "She's in a bad way over here!"

"Don't worry Anderson," he said. "You'll be ok."

"Easy for you to say!" She shouted in pain. You don't

have a fucking stick jammed into your leg!"

"Come on, guys," said Trooper Barry. "We need to get her out of here now."

While Barry and the other troopers began carrying Anderson out of the forest, Walter had a sorrowful expression on his face.

"Damn it, James," Walter uttered to himself as he hung his head toward the ground. "Why can't you just let it go?"

"What do you mean?" Jones asked, giving him a mystified look.

"What do I mean?" Walter added. "My brother is ex-Special Forces. He did black-ops for the government. He is trained to survive and elude people like you. That's what I mean."

"Oh. I see," replied the Marshal.

"The only people here who stand a chance against him are these boys standing beside you," he continued, pointing at Roger and buddies.

Walter's tone went from somber to bitter as he walked a few feet in front of the search party. He took a peek around through the branches sparkling underneath the moonlight, wondering exactly where his brother was, knowing he was somewhere nearby.

"James!" He yelled. "I know you can hear me! Why are you doing this?"

James was taken back by the old, familiar sound of that voice.

"What the? Walter?" He thought to himself. "What in the hell is he doing here?"

Walter was reasonably sure that James would never give up his position. But, it was worth a try.

"What in the hell are you doing?" Asked Jones.

"Trying to save your ass," he replied. "Nobody else needs to get hurt, brother. Just give yourself up!"

He was assured that James wouldn't go for it. Though, at that point, Walter had absolutely nothing else to lose. Except, of course, his life.

"Because of you, I'm being hunted!" He shouted at James. "Because they can't get to you, they are coming for me, asshole!"

That was the first time they'd ever seen Walter show his temper in that way. Roger was glad that it appeared he had finally had enough. James shook his head for a moment, trying to make sense of what his brother had just said. But, it made no sense to him. Walter was the last person he'd ever expected to show up out there.

"He's listening," Walter said, looking out through dreary backwoods.

"How do you know that?" Jones asked.

"I just know."

James didn't understand why Walter was involved in the first place. He never expected the Aryan Brotherhood to go after anyone, but him. But, he wasn't about to respond to him. Nor give up, as his brother pleaded for him to do. Instead, he dropped down to the ground, silently moving further away from them as the ambulance rolled in to evacuate Trooper Anderson.

He had all of the signs of a desperate man. James was intent on making it out of there, no matter what. Everyone was the enemy to him at that point, even his brother. Trusting people just wasn't an option for him anymore. If he had stayed in prison, James would have nowhere to hide. His worst fear was that the Aryan Brotherhood would kill him in his sleep. But, out there, he was king. The forest was his domain. The police would have a challenging time trying to beat him at his own game.

"You guys were special ops," the Marshal said to Roger. "You want to take point?"

"Be glad to," he replied, swinging his AR-15, slung on his back, around to the front of his body. "Right guys?"

"Damn straight," Frank commented.

"Hell yeah," said Shane.

"Let's do it," Lamar added.

Jones directed Roger, Frank, Shane, and Lamar to the front of the file.

"After you," he stated.

Roger led his men further down the trail in staggered formation, with Lamar taking upon the back.

"Look out for more traps," he urged them.

Walking guardedly down the forest path and shining their tactical lights against the frosted terrain, Trooper Barry heard something move behind the trees. He jumped backward, disturbed.

"What was that?" He asked.

"I think it was just an animal or something," Roger said. "Don't piss yourself just yet."

"Man, that's not funny," replied Barry. "I'm not an outdoorsy kind of guy."

What they didn't realize was that James had a plan. He was going to wait in the dense vegetation until they passed him by. Then, he'd double back the way he came and slip out, undetected. But, Roger was smarter than that. He knew by now that James was a tricky bastard. He held one hand up, halting the formation.

"Marshal," he called out in a whispering voice.

Jones stepped toward the front of the formation.

"I think we need to split up," Roger continued. "Half of us keep following this pathway. The boys and I will move back near the road in case he tries to escape that again."

"Good idea," said Jones.

"Come on, guys," he said, as they turned back toward the entrance to the trail.

"Let's hide in the bushes and wait," Lamar said.

"I hope this prick decides to come back," Frank mentioned. "I'll tackle his ass to the ground."

Although he was surely armed, James wouldn't kill unless he had to. If they backed him into a corner, though, he wouldn't hesitate to use force. However, James just wanted them to back off. The last time he lost his temper, he killed someone and ended up in prison. He'd been trying to turn his life around. But, conditions in that prison didn't exactly allow for that. Notably, when the guards turned a blind eye. Many of those prison officers were dirty, anyway.

James was making his way back to the highway truck stop. He remained, camouflaged, watching as they waited to spot him. If he were going to make it out of there, he'd need to subdue half of the search party or create a disturbance long enough to slip away. With the search unit only fifty yards from his location, James began poking around in the dark. Looking for something to use, he spotted a pile of trash a little further off the path.

"That should do it," he thought, removing the lighter from his pants pocket.

Reaching into the pile and finding a piece of dry cloth, he set it alight. Crawling further away from the impending flame, he waited in the vegetation for his plan to unfold.

Near the edge of the tree-line, Shane had noticed black smoke rising high against the full moonlight.

"You guys see that?" He asked them.

As Roger took a closer look, he could see the orange glow of flames growing higher.

"Shit," he continued. "Something isn't right."

"Yeah," Walter replied. "My brother isn't right."

"We got fire over here!" Roger shouted.

"Marshal," Barry said over his radio. "We have fire coming from the brush."

The remainder of the unit descended on the flames, looking for signs of James.

"Damn it," said Jones. "We need to call the fire department before this spreads!"

James moved slowly away from the unit, heading to

another opening just down the way from there. He made his way to a drainage ditch and spotted an old lady approaching her vehicle from the cabin site. The car was an old, rusty sedan, and didn't look like it would go very fast. Still, it was his only choice.

"Here's my chance," he told himself.

Desperate, James withdrew the handgun from his pants and approached her quietly from behind, pressing the barrel of the weapon to her back.

"Don't move," he said calmly.

"Oh my God," the woman said, frantically dropping her purse to the ground. "I don't have any money, mister, if that's what you're after."

"I don't want your money," said James. "I need your car."

"Take it, mister! It's not worth dying for!" she said. "Take it, please. The keys are in my bag."

As James escaped the scene, Roger heard the squealing tires from his position not far away.

"Oh, no!" Roger yelled. "You hear that?"

"Sure did," Frank remarked.

With the glow of fire truck lights coming into view, Roger and the rest of the party ran toward the highway just in time to catch a glimpse of the old car moving out of sight.

"It was a diversion," said Roger, glancing over at the poor old lady standing confused by the side of the highway. "I'm starting to think it would just be easier to kill this fucker!"

"Well," said Jones. "If this gets much worse, I may just give you boys the green light."

James was making the police look like fools. He had eluded them at every turn. But, he was running on borrowed time, and it was only a matter of time before the situation turned deadly.

"Let's go!" the Marshal shouted as they all dashed for the vehicles. "Come on! We need to hurry!"

As they scrambled down the dark roadway with the rest of the Marshals and troopers trailing behind, Jones shined his bright spotlight far ahead of them, searching for tail lights.

"Anybody see anything?" He asked them.

"Nope," replied Roger. "He probably got off somewhere."

"Damn it, man!" Said Jones. "I'm going to have a hard time explaining this to my boss!"

Marshal Jones could see his spotless record slowly slipping away from him. James was, by far, the most elusive, slippery fugitive he'd ever tracked. He was starting to believe that the only way they were going to end it would be to kill him. As a law enforcement officer, his primary responsibility was to uphold the law. But, if James kept wreaking havoc and threatening people across the state, he would leave them with no other choice.

As the men continued searching for the vehicle, the Marshal's cell phone started to ring.

"Shit," he said. "It's her."

"Who?" Asked Roger.

"My boss."

Answering the phone, he could hear the authority in her voice.

"Give me an update," she ordered.

Stacey Milton had been the director of the U.S. Marshals Service for a little over five years. At five-foot-eight, she was fairly tall for a woman. But, she could hang with the toughest of men. With a flawless service record, Milton commanded authority from everyone under her command. Nobody wanted to be on her wrong side. Jones understood that she would not be happy about the status of the case.

"He got away, madam director," Jones told her.

"What do you mean, he got away?"

"We had him, and he just slipped right through our grasp."

"We need to have a meeting," she continued. "I have some information about this case that I don't want to mention over the phone. Meet me at the Billings office at once."

"Yes, madam," he replied. " I'll be there as soon as I can."

Marshal Jones hung the phone up, tossing it onto the center console.

"Shit," he uttered.

"What do you think she wants?" Roger asked him.

"Whatever it is," he answered. "It can't be good."

Fearing the worst, he was slightly nervous about meeting with her. Usually, when the director called on him, it wasn't great news. As the supervisory Marshal in the field, this case was his responsibility. If he couldn't achieve the desired outcome, he had no idea how he was going to explain it to her.

Jones snatched the radio receiver from the center of his car, squeezing the call button.

"Guys. The director needs to see us," he said to the rest of the Marshals. "Follow me."

They left the state troopers to continue the search for

James, and went straight for the Billings field office, total-ly unsure about what they were getting ready to walk into.

CHAPTER 21
SOLUTION

Marshal Field Office, Billings, Montana

THE MARSHALS ENTERED the office, and Jones told Roger and his boys to wait for them in the lobby. He was nervous. Inhaling deeply, he and his subordinates headed through the double doors leading to the conference room. As they walked in, they spotted the director and another gentleman standing next to her.

"Hello, madam director," Jones said as he moved closer to the table.

"Hey, Jones," she replied. "So, I am guessing that you are wondering why I called you out of an operation."

"It crossed my mind, yes," he answered. "We are so close."

"Well, to put it bluntly," she said. "We have a

problem."

"I know we have a problem," Jones replied in a bitter voice. "We have a maniac running lose out there, and I'm in here."

"Take caution in your tone," she said. "This isn't my first rodeo, you know?"

"Sorry, madam director," he continued. "I'm just frustrated."

"I get it. I do," she told him. "Who are these other guys? What are they doing here?"

"It's complex," he said. "But, they are all former special ops guys. They can help us."

"Well," she said. "You might need them."

"What do you mean?"

"Just have a seat, would you?" She asked. "Something needs to be explained to you that they just brought to my attention."

The marshal took a seat at the conference room table as he glanced curiously at the mystery man standing silent behind the director. Then, he spoke.

"Hello, Marshal," he said. "My name is Joshua Durant. I am with another agency."

"Ok."

"I have specific knowledge of the man you are hunting," he added. "I felt obliged to fill you in on just who you are dealing with. It's on a need to know basis. You understand?"

Durant had the look of an old spook, quite possibly C.I.A. His mysterious persona was evident the more he talked. Jones gave Durant an odd look.

"No, I don't understand," said Jones. "We are doing what we do, chasing a fugitive. He's just another desperate jail breaker."

"Marshal. I don't believe you quite get what I am saying," continued Durant. "You wouldn't. Apart from the Army, his background is sealed. The man's own family doesn't even know about it. I was sent here by the United States Government for the sole purpose of informing you of who you are after."

Jones was surprised and speechless as he was waiting for mister Durant to continue.

"James is a dangerous man, Durant affirmed. "He was recruited by the C.I.A. straight out of Special Forces after the Vietnam War ended. He was an assassin, trained in killing and espionage. He may be old now. But, do not underestimate him. I am telling you this because I don't want anyone else to get hurt. You understand what I am saying now, Marshal?"

"I think so," said Jones.

In the lobby, Roger had been eavesdropping on their discussion through the conference room doors. He couldn't help but feel that the Marshals were in over their heads.

"What are they saying?" Asked Frank.

"Hard to make out," said Roger. "Something about James being a dangerous man."

"Dangerous?" He added. "We'll show him dangerous."

"All they need to do is just let us loose," Shane answered.

Roger pulled up a chair next to Lamar.

"I'll tell you what," Lamar said. "You give me a direct line of sight between me and the target, anywhere up to eight hundred meters, I'll put a bullet center mass of his chest."

"I worry that is what is going to happen," Walter said. "He isn't going to give up."

Back in the conference room, the Marshal, in a slight state of confusion, had been trying to take in all of the information that he'd just learned. He was starting to feel like he was a little out of his element. He'd never pursued a target like James before. He was beginning to figure out that treating him as if he were any other fugitive just wasn't in the cards, anymore. He wasn't just another guy.

"So, Now that you know, you need to be extremely careful," the director said. "The safety of you all, and the public is my main concern. If you have to kill him to end this, then do it."

"Yes, madam director," Jones replied.

"Marshal," Durant said. "You need to tread very carefully. He's not just another fugitive."

"Right."

"That is all, Jones," Director Milton continued. "You're dismissed."

"Yes, madam."

They met Roger and company, who were waiting impatiently in the hallway. Roger was concerned that the situation was going to end up killing Walter. He knew he couldn't save his brother. At that point, Roger didn't want to. He was so angry that he didn't care anymore. To Walter, James had a special place in hell for what he had put him through, unknowingly or not. He'd be dead if it weren't for Roger and his friends. Walter owed them a debt that he could never repay. Although he knew they didn't expect anything in return. It was the kind of men they were.

"So, what's the story?" Roger asked.

"Well, It isn't good," the Marshal told them.

"I guessed that much," continued Roger.

Has any of it been helpful? Roger just wanted it to end. He was tired of chasing this man all over the place and just wanted to be with his family. But, there would be no peace until the matter was laid to rest. They were in too deep. As they headed back to the car feeling less than confident, Marshal Jones was reasonably sure from everything he had just heard that James wouldn't go down without a fight. He was beyond doubt if they were going to catch him alive.

James was a survivalist. He knew how to live out in the wilderness. He had to live alone in the jungle for months at a time, surviving on food that he could catch or kill. A man like James was the most challenging kind of man to track. But, he was a lot older now, and not at all in the shape he used to be. Surely, Roger and his men could get the job done. After all, they were highly trained ex-Army Rangers, and pissed, nonetheless.

As they rode into the black night, silence filled the vehicle. Nobody had much to say. But, Roger was deep in thought. As soon as he got the chance, he and his boys would stop James forever. All they needed was the chance and one clean shot. He hadn't overlooked about the

Aryan Brotherhood either. That was a different matter. They still needed to deal with them. But, there was no way Paul and his guys would engage a group of law enforcement officer's out in the open. At least, they didn't think so.

Cruising down the open road, suddenly the Marshal got a radio call.

"Marshal," Barry said from the other end.

"Go for Jones."

"Sir," Barry added, standing next to a smoking car. "We found the stolen vehicle. It broke down at the foot of Red Lodge Mountain. He must have fled on foot from here."

"He went south?" Jones asked.

"Yes, sir," answered Barry. "Maybe he wasn't going for Canada, after all."

"Or, maybe he's just trying to confuse you," Walter added. "It's what he does."

"Copy that," Jones said to Barry. "Don't do anything until we get there. And, don't touch that vehicle. We're twenty minutes out. I'll fill you in when we arrive."

"10-4. We'll be here."

Red Lodge Mountain, Montana

"Which way did he go?" Jones asked as they pulled up beside Barry's patrol car.

"I have a witness who said she saw a man ditch this vehicle and run straight for the hills," said Barry

"Ok," Jones replied. "Wait here in case we need to call for backup."

"10-4."

While making their way toward the base of the mountain, Walter stopped Roger in his tracks.

"Holy shit," he said. "I think I know where he's going."

"How?"

"Well," Walter replied. "There's a place up there we used to go to when we were kids. I think it is still there."

Walter was convinced that James was heading to an old cabin at the top of the mountain. It was the epitome of the Montana wilderness. With rugged and steep rocky trails, the place was tough to navigate. James knew that, and he was undoubtedly using it to his advantage. Still, they were so close to catching him, or so they believed, that it wouldn't make sense to stop now.

Ok, Walter," said Roger. "You stay here with Trooper Barry. I don't want you there when the shit hits the fan."

"Mister O'Neil," said Jones. "Let's split up. You and your boys go around to the right. My men and I will take the left side."

"Roger," he replied. "I mean, 10-4."

"You guys have night vision?" Frank asked him.

"No," said Jones. "We have flashlights."

"He'll see you coming a mile away."

"I think we'll be ok," Jones answered.

"Alright. It's your head."

Pulling NVG's (night vision goggles) from their bags and mounting them over their heads, Roger and his buddies continued in a column up to the right side of the mountain, moving stealthily, as they had done so many times during combat. They were one unit, unlike the Marshal's. They were used to it. To them, it was as natural as breathing. As Rangers, they had trained repetitiously to the point of becoming a reflexive action.

Roger held a hand up and halted the four-man formation, trying to get a feel for their surroundings.

"What you got, boss?" asked Lamar.

"Nothing. Just checking," Roger said. "Let's keep moving."

As they continued up the hill, they could see the flashlights beaming from the Marshal's position a couple of hundred meters to the left of them.

"They are giving him a target to shoot at," Roger said. "Do they know what the word tactical means?"

"At least we can say we warned them," Shane added.

Further up the mountain, James had been lying in wait. He could see the glow of flashlights bouncing with every step as the Marshals made it closer to the top. Tired of playing around with these men, he glanced down the sites of his bolt-action rifle, aiming directly for the bright beam.

As Roger and his men nearly made it to the top, he could make out the outline of James' head through his night vision as he pointed his rifle at the search party.

"Marshal," he said into the radio. "You need to turn those flashlights off!"

But he wouldn't listen.

"We are almost there," Jones replied.

Roger knew that one of them was about to get shot.

James started squeezing the rifle trigger. At the very moment the round began to fly through the barrel, Roger fired a shot from his weapon straight into the window.

"Shit," James said to himself.

The bullet only missed his head by a centimeter as he quickly ducked below the window sill, not knowing exactly where the shot had originated. The Marshal's were not so lucky. Brian Harrison, a young rookie Marshal in his late twenties, had been struck in the side of his face.

"Damn it!" Roger shouted as they darted for the Marshal's position. But, it was too late for the young man, killed by a single .308 shot to the head.

"We told you to switch the flashlights off!" Roger told Jones.

"Who in the hell do you think you're talking to?" The Marshal asked. "You're not in charge here!"

"Neither are you!" Shouted Roger. "You just got your man here killed!"

"Let me be clear," said Jones. "If you guys are to be here you will follow my orders, no question. Got it?"

"Does that involve endangering lives, needlessly?" He asked. "You're dealing with a guy who has a lot more training than you do. We won't take part in any blunders."

"I'm not going to repeat myself," the Marshal reiterated.

"Fuck it," Roger told him. "Let's go, guys. We'll do this our way. At least we know how to stay alive."

"We can't allow vigilantes, Mister O'Neil!" The Marshal yelled as Roger, and his men parted ways with them. "I don't care who you are!"

But, they weren't listening. Roger knew they had a better chance of getting to him, anyway. He and the guys left the Marshals to deal with the evacuation of their dead colleague, as they advanced toward the cabin where James was holed up. They had the element of surprise since James couldn't see them in the pitch darkness. But, he wasn't about to stick around after that. As the men stacked on the cabin door, Roger pointed Frank to the front of the file.

"Do your thing, man," he said.

"Roger that," Frank replied as he positioned himself in front of the wooden door.

With a strong kick of his foot, the door jam broke and flung open with incredible force. The men entered, pointing weapons to clear the structure. But, James was nowhere in sight.

"Look," said Lamar, pointing to a back door that was left wide open. "He fled through there."

"Come on," Roger said. "Let's get this asshole."

Roger led the men out, following a set of boot prints in the snow.

"Looks like he went down the other side," he added.

They proceeded down the hill, searching up ahead for any sign of James in the distance. The breeze began to pick up, and shortly, those tracks would be much more difficult to follow.

"You guys see anything?" Roger asked.

"I don't see a damn thing," replied Frank.

"Hold up a second," said Shane. "I think I see something.

"Where?"

"Between those trees down there, about three hundred meters."

"Oh, yeah," Roger answered.

As he raised his rifle and pulled it tightly into his right shoulder, glancing through the night vision scope, Roger let a round go.

"I got him!" He said as he watched James clutching his left shoulder.

But, from that distance as the wind steadily blew from side to side, visibility was becoming an issue, and it was hard to tell exactly how bad it was.

"Come, on guys," Roger said. "Let's go!"

They ran straight for James' location. However, when they arrived, the only evidence they could find was a trickle of blood on the snow-white ground.

"Well, at least we know he's hurt now," Roger said.

"Wait for a second," said Frank. "There's a trail. It's

small, but it's there. You see it?"

"Yeah," he replied. "It leads that way."

They began to follow the trail of blood further down the mountain. But, as the men got closer to the roadway, suddenly, all signs of him just disappeared.

"What the hell?" Roger asked. "Where'd he go?"

"I hope he didn't hijack some poor bastard again," said Lamar.

"Don't worry," Roger told them. "We'll find him soon enough."

Just as fast as James appeared in the dark, he seemed to vanish just as quickly. But, at least they knew now that he was wounded. They would have to put off killing him for another day. But, everyone gets his due, eventually. It was just a matter of time.

CHAPTER 22

TORMENT

Outskirts of Bozeman, Montana

KATE AND THE CHILDREN had been stuck at home, worrying about Roger. With guards present on a rotating basis, she wasn't particularly concerned about anyone getting to them. But, they hadn't heard from him in over twenty-four hours, and it wasn't like him not to check in. She continually paced throughout the house, hoping and praying that he was alright. She wasn't the no news is good news type.

"Mommy," Emily said as she was eating her morning oatmeal. "When is daddy coming home?"

"Soon, baby," Kate told her. "Very soon. I hope."

"Are the bad men going to get him?"

"No, honey, " she reassured Emily, stroking her hair.

"Don't you worry about that."

In her mind, she wasn't very sure. But, she had children to think about. Her husband knew what he was doing. But, that didn't keep a loving wife from a feeling of uncertainty. She had been worried sick ever since they left the cabin. Still, she believed in Roger. He'd been through far worse before. She knew that he would do it all over again to keep his family safe. And, she loved him for that. It was that stubbornness and unwillingness to quit that kept him alive in Afghanistan.

Finally, as she sipped her morning coffee, the phone began to ring. Kate hastily set her cup down, knocking it over and spilling half of its contents on the table while bustling to pick it up.

"Roger?" She answered anxiously. "Please, tell me it's you."

"Hey, honey," he said.

"Oh, thank God. We were so worried. I was about to call the damn hospital!"

"We're fine," he told her. "Just drained. The boys send their regards."

"I heard some stuff on the news," she added. "I couldn't sleep at all."

"Don't worry about what you see on TV," Roger told

her. "Trust me. It's nothing we can't handle."

"Alright, honey."

All of a sudden, Kate overheard one of the guards arguing with someone outside.

"Babe? Who is that?" Roger asked.

"I'm not sure," she replied. "Sounds like a couple of the deputies."

"Oh, ok."

While Roger thought of anything else to say to comfort his wife, a popping noise came from the direction of the front door of the large home.

"Kate. What was that?" Roger asked.

She glanced to her left, and, almost as if in slow motion to her, a single guard who had been watching the front of the house fell back against the door and onto the hardwood floor, a single gunshot wound to his forehead.

"Oh, no!" Kate said as her grip loosened, dropping the phone to the floor.

"Kate?" What's going on?" Roger asked. "Kate!"

But, there was no answer. Instead, the other end fell entirely silent.

"Shit!" yelled Roger, slamming his phone down on the counter.

"What is it?" Asked Frank. "What's wrong?"

"Its Kate! I think they're in trouble!"

Roger, in fear for his family's safety, continuously attempted to call her back. But it was no use. The call wouldn't go through.

BACK AT THE HOUSE, Kate was shaking as she hid behind the china cabinet in the dining room. Suddenly, two more shots came from somewhere out in the yard.

"This can't be happening," she mumbled, scared.

Stepping over the dead man's body and making her way to the kid's bedrooms, she began ushering them into the enormous walk-in closet in the master bedroom.

"Come on, kids," she said. "Come on. Let's go!"

"Mom? What is it?" Asked Patrick. "What was that noise?"

"Just get in here, now," she told them. "Hurry!"

"Mom," Emily called out as Kate shoved them behind a tall rack of hanging clothes. "You're scaring us!"

"Just stay right here," she said. "Stay here and don't make a sound. I'll be back to get you."

"Mom. What is it?" Patrick asked. "Are you going to tell us what's wrong?"

"Just do it!"

Kate turned the light off and quietly shut the closet door before tip-toeing her way back toward the hallway that led to the front, where the main entrance had been left standing wide open by the fallen deputy. As she took cover behind the wall, still wearing her nightgown, she took a peek through the window just in time to see another slain officer lying face down in the snow.

"Oh my God," she uttered. "Get yourself together, Kate."

One more glimpse through the glass, and she spotted three unidentified men wearing black balaclavas on their heads and walking up the sidewalk toward the front porch.

"Come on, Kate."

Before they could make it to the entrance to the house, she snatched a hardcover book from her bookshelf and brought it down to her side.

"Ok, Kate. Ok," she said to herself. "You can do this."

As the first man reached the doorway, Kate brought the book behind her back and then swung it forward as hard as she possibly could.

"Take this!" She balked.

But, the man spotted the book just before it reached his face and quickly grabbed her by the arm.

"Oh, no, you don't!" He shouted, forcing her hands behind her in a violent struggle as the other two men laughed. "You're coming with us!"

They forced Kate into the living room and onto a wooden dining room chair they brought into the center of the room.

"You're staying right here!" He said, shoving her down and binding her arms and legs to the chair with a piece of rope. "You Bitch! Where is your husband at now, huh?"

"When he gets here, he's going to kill all of you!"

"I'm just so frightened," The man said to his buddies as they laughed at her. "Don't I look like I'm shaking?"

"Yeah, boss," another man said. "Real scared."

"But, you see," he continued. "This is payback now. Your Ranger, pansy ass of a husband just had to play the hero. Now, he's gotta deal with the consequences."

The man knelt in front of Kate, stroking her hair and slightly pulling down her nightgown to expose the top of her breasts.

"Too bad he ain't here, though," the man said. "This is going to be fun."

"Get your grubby hands off me!" She screamed.

"Oh, no," he added. "I can't do that. I'm taking full advantage of this situation."

"What do you want from us, asshole?"

"Asshole? That's no way to treat a guest," he said,

slapping her with an open hand across the right side of her face and leaving a red hand print on her cheek. "You know what we want, Mrs. O'Neil."

As Kate held her palm against her face, she began to struggle in her chair, trying to break free.

"It's no use," he told her. "I got 'em on nice and tight. You ain't going anywhere."

"What did you do to the guards?" She asked.

But, the unknown man behind the mask just laughed at her.

"I think you should be more concerned with what we're going to do to you, Mrs. O'Neil."

He paused for a moment to take a glance around the room.

"Find those kids and get them in here!" He said to the others.

"Right boss."

"No, please," Kate pleaded. "Leave my kids out of this. They are innocent children!"

"Sorry. Can't do that."

The men began searching through the house, one room at a time, starting with their bedrooms. They went through Emily's room, peering into the closet and underneath her bed.

"Come out, come out wherever you are," one of them said.

They continued into Patrick's room, repeating the same process. But, the kids were nowhere in sight.

"Come on. I know you're here."

They advanced down the hall and into the master bedroom, looking around the room and the spacious bathroom.

"Where in the hell are they?"

"No idea."

But then, one of the men heard a slight noise.

"Hey," he said, pointing at the walk-in closet. "I think it came from in there."

They progressed toward the closet door, and one of the men began to turn the doorknob slowly. As he opened it, they peeked down to the floor and noticed two sets of sneakers sticking out from under a row of hanging clothes. Looking at each other, they prepared to yank them both out.

"Gotcha!" One of them yelled as they grabbed both children by the feet and began dragging them, kicking and screaming from the closet and across the bedroom floor to the hallway.

"Where are you taking us?" A terrified Patrick asked. "What have you done with our mom?"

"Shut up, you little brat!" One man said. "You and your sis are going to join her right now."

Pulling the children into the living room, they shoved them both down into chairs and tied them up right beside their mother.

"Now," the man said. "One big happy family."

"Except for one," another said.

"Yeah," he continued. That reminds me."

The man picked Kate's cell phone from the living room floor and turned it back on.

"Now, this is what you are going to do, Mrs. O'Neil," he told her. "You are going to call your husband. You are going to tell him to hand Walter over. If he doesn't, things are going to get much worse for you, I promise."

He untied Kate's right arm and handed the phone over to her. She was so scared and nervous at that point that her fingers were barely able to remain still long enough to dial a number. Somehow she managed to hit the final digit.

"Put it on speaker," the man ordered her as all three men stood in front of them, pistols in hand.

Kate hit the speaker button just as the phone began to

ring. She wasn't entirely sure what she would say once Roger picked up the call. More importantly, Kate wasn't positive of what Roger would do once he found out what was happening. But, if she knew her husband, he was almost certainly already on his way. She knew that these guys had no clue of what they were getting into.

Roger was one in a long line of war heroes. He and his buddies had seen enough combat to last for an entire lifetime. If they wouldn't be intimidated or defeated by the Taliban or al-Qaeda, they sure as hell weren't going to give in to a bunch of white supremacist NAZI's. Paul was the target. He would pay for what he has done to this family. As far as Roger was concerned, his fate was absolute.

"Hello? Kate?" Roger answered as they scrambled for the home in Frank's pickup. "You guys, ok?"

"Listen to me carefully, honey," she replied. "They have us."

Right at that moment, with a lump lingering in the back of his throat, it seemed as though Roger's worst nightmare had come true. At that instance, he began to regret the decision he had made to help a man in need. Not bothering to ask Kate who she was talking about; he already knew.

"Have they hurt you?"

"No," she replied. "But, we're tied up in the living room."

"What about the guards?" Asked Roger.

"They're all... dead!" She cried out.

"Enough of this shit!" The man shouted, snatching the phone from Kate's hand and switching the speaker off. "Either you give us Walter, mister O'Neil, or we're going to start having some fun over here. Starting with your beautiful daughter!"

"You lay a hand on her," Roger yelled into the phone. "And, I swear to God, I will cut your damn balls off myself!"

"Bring it on, partner," the man said as he and his buddies laughed at them.

"This is war, now!" Roger told him. "You will regret ever going near my family, shit head. That's a promise!"

The man didn't respond. Instead, he threw the phone against the hardwood floor, busting it into pieces.

"Damn it! That husband of yours is barking up the wrong tree," he said to Kate.

"You won't be talking anymore when he shoots you right between your beady eyes!" She said."Asshole!"

As he and the boys whizzed down the road as fast as

Frank's pickup would take them, Roger began loading his rifle with hollow-point ammunition. This time, Paul's men made a colossal error. Going after his family was the only excuse he needed to go to war. This time, it was personal.

CHAPTER 23

THIS IS WAR

AS THE TRUCK CAME to a standstill next to a wooded area beside Roger's property And hidden out of view from the house, the men hopped out and expeditiously made their way into the trees, trying to come up with a plan of attack. With Walter hidden in the back, they weren't too worried about anyone spotting him from the large timber frame home.

Lamar, with his bolt-action, .338 sniper rifle in hand, noticed a hill just across the road and within five-hundred meters of the front door. With a good vantage point and the ability to see through the large windows in the front of the house, it should be an excellent spot for a skilled sniper to lie-in-wait.

"I could get in position over there and provide overwatch," said Lamar. "It's got a direct line-of-sight to the front of the house."

"Yeah," Roger replied. "That's a good spot. Move along the ditch, so they don't spot you."

"Roger that," he said, putting in his earpiece and cocking the long gun as he withdrew across the snow-covered road and into the drainage ditch on the other side.

"Radio check. You guys reading me?" He asked over the radio."

"Lima-Charlie" (Loud and clear), said Frank.

"Roger," Lamar replied as he low-crawled up the frosty embankment.

Flipping the bipod open and resting it on the ground, he brought the butt of the rifle firmly into his shoulder and glanced through the twenty-four power, variable scope.

He zoomed his scope, pointing it straight for the living room window.

"Where you at, asshole?" He said to himself.

Spotting Kate sitting in the center of the room, one of the men entered his field of view.

"What you got, Lamar?" Roger asked over the radio.

"I see them,' he replied. I have one guy standing over Kate."

Lamar closed his dominant eye and gazed back through the glass.

"Wait," he continued, as the other men came into view. "I got three men standing by them in the living room. It looks like one of 'em is harassing her pretty good."

"Fuck," Roger said. "Alright. Frank and I will take the side door. Shane, you go around the back of the house just in case they decide to run."

"You got it, boss," Shane answered as he peeled away through the trees and toward the back of the property.

"Lamar. If you get a shot, take it," Roger told him over the radio. "Let's punish these fucking pricks."

"Roger that," said Lamar. "One shot, one kill."

While Lamar maintained his overwatch position, Roger and Frank got down low to the ground and made their way to the side door of the spacious home. Roger was in a hurry to get inside the house and free his family. But, he also knew that trying to rush through could lead to mistakes and put his loved ones in even further danger.

As he and Frank reached the door, Roger radioed back to Lamar.

"Alright, man," he whispered. "What you got in the scope?"

"I still see three men," he replied. "If you guys can

sneak up on the other two, I'll keep the glass trained on the one behind Kate. When he makes a move, I'll drop him."

"Roger," he answered. "But, wait until you see us before squeezing that trigger. Too soon and they might hurt them before we can get there."

Roger and Frank hung their AR-15's, removed their handguns from the holsters, and prepared to enter. Meanwhile, Shane was in the back of the house, waiting on word to make his move.

He had done this so many times before. Kicking in doors was Roger's occupation. Sadly, it momentarily reminded him of his last mission as a Ranger.

HE AND HIS RANGER unit were part of a joint task force sent to the outskirts of Jalalabad, Afghanistan to rescue a group of supply soldiers who'd been taken hostage by members of the Taliban while driving their convoy through a Taliban friendly village.

Roger and his squad were the first ones to reach the door of the compound. Some members of that unit were killed in the ambush. But, three of them were held in some underground area that looked like the remnants of an old jail cell. They were no doubt getting prepared to torture them. Roger and the others could hear the screams coming through the large, steel door. They weren't a combat unit. They didn't have much of a chance against a large group of heavily armed Taliban fighters.

Unfortunately, they were only able to save two of the three hostages. That mission had an eerie comparison to the Jessica Lynch story so many years before. It was that day that Roger swore to himself that he would never allow the evil to prey on the weak as long as he could do something about it. Still, he never predicted in a million years that it would be his own family that needed saving.

"You ready?" Roger asked Frank.

"Always," he replied. "Let's do it."

"Lamar," Roger called out over the radio. "We're going in."

"Roger that," said Lamar. "I got eyes on."

"Shane," Roger added. "On my mark. Ready, go."

Roger began slowly turning the doorknob as he and Frank slipped silently into the long hallway that led to the living room on the other side of the house. As both men hugged opposite walls, they continued slowly down the corridor, sticking to the shadows. Simultaneously, Shane had taken cover behind a large bookcase, waiting for the two to make their move.

While progressing gradually toward where his family

was located, Roger began to hear one of the men shouting.

"We're going to have a little fun with you!" The man said to Kate. "A pretty thing like you needs a real man, anyway."

"Go to hell!" She yelled back at him.

"Oh, no," he added. Your husband is the one who's in hell. But, you won't have to worry about that for much longer!"

"Fuck," Roger said silently with his mouth, not wanting to make their presence known just yet."

He quickly glanced over at Frank and gave him the Rangers well-known hand signal to hurry.

With weapons pointing forward, the two advanced to the end of the long hall and rushed around the corner as Shane followed behind them, aiming guns directly at the three men standing over the family.

"Don't fucking move," Roger told them. "You piece of shit."

"Well, there you are," one of them said. "We've been waiting for you."

Roger pointed his .40 caliber handgun straight for the man's head.

"You know you are about to die, right?" Roger asked.

"What is this?" The man asked laughing. "Gunfight at the OK Corral?"

But, then, in a split-second, he grabbed Kate around her throat, the barrel of his gun pressed hard against her temple.

"What you going to do now, Mr. Ranger man?"

"I swear, if you don't let her go, I'll kill every last one of you bastards!"

"Doesn't seem to me that you are in a position to do much of anything right now," the man said.

At the same time, Lamar had been watching the events unfold through his rifle scope, hundreds of meters away. He was following the man's every movement, waiting for the right moment to squeeze the trigger.

"Come on, asshole," he said to himself. "Just give me one clean shot."

Roger could hear him over the radio, and moved out of the way of Lamar's line of sight, glancing through the window to the hillside far across the snow-covered road.

"What are you looking at?" The Brotherhood member asked him.

As the man glared back through the window for a brief second, gun still pointing toward Kate, Lamar saw his chance.

"That's it," he said. "Perfect."

Lamar positioned his reticle right over the man's forehead, squeezing the trigger with dead-on accuracy. As the round was sent hurling forward at 3,300 feet per second, it shattered the high window glass and entered the man's head with devastating force, silencing him forever.

"One more dead racist," Lamar said.

As the other two men watched their buddy fall to the floor, they quickly brought their guns up. But, not before Roger and Frank sent bullets flying into their torsos, causing them to double back, blood splatter littering the log wall behind them.

Roger, Frank, and Shane hurried to free Roger's family from the ropes.

"You guys, ok?" Roger asked as he wrapped his arms around all three of them.

"We're fine," answered Kate, a tear rolling down her cheek. "I thought they were going to rape me."

"It's ok babe," he said, squeezing them tighter. "You guys are ok now."

As Lamar slid the bolt of his weapon and flicked the safety, he spotted an old, rusty pickup speeding down the white road toward Roger's house and slipping to a standstill at the beginning of the driveway a couple of hundred meters away.

"Guys," he said into his headset. "We have a problem."

"What is it?" Roger asked.

"I count eight more guys, and they are coming your way with AK's!"

"Shit," Roger said as he glanced through the broken window. "Let's get them out of here!"

"I guess this fight ain't over yet!" Shouted Frank. "Just like Afghanistan!"

"I guess not!"

Roger handed his family off for Shane to escort them downstairs.

"Get them down there, lock the door, and meet us back up here!"

"Roger, boss," Shane replied as he hurried the family down into the basement.

"Lamar," Roger called out. "Is Paul out there?"

"I don't see him," he said. "But they're moving to you pretty fast."

"Damn it. He sends his cronies to do his fucking dirty work."

Roger and Frank locked all of the doors to the home and met back up in the living room area. As Shane made his way back upstairs, Roger stopped him.

"Take up a position near the back door," he told him. "We'll cover up here."

"Roger."

As Roger and Frank took cover behind the living room walls, they could hear the sound of footsteps walking onto the front porch. Lamar, still on the hillside, repositioned his rifle and aimed.

"Mister O'Neil!" One of the men yelled. "We are here for you!"

"Oh yeah?" Said, Roger. "Your buddies here didn't have any luck. What makes you think you assholes will?"

While the two were bantering back and forth, Lamar was going through his tactical breathing, as he had done so many times in combat.

"Get ready for a gunfight," he said into the radio. "I'm taking the shot."

He steadied his scope on the one who was arguing with Roger. Upon squeezing the trigger, the round penetrated the man's chest, exiting his body and leaving a gaping, bloody wound on the other side. The force of the blast threw him against the wall and dropped him straight to the ground.

Suddenly, half of the men began shooting toward the hillside, Lamar rolling onto the other side of the mound.

The other half started sending bullets into the wooden walls at the front of the house and the living room.

"Get down!" Roger said as he and Frank dove for cover behind the large sofa in the middle of the room.

Shane, with quick thinking, exited through the back door, peeking around the corner and popped a shot off with his rifle to draw their fire away from the two. As he turned around, the men began chasing after him, just as he had hoped. While they had time, Roger and Frank jumped from the floor and headed through the front door to back Shane up.

Shane took cover behind the outbuilding, firing at the men as they positioned themselves behind a row of trees. Just in time, Roger and Frank came around the side of the house and began shooting into the gaggle of men, dropping four of them.

"Damn, that was ballsy!" He shouted to Shane.

"You're welcome!" Shane yelled back at them.

The rest of the gang members ran into the forest, with Roger and his friends commencing the chase.

"Come on," said Roger. "We can't let those bastards get away!"

All three of the men dashed through the timber, trying to close in on them.

"They are running back toward the road!" Frank said.

But, before they could catch up to them, Roger heard an engine start. The group of men had gotten back into their truck and were peeling off back down the icy road.

"Guys," Lamar said as he was trying to get a decent shot on the moving truck. "We have a real problem over here!"

"What?" Roger asked.

Another one came out of the woods and snatched Walter!"

"Say that again," he said.

"They got Walter. They just dragged him out of the truck!"

The lone man had come running from the trees, snatching Walter and tossing him into the back and jumping into the bed of the slowly moving pickup as it increased speed and got away. Lamar, following the vehicle through his rifle scope, managed to get a shot off and busted the rear windshield glass as they fled the scene.

"Watch out!" Roger said. "You don't want to hit Walter!"

As Roger, Frank, and Shane made it to where the driveway met the road, they caught the tail lights of the old truck as it went around the corner and out of sight.

"Damn it!" Roger screamed as he punched his mailbox. "We have to save him!"

"We will," said Frank. "Come on. You need to go check on your family."

"Sorry, man," Lamar said as he crossed the road to meet them. "Don't worry. We'll bring hell raining down on those skinhead bastards. It isn't over by a long shot."

"You got that right," Roger replied, staring profoundly down the winding road. "Every last one of them will die."

CHAPTER 24

RETRIBUTION

ROGER WAS WAITING by the road when the bright, swirling lights of police cars came zooming around the bend. He hadn't wanted to call them. And, he wouldn't have if his wife hadn't urged him to. She didn't want her husband to be some angry vigilante. But, he didn't care.

The cops weren't able to defend his loved ones against a group of insane, murderous gang members. Although, it seemed that Roger and the guys weren't able to keep them from kidnapping Walter, either. Perhaps his focus was on saving his family. It was understandable. Still, they were faced with a severe problem that they needed to find a solution for quickly. Roger didn't believe that Walter's frail body could survive the torture. That was almost surely what they had planned for him.

As the multiple Montana State Police cars and an ambulance pulled into the long driveway to Roger's home, he spotted Trooper Tillman sitting in the driver's seat of the first vehicle.

"Anything left for us, Mister O'Neil?" Tillman asked as he braked next to Roger. "The Marshals briefed me over the phone about the situation after I got the radio call."

"Just bodies," he replied. "But, they killed the four deputies before we got here."

"And your family are all ok?"

"Yeah," said Roger. "Thankfully, we got here in time. Bastards were going to rape my wife in front of my children."

"I'm so sorry to hear that, Mister O'Neil," Tillman added. These assholes are a blight on civilized society. They'll get their due, soon enough."

"Oh, for sure they will," Roger answered. "Very soon."

Of course, he wasn't referring to the police. Roger deliberately withheld Walter's name. They weren't the ones who were going to be going after the Aryan Brotherhood. Roger and his friends would take that responsibility. They were the only ones who stood a chance against them. Secretly, he believed that the police knew that. He figured it was the only reason why the cops weren't standing in their way. Nonetheless, they preferred it that way. If they could rid Montana of a massive drain on society in the process, then, so be it.

While EMS personnel removed the dead bodies from the scene, Roger retreated into the home to check on his family. He knew they were still pretty shaken up by the experience. Roger would comfort them any way that he could. Though he also needed to get them out of there soon, just in case they decided to show back up there after eliminating so many of their men. Given the opportunity, they would kill many more, the recoil of their rifles being the only thing they felt when sending those Aryan bastards to hell.

"Honey," Roger said as he embraced his wife softly. "You sure you guys are ok?"

"Yeah," she replied. "But, I can't get that man's evil eyes out of my mind! If you hadn't shown up when you did, I don't know what would have happened."

"It's over," he continued. "It's all over now. We need to get you guys far away from here. The sooner, the better."

"What about you?"

"Don't you worry about us," he told her. "We'll be fine. But, we have work to do before we can put this to rest."

Roger was sitting next to her on the sofa when Trooper Tillman approached them from behind.

"We need to get you guys out of here," he said. "This is a crime scene now, and we need to rope it off."

"Ok," replied Roger. "Let's go, guys."

As he, the family, and the boys proceeded to step outside to let the investigators do their work, Tillman pulled Roger to the side.

"Come here for a second," he said. "I need to talk to you."

"Alright," Roger answered as they walked to the side of the drive. "What's up?

"Well, I just got off the phone with one of my contacts who know the Aryan Brotherhood in this area pretty well."

"Ok," said Roger. "And?"

"He's a police informant who has helped us to put away some pretty bad people."

"Ok."

"And, we believe now that we know where they have taken your friend," Tillman added. "There is a particular place, pretty remote, where they like taking guys who, we believe they like to torture to death."

"Fuck!" Roger said.

"My thought's exactly, Mister O'Neil."

"You going to tell me where it is?"

"Well," Tillman continued. "It's better if I show you. Let's go to my car. I have a map."

Roger waved his hand for his buddies to come over, and they followed the Trooper to his vehicle. It seemed to him that the police were now basically giving them the green light to wreak havoc on the Brotherhood. Not that they were waiting for their blessing, in the first place. But, at the very least, it meant that the authorities were not going to interfere.

Roger eyeballed Frank as Tillman snagged a Montana State Map from his glove box and laid it out across the hood of the car.

"Ok. We are here," the trooper said, marking a spot just outside of the city limits of Bozeman.

"Yep," replied Roger.

"And, the place where we think they have taken him is right outside of here," he added, pointing to the town of Whitehall, Montana.

"There is an abandoned factory just outside of town and hidden from the road right about here," he continued. "We've had problems with drug making and gun-running taking place from there. That is most likely where he is."

"Well," Roger said. "Thanks for the info."

"Also," the trooper added. "We have arranged for your family to be put into a federal protection program until it is ok for them to return home."

"You can promise me they are going to be safe this time?"

"Don't you worry about that anymore, Mister O'Neil. They'll be in a safe house far away from here until then. They'll have rotating guards and twenty-four-hour surveillance. Won't be local deputies this time. Nobody will get to them."

"If something happens, I know where to find you," Roger told him, grinning.

He gave his wife and kids a goodbye kiss as they climbed into the back of the trooper's squad car, hoping they would finally be together for good, shortly.

"Be good, guys," he said to his children as he watched them Begin to roll away.

"You sure you guys don't need help?" Tillman asked through the driver's side window.

"I promise you, buddy," Roger answered. "Us is all we need. Too many people and they'll see us coming."

"Ok. Just be careful. Those guys don't care who they

hurt."

Roger watched as Kate blew him a scared kiss while backing through half a foot of snow and out to the road. It was apparent that she was fearful for him. But, there was no backing out now. They were in it too deep. Putting his family in danger was not something Roger was willing to let go. With his team standing by his side, he would walk right through hell.

Observing the car as it moved out of sight, he had a unique feeling come over him. The guys needed to make a beeline for that place before those delinquents had a chance to hurt him seriously. Roger hoped, for Walter's sake, that Tillman was right. With speed and enough luck, they would be able to get there in time.

Whitehall, Montana

The truck rolled to a stop in front of a pathway that was barely visible from the road. It was pretty evident that it hadn't been used for its intended purpose in years. High vegetation and low hanging tree branches littered the trail as far as they could see. The only sign of use was a set of freshly made tire tracks that had compacted the mountain of snow covering it.

"You see that?" Asked Frank.

"Yep," replied Roger. "Let's park this thing out of sight and grab our stuff. I don't want anyone to notice it."

Frank slowly moved the vehicle into cover within the densely wooded area, put it into park, and shut the engine off.

"Guys, we need to be very careful," Roger urged them as they got their rifles ready for action. "If he is here, and they notice us coming, Walter is as good as dead."

"You got it, boss," said Frank.

Roger loaded a fresh magazine into his AR-15 and handgun and hopped out of the truck, slipping the pistol back into its holster. As the boys covered the bed of the vehicle with fallen limbs and forest debris to camouflage it somewhat from the road, they decided to wait for nightfall to advance on the building.

As they sat in the bushes, monitoring the building from a reasonable distance, Roger felt like they didn't have a lot of time. He knew Paul. Roger knew how the man operated. He wasn't what one would call level-headed, as most criminals are not. But, this was different — a more cutthroat and savage son of a bitch he never had seen.

The men hunkered down in the snow, sitting quietly among the brush and waiting for night to fall.

Thirty minutes later

THE SUN HAD SLOWLY disappeared beneath the vast, forest landscape. Roger swiped his tactical binoculars from the front pocket of his camouflage coat, and they advanced toward the edge of the woods to recon the old factory. It seemed as if the place was deserted, except for tire tracks that led directly to a large, sliding metal door at the front of the site.

"What do you see?" Lamar asked.

"Just tracks," replied Roger. "They must be inside."

Lamar aimed his sniper rifle toward the building and peeked through the night vision scope. As he raised it higher, he noticed movement coming from the top of the metal steps that led to a rooftop platform.

"Wait," he said. "I got something. Somebody's up there."

Roger glanced through his binoculars once more while Lamar screwed a suppressor to the tip of his twenty-six inch .338 rifle barrel.

"I see 'em," Roger said. "Don't do anything just yet. Let's see where he goes."

"I want 'em, boss," Lamar stated. "I want 'em bad."

"I know, man," Roger answered. "I know. You'll get your chance."

Watching the man begin to move toward the steps that led to the ground below, the men started to inch forward under cover of darkness.

"Come on," said Roger. "Let's move."

They followed the tree line going around to the other side of the structure, as quiet as a mouse but as vigilant as an Eagle, until they reached a spot that faced directly toward the bottom of the stairs.

"Here he comes," Roger whispered. "Lamar. He's yours."

"Roger that," Lamar replied, pulling a .40 caliber, suppressed pistol from his side.

He sat, patiently waiting for the guy to get within a decent range. Pointing the handgun, Lamar squeezed the trigger, and the bullet flew forward with enormous velocity, piercing the man in the center of his chest and sending him tumbling down the remaining steps to the snow-covered ground below.

"Got him," said Lamar. "That's one down."

He made his way to the man's body, pulling him by the arms into cover behind the nearby trees.

"He was guarding something up there," Shane said.

Frank pointed the night vision optic on the top of his weapon toward the very top of the abandoned factory.

"You're right," he answered. "I think there's an entrance up top."

"That may be our way in," Roger added. "Follow me and stay low."

The team moved forward and up the metal staircase in column formation, With Shane taking up the rear of the file. As they reached a single door on the top of the platform, Roger gripped the doorknob and attempted to turn it slowly.

"It's unlocked," he said. "We're good. Move on me and stay close."

The men entered the building and crouched, weapons at the ready, moving along the second-floor scaffold at a snail's pace. Glancing down, Frank spotted four men below them, wearing masks on their faces.

"Holy shit," said Frank.

"Looks like the trooper was right," Lamar whispered. "This must be where they're making the drugs."

"Yeah," replied Roger. "But, I don't see Walter."

As the men continued forward toward the steps that led below, a loud noise came from the front of the building.

"What was that?" Asked Shane.

"Shit. Someone's coming," Roger continued as the big

metal door slid open, and another truck entered the premises.

"It's Paul," he added, staring into the cab of the vehicle.

"We should kill that racist bastard right fucking now," Lamar stated.

"We can't," replied Roger. "At least, not until we find out where they are keeping him. If we shoot now, we'll probably never find him."

As Paul and three of his men got out of the vehicle, they approached another group standing within earshot directly below Roger and his buddies.

"Shh," said Roger," holding a finger to his mouth and pointing down below as they hid in the shadows.

He was trying to listen in on the conversation that was happening beneath them.

"Has he talked yet?" Paul asked one of them.

"No, sir. But, he will. It's only a matter of time."

"You make sure he does, you hear me? I don't care what you have to do. I want the brother. After that, feel free to kill him any way you want."

"Yes, sir. It will be done," the man replied.

"We also need to get those asshole Rangers for what they did to our guys," Paul added.

"I'm sure they will come for him, boss," he continued.

"Yes," Paul said, getting back into his truck to leave the area. "And, when they do, be ready!"

"Yes, sir."

There was no doubt now that they were doing a number on Walter. The question was, where in the hell was he? Roger had already figured that they were planning to kill him, eventually. Paul's orders suggested that they were trying to use him to get to his brother. But how? He hasn't had any contact with James in years.

As the man walked away, Roger began following him from above, his men trailing closely behind. They were going to find out where Walter was, one way or another. Without definitely knowing where he was located, they could have quickly executed the man before Roger and his friends were able to get him out of there. Time was not on their side.

CHAPTER 25

ONE FOR ALL

ROGER AND HIS TEAM exited the structure the same way they had come in. They needed to figure out where Walter was being interrogated before it was too late. Roger didn't want to involve the police. Having a dozen cars rush in with sirens blaring was simply out of the question. They would most likely kill Walter before anyone had a chance to get close to him. Roger knew that Paul wouldn't be reasoned with, especially by the cops.

It seemed to Roger as though the only real chance they had of getting any accurate information of his whereabouts was to catch one of those pricks off guard, away from the rest and make him talk. As the team moved swiftly across the lot under a glimmer of moonlight, they made a position toward the rear of the complex, hidden away in the brush.

"This should do," Roger said as he got down into the prone position, binoculars in hand.

"What do you want to do, boss?" Asked Shane.

"We are going to wait until one of these guys comes out to smoke," he added. "Then, we will snatch his ass."

"Hell yeah."

"And, since we all hate racist's, but one of us in particular," Roger continued. "That honor goes to Lamar."

"Damn straight," Lamar answered. "I'll get my hands on as many of 'em as I can."

The men waited there in the bush, what seemed like forever, for one of those guys to pop his head out. Finally, almost an hour later, Roger spotted a man standing in the corner by the back door, lighting up a cigarette.

"I got one," he said. "It's about damn time. I was starting to seriously consider just going back in and shooting up the place."

"Where?" Frank asked. "I don't see anyone."

"Right over there by the rear," Roger replied. "You see the orange glow?"

"Yep. I see it."

"What do you want to do?" Asked Lamar.

Roger glanced back through his optic, noticing how

close the man was to the open door.

"We need to get him away from that entrance, some-how," he said. "We don't want anyone to hear him."

"I have an idea," Lamar said, as he snagged a rock from under the snow. "We just need to get his attention so he'll walk away from there."

Lamar gripped the large rock in the palm of his hand, bringing his arm back and throwing it against a tree ten meters in front of their position.

"I think that did it," Roger whispered as he watched the man toss his cigarette onto the ground, seemingly alert to the sound that Lamar had just made. "He's coming over."

"Wait here," Lamar told them, sliding to the ground and low crawling toward the direction the man was heading.

Lamar came to a stop at the edge of the forest, waiting for the man to get close enough for him to grab.

"Come here, you bastard," he thought to himself.

As the man shined a flashlight around the edge of the tree, Lamar prepared to pounce on him. Suddenly, he turned, facing away from the trees. Lamar reacted in a split-second, grabbing him in a choke hold and wrestling him to the ground.

"Got you, you son of a bitch," he said, wrapping his arm tightly around the man's neck.

He couldn't breathe, trying to speak as his face was flushed red.

"Did I say you could talk yet, jackass?" Lamar asked, pulling a rag from his back pocket and shoving it into the man's mouth.

While the rest of the guys met up with him, Lamar took a set of twist ties from his bag and scrunched them tightly around the man's wrists.

"What do you want to do with him?" He asked Roger, holding his new detainee by the shirt.

"Oh, we're going to have some fun with this guy," Roger answered. "Bring his ass over here."

The men escorted him further into the woods and Roger tied him up with rope to a large evergreen tree.

"How's that feel, asshole? He asked. "You like harassing innocent people?

Roger glared into the man's eyes as if he was searching for something that wasn't there. With no warning, he balled his fist up and hammered the guy right in the stomach, watching as he cringed in pain.

"You like that?" He asked, punching him in the gut one more time. "How about that?"

"Come here, Lamar," said Roger. "I know you want to.

"Damn right, I do."

Lamar raised his big size thirteen boot and kicked him straight in his groin as the man wailed and cried through the rag in his mouth.

"Please stop!" He squealed, barely audible.

"What, bitch?" Lamar said, snatching the rag from his mouth. "Where is our friend?"

"I-don't-know," he said," struggling to get the words out. "They are going to come after you when they find out I'm missing."

"And, we welcome them," Roger told him. "But, I bet they don't give two shits about you! Now. I'll ask you one more time. Where is Walter? If you don't answer me, this is going to end horribly for you."

"Who in the hell are you guys?" The man asked.

"We're the exterminators," said Frank, spitting a stream of tobacco in the man's face. "We get rid of pests."

"I swear, I don't know what to tell you. I don't know anything."

"What's your name?" Lamar asked him.

"Uh, Joey," he answered. "Why?"

"Well, Joey. Lamar added. "If you don't cooperate with

us, we will take you apart, piece by piece. You understand? Nobody will ever find you."

"But I don't know anything!"

"Oh, I think you do, my friend," said Roger. "I think you know exactly where he is."

Joey remained silent for a moment, trying to come to terms with his fate. He didn't want to die. And, the guy sure didn't want his life to end for something as stupid as a kidnapping. It seemed that he was the exception, not the rule. But, he was scared as hell of Paul, whom Joey knew would kill him instantly if he found out that he talked.

"Listen, man," Joey said after giving it some thought. "If I tell you where he is, Paul will kill me."

"And?" Said, Roger. "You guys threatened my fucking family. Now, you kidnap my friend? Why the hell should I care if they kill you?"

"If you don't tell us where he's at," Frank added. "We'll kill you right here!"

"Look," Joey continued. "I swear to you, I had absolutely nothing to do with that!"

"Bullshit!" Said Shane. "He's lying."

"I'm not lying!"

"How about this?" Shane said as he kneed Joey in the gut, causing him to throw up a little.

"Listen," Joey added, wiping his mouth as he tried to gain composure. "I'll tell you where he is. But, you have to promise to protect me from Paul."

"The only thing I promise you," Roger said. Is that if you lead us to him, we won't kill you. That's it!"

"You need to be hammered some more?" Lamar asked. "I'll be happy to loosen up your tongue!"

"No," he spouted. "No. I'll tell you. But, then you drop me off far away from here."

"Fine then. Spit it out!"

"He's not here," said Joey. "They moved him to the basement of Paul's house and tied him up to the ceiling. That is all I know!"

"What about James?" Roger asked him. "The brother. How is he tied into this?"

"They are using Walter to get to James, hoping he will draw his brother out," he answered. Too much police. They haven't been able to get to him."

Roger knew the Aryan Brotherhood is known for going after entire families of their victims. It was all beginning to make sense now to him and the boys. But, this time the Brotherhood drew the short straw. If it weren't for these men, nobody would be going to rescue Walter. This group of special ops guys was not about to back down or bow to them. It just wasn't going to happen. They were willing and able to do things the police couldn't, or wouldn't.

"Let's go," Roger said to them as he began untying the man from the tree. "You're coming with us."

"Remember what you promised me," Joey said. "Drop me off anywhere but there."

"Listen," Frank told Joey, clutching the man by the throat. "We'll hold up our end of this. But, I swear on my grave, if you are lying, we'll kill you and dump you for the wolves! Got it?"

"Uh-huh," he said trembling.

"Then, let's go," Roger said, tugging him by his shirt.

The men made their way around the long stretch of woods and back to the truck, pulling their new captive along. As Lamar basically tossed Joey into the back seat between them, Frank hopped into the driver's side, cranking the engine and busting through the brush, jumping the ditch to the road on the other side.

"Hit the gas, man!" Roger said. "I don't think we have a lot of time."

Springdale, Montana

After a long drive into the early A.M. hours of the

next day, Frank shut the lights off and pulled his pickup into a small trail a few hundred meters from Paul's home. As they got out of the vehicle, Roger motioned for them to huddle near the rear of the pickup while Frank tied Joey's hands to the steering wheel.

"Hey, man," said Joey. "Is that really necessary?"

"Yep," Frank replied. "It is. If he is here, as you said, we'll let you go. But, not before then."

"Fine. Damn it."

Roger and the boys grouped up next to the truck to come up with a plan for entry into the house.

"Listen," Roger said. "We're going dark. No radios. Hand signals only. We stick close together in a tight formation and hit that place the way we know how."

"Roger, that."

"And hope that we can get to him before they have a chance to do too much damage. Walter needs a savior right now. Tonight, that responsibility falls on us."

It was almost as if the boys were heading into another one of many Ranger missions. They had done this so many times, it was like clockwork. The Rangers never leave a man behind. And, they weren't going to leave Walter behind, either.

"Weapons ready?" Asked Roger.

"Check."

"Everyone good to go?"

"Roger."

"Alright," he continued. "Fall in behind me. Let's get our boy and kill this bastard."

The men pressed on with the slyness of a cat, moving across the field next to the property as a single unit, each man remaining alert as to what lay before them. They didn't plan on getting spotted.

As they got within two hundred meters of the house, Roger held a fist up to stop the formation. He glanced through his binoculars, noticing a single individual standing on the deck, smoking a cigar and holding what looked to him like an AK-47 under the front porch light. Roger pointed toward the man, and Frank gave him a tap on the shoulder to signal that he had also seen him.

The men held the position as Roger surveilled their surroundings, trying to get a feel for what they were up against. Roger was known for making decisions on the fly. As a Ranger, he led his men into combat on numerous occasions, earning many awards for his leadership and bravery in the face of the enemy. This was different, however. The stakes were higher.

America is a place where people should live in peace.

That can never happen as long as lawless thugs endanger the safety of innocents. It was enough to make Roger boil over with anger. All he wanted was to take his family on a peaceful holiday. That should have been the end of it.

It was a case of being in the right place at the wrong time. But, he didn't blame Walter. No. That burden was on James and the Aryan Brotherhood. Walter was just caught in the middle. That region of Montana had long been tired of the Brotherhood, which most likely explained why nobody was standing in their way. Now, it was eradication time.

Roger continued scanning the vicinity with his night vision binoculars, getting into position to see the front and back of Paul's house. He needed to determine how many guards were roaming around the grounds. As he turned his body to the left, Roger noticed two more men posted at the entrance to the driveway and pointed at them.

The four men all mounted their night vision goggles onto their faces and screwed suppressors to the end of their rifle barrels. Roger gave the signal to move forward, and they all proceeded, inch by inch toward the front gate. Swiftly Roger held up a fist, and the guys froze in their tracks with weapons at the ready.

As Lamar and Shane stood fast, Roger and Frank moved a little closer to the two men standing guard. Within one hundred meters, the two halted and lined their ACOGs (Advanced Combat Optical Gun sight) crosshairs on the enemy. Almost simultaneously, having neither seen or heard them coming, the men squeezed their triggers and dropped the sentries right where they stood. Roger and Frank dashed for the front drive, yanking the men by their legs and laying them across the ground in the middle of the high, dead brush on the side of Paul's property.

Under cover of a dark, moonless night, the men advanced back to their last position, ready to move in on the house. Roger signaled for them to continue on and they made their way right to the edge of the clearing surrounding the building.

As he watched the front door guard, cigar hanging from his lip and walking over his own footsteps in the packed snow, Roger decided to give this one to Shane. Giving him the sign, Shane waited until the sentry had his back to them. As the man began to turn, Shane progressed toward him at a steady pace. Pulling his knife from his tactical vest, Shane pressed one hand hard against his mouth as he struggled to break free. With the other, he jammed that knife straight into the man's chest as blood spurted out onto his arms and the cold ground below.

No sooner than the man had fallen, Shane hoisted him over his shoulder and rushed away, dropping him head-first into a thick patch of vegetation. Crouched, Shane darted back to the others, Lamar giving him a congratulatory pat on his back. The men got all set to move again, and Roger led them into the blackness at the rear of the premises, and they stacked on the door.

It all seemed quiet, at first. But, as Roger slowly turned the knob and cracked the door open slightly, a large man, and one of Paul's top lieutenants, kicked it hard, with his huge foot, forcing Roger to plunge behind onto the slick ground.

"Mother fucker!" Roger roared.

The stout man stood over Roger, his large frame barely visible against the pale sky.

"I know who you are," he told them. "You should not have come here!"

As the guy began kicking Roger in his side, Lamar ran toward him, tackling him to the ground like a linebacker.

"Come on, you racist bastard," Lamar said. "Let's play."

The man pulled a knife from his pocket and began to charge at Lamar. Stepping to the side to avoid being stabbed, Lamar kicked him in the groin and watched him fall down to his knees, groaning and moaning in absolute pain.

"How's that feel, ass swipe?" Lamar asked.

Lamar swiped his suppressed .40 caliber Glock handgun from his holster and pointed it straight at the man's head.

"Now, it's payback time," he said, just before squeezing the trigger and watching him fall forward to the ground, lifeless.

"The only good racist is a dead one," he uttered.

Lamar held the gun at his side, spitting on the man's body.

"You alright, brother?" He asked Roger.

"Yeah, I'm fine," he replied. "Fucker kicked me in the ribs."

Before they could make another move, the outside light came on, and a group of guys appeared in the doorway.

"Who's there?" One of them asked just before noticing the corpse sprawled out on the icy ground.

"Shit!" He said. "It's Randy!"

Roger and the boys took cover behind a woodshed, getting ready for a long-drawn fight. As the gaggle of men continued toward their dead friend, Roger and Frank peeked out from the side of the small building.

"Go loud!" He yelled as they began firing into the gaggle of men.

One by one, they fell to the ground, and the guys advanced toward the backdoor steps.

"Let's get this over with!" Said, Roger. "I'm tired of this shit!"

They resumed into the back of the residence, getting ready to clear it room by room.

"Move quick. Be deadly," Roger said to his men.

As they moved into the long hallway, two men came walking around the corner. Pointing rifles forward, both Roger and Frank dropped them before they had a chance to aim their weapons.

"Good kill," said Roger. "Keep moving."

The guys turned the corner and into the dining room area. Just as they entered, two men began firing automatic sub-machine guns in their direction, ripping holes into the wall around them.

"Get down!" Roger shouted, all four men diving for the floor.

"We are not here for you!" Roger yelled to the shooters. "We are here for your boss! Just walk away, and we won't kill you!"

"He ain't here, you fool!" One of them said as he laughed at Roger. "You have to deal with us!"

"Damn it," Roger stated, glancing back at his boys. "So be it, then. But, we're walking away with Walter!"

The guys began firing rapidly at Paul's men, sending them falling to the hardwood floor, one at a time with a loud thud. One of them, still alive, reached for the weapon that he had dropped onto the floor. Roger walked up to him, resting his combat boot on the man's hand and stomping it.

"What do you think you're doing?" Asked Roger, kicking the weapon and sending it sliding across the room. "I don't think so, mister."

"Now," Roger declared, pointing his AR-15 at the man's head. "You tell us where Walter is, and I won't send you to hell."

"He's in the basement, mister. Down those steps," he replied as Roger kept his rifle trained on the man's head. Now let me go. I need a hospital!"

Roger glanced back at his team, standing directly behind him.

"What do you say, boys?" Roger asked. "Should I let him go?"

"Personally," Lamar answered. "I would send his bigoted ass six feet under."

Roger looked at the man on the floor with a half-grin.

"Sadly," he said, wrapping his finger around the cold trigger. "I agree."

Roger aimed his rifle and fired off a single shot, and another member of the Brotherhood could speak no longer.

"I hate all you bastards," Roger uttered aloud. "That's for my wife and Walter."

Roger headed straight for the basement steps, his team trailing closely behind him. As they made it to the bottom, there was a concrete floor and the smell of blood lingering in the air.

Roger rounded the corner, and, there he was. Walter's arms had been chained to the ceiling, his feet hardly touching the ground. He had been roughed up pretty critically.

"Walter," Roger said. "Can you hear me?"

But, Walter just hastily nodded his head. Roger grabbed Walter's face and looked into his worn, beat up eyes.

"Come on," he continued. "We're going to get you out of here."

Frank released the chain from the ceiling, and Roger caught Walter to keep him from hitting the cold, damp, floor.

"I-feel-like-I'm-dying," he grumbled, barely understandable.

"Hang on, man," said Roger. "You're not going to die. We'll get you help."

Walter was not in excellent condition. He could barely speak and was going in and out of consciousness. He smelled of blood and old urine and had cuts all over his body and through his shredded clothing. They needed to get him to a hospital as soon as possible.

Roger placed Walter on his shoulder, and they transported him to the waiting vehicle in haste to get him to the closest emergency room.

"Get out of here!" Frank said to Joey, releasing his hands and yanking him from the vehicle as he fell to the ground.

"You said you would drop me off away from here!"

"I changed my mind," Frank responded. "Now run away from this place while you still can. Or you'll be one of them!"

As Joey moved out of sight, they quickly loaded Walter into the backseat and drove away into the night, hoping and praying they could make it in time.

CHAPTER 26

VENGEANCE

Livingston General Hospital, Montana

FRANK SWUNG THE VEHICLE into the hospital entrance, jumping the curb and coming to a rest in front of the large double doors to the emergency room. Although they had given him first aid, the guys had no idea of Walter's real condition, yet. He had passed out on the way to the hospital. But, they hoped that he was just in shock.

"Help!" Roger shouted as they pulled Walter from the truck. "We need help over here!"

As Frank and Roger carried Walter by his limbs up to the concrete ramp, a petite Hispanic woman rushed through the door and to their side, pushing a wheelchair down the incline.

"I'm nurse Garcia," she told them, helping them to set Walter into the chair. "What happened to him?"

"He was hurt by some evil men, miss," Roger replied. "We don't know the extent of his injuries."

"Do you need me to call the police?" She asked him.

"Nope. We got it covered."

"If you say so, mister," she said reluctantly. "I'll get him to a room, right away."

"Thank you, mam."

Roger and his partners stepped into the deserted waiting area, both dead on their feet and apprehensive of what the doctor might tell them. They'd been awake for close to a full day, and Roger was trying to fight the urge to fall asleep. But, they had work to do.

He didn't want to rest until the perpetrators of this horrible incident got what was coming to them. Especially their ring leader, Paul. Roger hated that man more than he thought was ever possible. People who prey on the weak and defenseless have a special place in hell, according to him.

As Roger sat, motionless and counting the tiles on the ceiling above him to remain awake, his weariness got the better of him, and he gradually slipped into a restless slumber. Roger's mind simply couldn't escape the realities of his past. Like so many times before now, he just could not shake it.

KABUL PROVINCE, AFGHANISTAN, 2008. Roger was right back in the middle of the action with his team. It was a night-time raid to rescue an embedded news reporter who'd gone missing a couple of weeks earlier. They had gotten intel reports that she was being held by al-Qaeda operatives in a neighborhood in the center of the city of Kabul.

Military vehicles rolled onto the surrounding neighborhood streets at 0100 hours, blocking off any accessibility from the outside. The plan was to catch the terrorists off guard. They couldn't send a JDAM (Joint Direct Action Munition) bomb, or a Hellfire missile into the building complex—Too much collateral damage, even though most of the residents were reported to be al-Qaeda sympathizers. Plus, without knowing exactly which building she was being held in, they would risk killing the reporter herself.

They had their mission. Team by team, the Rangers advanced on the small neighborhood as vehicle gunners kept watch with their .50 caliber, mounted machine guns. Moving away from the amber glow of street lights, they hugged the walls as they progressed into the dark, narrow alleyways and prepared to launch their assault and rescue the captive woman.

Roger's team came to a pause as they got ready to breach the apartment door. He silently gave the signal, and Shane ran up to the front of the file, sledgehammer in hand. With one mighty swing, he busted the lock from the metal door and kicked it in with his combat boot.

"Go, go, go," Roger ordered.

As they cautiously entered the residence, three civilian ladies jumped from the floor and began shouting at them in the Dari language.

"What are you doing here?" One of them said. "Why you break my door?"

"Get down!" Roger yelled, pointing downward. "On the floor! Now!"

But the women didn't seem to understand what he was saying to them.

"Guard them," Roger said to his most junior Ranger, Specialist Mike Mendoza, a Hispanic Soldier formerly from Mexico. "Don't let them out of your sight."

"Roger sergeant."

While Mendoza stood watch in the living area, the rest of Roger's team began searching throughout the dwelling, determined to find any information on the reporter's whereabouts. As they made it to the last room, Roger could hear some commotion coming from the other side of the closed entryway. He held a finger to his mouth and pressed his ears to the door.

"Sounds like she's in there," he muttered. "I hear a female voice."

"Get ready," Roger continued. "On my go. I'm going to blow this door open."

He held his fingers up and counted. 1... 2... 3...

The rounds from his M-4 sent the door lock tumbling to the floor, and the team entered the home very confident they would get her out of that place. However, her fate had already been sealed.

As soon as Roger and his team began sending bullets flying through the bodies of those men, one of them managed to get a shot off from his AK-47 before he slumped over, and struck the poor woman in the neck as Roger dove to push her out of the way.

"No, no!" Roger squealed as he landed on the floor on top of her, trying to put pressure on her bleeding wound. "Fuck!"

Frank stepped toward Roger and the reporter, holding two fingers on her carotid artery.

"She's gone, man," Frank said, shaking his head.

"Nothing more we can do for her."

Roger never truly got over that mission. His unit had lost numerous Rangers to combat operations. But, it was the first time he'd ever lost a rescue. An innocent woman's life had been in their hands. For a prolonged time, he blamed himself for the indiscretion, like it was his fault that she had died. He questioned himself, wondering if he made the right call. It was a moment in time and his career as an Army Ranger that would come back to haunt him time and time again, as many others have over the years.

A COUPLE OF HOURS later, as Roger sat, head tilted back on the waiting room sofa, he slowly wakened to a voice calling him in the background. It was an older man, short gray hair, and wearing a long, white coat.

"Mister O'Neil," The man said, tapping him on the shoulder. "Mister O'Neil."

Roger's eyes slowly opened, and he caught the gentleman's face glimpsing down at him from above.

"Mister O'Neil?" He continued.

"Yeah," Roger answered, sitting upright in the chair and rubbing his eyes with his sleeve. "That's me, mister."

"Mister O'Neil," he said. "I am Doctor Richards. I have an update on the gentleman that you guys brought in this morning."

"Ok," Roger replied, as the boys all gathered around the doc. "What's going on?"

"Well," the doctor added. "I am afraid that he has suffered a heart attack. It most likely happened while he was captive. The cuts he has, although unfortunate, aren't too severe."

"Ok, doc," Roger mentioned.

"However," Doctor Richards continued. "Due to his newly found heart condition, we will need to keep him under observation for a while and conduct further testing."

Ok," Roger answered. "Thank you, doctor."

"My pleasure," he said. "I wish I had better news. But, if you hadn't found him when you did, he probably wouldn't be lying there."

As the doctor left them in the waiting area, Frank suddenly had a thought run through his mind. And it wasn't a good thought.

"Shit," he said.

"What?" Lamar asked. "What's wrong?"

"What's wrong?" Frank added. "You don't think they could get to him in this hospital, and finish him off?"

"Damn it," Roger replied. "You're right."

"Exactly," said Frank. "What are we going to do?"

"The only thing we can do, I guess," Roger told him.

"What's that?"

"Even though I don't want to," he said. "I'm going to have to call the state police."

"You trust them?"

"Hardly," Roger continued, stepping out into the bitter, cold morning. "But it's the only option we have."

Though he was reluctant, Roger snatched the cell phone from his coat pocket and began dialing Tillman's number.

"Hello?" Said the voice on the other end.

"Trooper Tillman?"

"Yeah. Who is this? It's five 'o clock in the damn morning."

"It's Roger," he answered. "I'm sorry to call you so early, but we have a situation."

"Uh, huh. Yep. I'm listening."

"Our buddy, Walter, is in the hospital. He was roughed up pretty bad, and we believe the Brotherhood will return to finish what they started."

"And you need a guard?"

"Yeah," Roger said. "Just until he can be released. Can you arrange that?"

"Alright. Give me some time to make a few calls," Tillman stated. "I'll give you a ring shortly."

"Sure," Roger said. "Thank you."

"Not a problem."

As Roger hung the phone up, he knew what they had to do. There was nothing or anybody who was going to stop them. Staring into the rising sun, a new day was beginning. His eyes filled with anger as he thought about Walter, lying there, helpless in his hospital bed. He thought about what they had done to his family. As Frank approached Roger from behind, he asked him the most pertinent question of all.

"What are we going to do, boss?" Asked Frank. "What's our next move?"

Roger glanced back at Frank and glared straight into his eyes as he balled up a fist.

"VENGEANCE," he said, without hesitation. "We are going to bring their world crumbling to the fucking ground."

"Hell yeah," Lamar responded. "Just give me a clear shot, and he's mine."

While the boys gathered around Roger, awaiting the arrival of the state trooper, he was preoccupied with revengeful thoughts. They were going to bring the world crashing down on that prison gang using their own brand of violence. As soon as they were able to leave Walter in their hands, they planned to find Paul, and make him pay for what he's done.

An hour and a half later

The boys were impatiently waiting so they could get to work, doing what they do. When, suddenly a patrol car entered the parking lot and came around the curve, stopping directly in front of them.

"It's about damn time," said Shane, as Trooper Tillman and another gentleman got out of the vehicle.

"Hello," Tillman said. "This is Trooper Harris. He's going to be posted at Walter's door for the next few days. We'll have another one relieve him at night, so they'll be rotating."

"Good," Roger replied. "That's great."

Harris was a reasonably large guy and looked like he could hold his own in a fight. With a short brown crew cut, he stood tall, at six foot two, and seemed to be in pretty good shape.

"How are you?" Roger asked Harris, shaking his hand with a firm grip.

"Good," he replied. "Nice to meet you all."

"You do understand this is only temporary, correct?" Tillman asked. "We can't allocate resources for longer than that."

"I understand," answered Roger. "That is all we need."

"Alright, then," Tillman stated. "Harris, you can go ahead inside."

"He's in room 211," Roger told him.

"10-4."

"By the way, gentlemen," said Tillman, retrieving a tiny notebook from his pocket. "I may have some information for you."

"What's that?" Roger asked him.

"A CI (confidential informant) of mine just informed me that the one you are looking for was spotted at a house in Clyde Park."

"Is that so?" Roger asked. "Do you have an address?"

"No," the trooper replied. "But you can't miss it. There is a swastika on the mailbox."

"It figures," Frank commented.

Trooper Tillman's RADIO began to squawk as he started to depart back to his patrol car.

"10-4," he answered into the RADIO. "Unit 57, responding."

"Alright, guys," the trooper continued. "I'll leave you

to it. I have another call to get to."

"Thanks for your help, Tillman," Roger declared.

"Sure thing."

Roger and the boys retreated to Frank's pickup, trusting that Walter was now in safe hands. They could lastly shift their focus to what really mattered, relieving the world of a white supremacist called Paul, and anyone else who stood in their way.

CHAPTER 27
WAITING GAME

Clyde Park, Montana

A SINGLE, THIN WHITE female pushed the chain-link gate open and continued up the concrete walk to the front door of the dilapidated residence. She had the look of a severe tweaker. With missing teeth, worn, broken out skin, and her constant fidgeting, she showed all of the signs of a user of methamphetamines.

It wasn't surprising, given the gang's history of narcotics distribution. The Aryan Brotherhood could care less about how many people they hurt, or that it was a societal epidemic, as long as they made their money in the end. The amount of cash they brought in for their illegal activities nationwide was rivaled only by Mexican drug cartels. The criminal justice system had a difficult time prosecuting many of the cases against them. Either that or they just didn't have the stomach to do what needed to be done. Somehow, eyewitnesses were always turning up dead. Somebody had to stop them.

The woman continued up the wobbly porch steps and knocked loudly on the old, faded door.

"Hey, man," she screeched. "Open up! It's me!"

Suddenly, a mysterious figure emerged, hidden behind the partially open door.

"Hey," the lady said. "I need some."

"Weren't you just here yesterday?" The mysterious man asked her.

"Come on, man," she added, bobbing back and forth on the wooden porch. "I just need some. I'm coming down."

"Fine," he answered. "You got enough money this time?"

The woman reached into her bra and pulled out a short stack of cash and presented it to him.

"This enough?" She asked.

"Enough for today," he replied as he counted the small wad of bills.

"Come on," she added, snatching a ziplock baggie from

his hand. "I'll hit you back."

"I don't give loans, bitch," the man informed her. "Now, get the fuck out of here, and come back when you have the money!"

The man withdrew back inside the residence, slamming the door in the woman's face.

"Fucking free-loading cunt," he said to himself.

"Who?" Paul asked, sitting at the kitchen table and counting mounds of cash.

"Oh, this stupid bitch," the man replied. "Expects a fucking hand out."

"Maybe we should just kill her ass next time, then," Paul answered, chuckling.

"By the way, boss," the man added. "I have some info on that Walter prick."

"What?"

"He's at a hospital in Livingston," he continued.

"Well," said Paul. "We can snatch him up as soon as they release him. We ain't done with that asshole yet or his new buddies."

"Damn right, boss."

"We should have murdered that guy when we had the fucking chance," Paul added. "That's on me."

Paul rose to his feet and stepped toward the window,

glancing out at the icy road in front of his yard.

THREE-HUNDRED METERS AWAY, Lamar was staring through the scope of his sniper rifle, all decked out in a snow-camouflaged ghillie suit, shooting gloves, and a matching boonie cap. He'd been lying in the prone on that hillside, waiting and observing the lady entering the property. Opening his dominant eye, Lamar had caught a quick glimpse of Paul as he stood, glaring through the window as if nobody was watching him. But, they were.

Stalking like a feline, they'd been monitoring every single move to and from that place for hours by now. They had all the time in the world to remain for the right moment to pounce.

"That's him," Lamar said. "Finally."

"You sure it's Paul?" Roger asked. "We need to get it right this time."

"I'm certain," replied Lamar. "I won't soon forget that ugly mug. Stupid of him to show his face like that."

"These guys are killers, no doubt," said Roger. "But, they aren't trained killers. That's their biggest downfall."

"They won't see us coming," Frank added. "That's for damn sure!"

"You got that right, bro," Shane added.

"Should I go ahead and take the shot?" Lamar asked Roger.

"No," Roger replied. "Not yet. Let's wait until we have a better idea of how many guys are in there. I don't want to be premature."

"Roger that."

"We'll just lay here and wait it out for a bit," said Roger. "See what we're dealing with. I want to send them all to their maker."

BACK IN THE HOUSE, Paul was becoming restless. He'd thought about just paying poor Walter a visit at the hospital. But, he knew that would leave far too many witnesses that he was comfortable with, plus video monitoring. There'd been a hit out on James for a while now. Now, Paul was attempting to figure out what to do next. He was worried that, if he didn't succeed, the higher-ups in prison would decide to take him out. They've done it countless times in the past.

He had people watching the cops, and every move that James made, from a distance. They knew that they couldn't get much closer to him. However, maybe they wouldn't have to.

As Paul was sitting, elevated in his lounge chair, pondering the situation at hand, suddenly his cell phone began to ring. He irritatingly snagged the phone from his side pocket, mashing the button hard with his thumb.

"What?" He answered in a loud voice.

"Hey, boss," said the man on the other end. "I think I got something!"

"What is it?" Paul asked him. "I'm kind of busy right now."

"Trust me, boss," the man replied. "You're going to want to hear this."

"Fine, then. Tell me."

"Ok, listen," he continued. "One of our guys heard on the police scanner that that asshole may be in this area, somewhere."

"Say that again," Paul told him.

"I think he's coming here!"

"You are shitting me, right?" Asked Paul.

"I don't think so, boss."

"Well, then," Paul said. "That might just make things a little simpler for us."

"That was my thinking," said the man.

"If the pigs get in our way this time," Paul added. "Then, so be it. I'm tired of pussy-footing around with them, anyway. It has to get done, one way or the other."

"Right, boss."

"Good job," Paul told him, just before hanging the phone up and tossing it onto an old, wooden end table.

"Well, fuck me then," Paul said to himself. "Maybe we won't need Walter, after all."

Paul flipped on the television, and talk of the chase was ongoing on the nightly news, along with an interview with the leader of the manhunt, United States Marshal, Jones.

"I'm going to end you, too," Paul murmured under his breath, as Jones spoke to the reporter about the continued pursuit of James. "Son of a bitch. You and anyone else who get's in my fucking way."

Paul continued eyeing the TV screen and was getting more and more pissed off by the minute. He listened as Jones called out the Aryan Brotherhood by name. He didn't like anyone talking shit about the Brotherhood. But, then, the Marshal mentioned him by name.

"The leader of the Aryan Brotherhood in this area, Paul Cabot, is suspected of being the hit man who is after our fugitive," Jones said to the reporter. "He's also a suspect in various other violent crimes, and needs to be stopped."

As if it couldn't possibly get any worse for him, Paul's

most recent mugshot was then displayed on the tube.

"Fuck!" Paul shouted. "Those cock suckers!"

Paul rose to his feet, grabbing a baseball that had been lying on the floor, and threw it as hard as he possibly could at the screen, busting the glass and sending shards flying all over the room.

"Damn it!" He yelled again, punching the side of the sofa.

"Boss, what's wrong?" One of his men came into the living room and asked. "What in the hell is going on?"

"Just get the hell out of my face!" Paul yelled at him. "I need to think!"

"But."

"But nothing!" Paul continued. "Leave me be, or you'll be eating through a straw, from now on!"

"Ok, boss," he replied. "If you say so."

Paul was beginning to feel that the world was closing in on him. He didn't want to go back to prison. But, if the man could get to James before then, it would be worth it to him. He wasn't about to bolt. Running from the cops just wasn't in the cards for the Brotherhood. The way Paul saw it, if he were going to be arrested, he would take as many of them down as he could, until the instant they slapped the cuffs on him.

For a brief bit, Paul had forgotten all about Roger and his friends. But, they sure as hell didn't forget about him. Paul seemed to believe that he would get away with all he and his cronies have done. Mostly, people were scared to death of them. But not those guys. They had been up against far worse, for sure.

The Aryans had been a peril to the citizens of Montana, and around the nation for far too long. Roger wasn't going to wait for any trial to take place, or for the authorities to come and arrest Paul. He might even lose his job for it. But, he didn't care. It was all about his family, this time.

OUTSIDE, the remaining sun was beginning to sink behind them, and Roger and his men had been lying in wait, observing every move in and around the home. They would remain until night time to strike from the shadows.

"What you got?" Roger asked Lamar. "How many?"

"So far, I count fifteen men," he said as he swiveled his rifle left and right on his bipod. "Not including our star."

"Ok," Roger continued. "Once we have pitch darkness out here, we'll make our move."

"Roger that, bossman."

The guys knew they had the tactical edge. There was no amount of time that they wouldn't endure there. They knew what was at stake. They weren't just avenging Roger's family, anymore. They were doing it for all of the countless people that the Aryan Brotherhood have screwed with their drugs, or killed over the years. The courts had failed their citizens. It seemed that Roger and the team were going to be the judge, the jury, and the executioner. That suited them, entirely.

"Wait," said Lamar. "I got a rover over here. He's coming down the side yard."

"Hold one," Roger told him. "Let's see where he goes."

"Looks like he's lighting up a cigarette."

"Too bad he didn't do that inside," Roger added. "He may have blown their meth kitchen, sky-high."

"That would have absolutely saved us all the damn trouble," Shane said.

"For sure," Frank replied.

"Oh, believe me," Roger maintained. "This is no trouble for me."

Lamar kept the crosshairs directed at the man in the yard when he spotted him walking through the front gate.

"Looks like he's going for a walk or something," said

Lamar. "He's on his way down the street. Should I subtract one?"

"Go for it," he told Lamar.

With his suppressed weapon, Lamar followed the man closely as he advanced further from the house.

"As soon as he gets around that corner, Lamar," Roger said. "Drop him. It's dark enough now that nobody should see the body."

"Roger that."

Lamar resumed following the guy as he stepped into the drainage ditch on their side of the road.

"Taking the shot," Lamar said.

"Send it."

Going through his tactical breathing, Lamar exhaled and held it for a moment. Squeezing the trigger calmly, he sent his. 338 caliber boat-tail bullet sailing toward the target at supersonic speed. The shot entered the man's neck and separated his spinal cord as it blew a giant hole near the rear of his head. As he plunged, blood splattered on the frosted ground around him.

"Tango down," Lamar affirmed as he slid the weapon bolt to the rear. "Damn near took his head off."

"Good shot," Frank told him.

"Well, that's one less bad guy," Roger replied. "Shane,

Get down there and drag the body further from the road."

"Got it, boss," Shane answered.

"We don't want them to know we're here until we want them to know we're here."

As Shane went to retrieve the man's corpse, the rest of the men kept their eyes steadfastly on the property, attempting to take notice of any other strollers around the house. They were all hunkering down, guessing they were in for a long night. Roger didn't want to put his team in the line of fire, without grasping, beyond a shadow of a doubt exactly how many they were dealing with.

CHAPTER 28

RESOLUTION

White Sulphur Springs, Montana

JAMES HAD BEEN RUNNING for far too long now. It appeared as though everyone in the state of Montana was out for him. He was turning more tired and weaker as the days rambled on, apparently with no end to speak of. Between the authorities and the gang who were after him, James wasn't wholly sure of which was worse for him, anymore. But, running just wasn't in the cards any longer.

However, he was at a crossroads now, it felt like to him. He'd been tearing across town in an old, black Thunderbird he had taken from a restaurant parking lot, trying to gain as much mileage from the cops as he could. Now, he was barreling down highway 89, Destination:

Clyde Park.

James literally had no plan what he would do once he got there. All he knew was that he had heard it through hearsay that the Brotherhood had a meth kitchen located someplace out there. James blamed his predicament on them. Knowing that eventually he would most likely be captured or killed, he wanted to get even.

With the wind whirling staunchly against his face through the car window, James began to reflect on his brother and questioned how it was possible that he got stuck in the midst of it all. He felt a sense of guilt, although they had been estranged for such a long period. He reminisced of his sister, Jessica, and had much grief for all that he'd put her through.

Maybe he was better off away from society. Possibly, they were better off without him. He'd considered killing himself to escape the constant, nagging feeling. Yet, James just couldn't bring himself to do it. He'd busted out of the joint to save himself. Maybe it would've been better for everyone if he'd remained. In any case, it was going to end. He would make sure of it. If he went down, he would ensure that he took at least a few of them with him.

Thirty miles behind

The Marshals and the state policemen were trying to pinpoint James' position. They'd found the victim of the carjacking ambling along the side of the road, looking distraught and afraid. But, too scared to notice his direction of travel at the time, she wasn't much use to them, except for giving the cops a description of the stolen vehicle.

Marshal Jones had come close to James on so many occasions. He was beyond baffled at this man for leading them halfway across the state. This time, he needed to make it count for his career's sake, and for everyone who'd been victimized by this fellow. The director was not pleased with the status of the manhunt. She'd made that perfectly clear. Nobody ever expects to incur losses. But, that's precisely what happened. He needed to get this man off the streets. It was do-or-die time for him.

"Hey, Jones," Trooper Barry called out, stepping out of his squad car. "I think I got something."

"What is it?" Jones asked as he finished wiping down his piece and placed it in the holster. "It better be good this time."

"Oh, it is," replied Barry. "I just got a call on my radio."

"Ok."

"Appears someone spotted a car matching the subject vehicle's description to a tee."

"Really?"

"Yep," Barry said. "And, that's not all. According to the witness, the car was seen speeding down highway 89, weaving around traffic. I think I know where he's going."

"Where?" Asked Jones.

"Clyde Park," he responded. "It's a known haven for drug distribution. There is only one gang that controls that area. See where I'm going with this?"

"I believe I do," the Marshal replied, as he snatched the radio from his leather belt. "Give me a minute."

"10-4."

"Eagle 3, Eagle 3," Jones said into the radio. "This is Marshal Jones. We are thirty miles outside of Clyde Park."

"10-4, Marshal," the pilot called out. "I read you."

"10-4," he replied. "We need eyes in the sky about halfway between here and Clyde Park. Our fugitive was spotted in a black Thunderbird, heading south at a high rate of speed."

"That's a good copy, Marshal," said the pilot. "We are

en-route to that location now."

"Copy that," Jones said. "Please, step on it. We don't know what he's planning."

As Marshal Jones shot for his unmarked vehicle, he wanted to rouse everyone one final time. He was planning to close in on James, no matter what he had to do.

"All units follow closely behind me," he said into his car radio. "Let's get this asshole. He's running out of real estate. I can feel it!"

With his newest man, rookie Marshal Todd Ferguson sitting beside him, they hurried down the highway at eighty-five miles per hour, trying to meet the police chopper near the fleeing vehicle.

Ferguson was sent to replace the poor soul that they'd lost to James, a week prior. He was six feet tall with an ordinary build. A greenhorn. Nevertheless, knowing that he'd been a military policeman in the Army, Jones was positive that he would be an asset to the team. Being thrown right in the center of pursuit as a newbie wasn't ideal. But, they needed all the help they could get.

BACK IN CLYDE PARK, Roger and the guys were continuing surveillance on the Aryan's Meth house. They'd watched as countless tweakers came and went from the residence. Roger wanted to catch the man outside. However, perhaps from paranoia, he hadn't ventured out in all of the hours they had been lying, hidden on that hill. He knew they were after him.

The men were getting tired of waiting. They were equipped to crash their party at any second. Paul was the primary target. Every other man was just an added bonus. Still, they would bring down as many of them as they possibly could.

"I got another one over here," Frank stated as he peered through his binoculars. "Looks like he's headed for that white Sedan by the road."

"Ok," Roger answered. "Lamar, it's your call. If you have a decent shot, take it. But, wait until he enters the vehicle. I don't want him sprawled out in the drive for everyone to notice. Not until we make our move."

"Roger that," Lamar declared, glancing through his night vision scope. "One dead bad guy, coming up."

Lamar followed the target closely as he continued down the path and onto the snow bank next to the parked car.

"I'll put all you jerk off's six-feet under," he said under his breath. "One shot, one mother fucking kill."

The figure of a man, tinted green by Lamar's night optic, got into the car and began to crank it up, having no clue of his impending fate. Lamar rested the tip of his finger firmly on the trigger.

"Night, night, asshole," he said to himself.

With one quick motion, he squeezed off a round and sent it soaring toward the mark, blowing away half of the other side of the man's head and collapsing him over in his seat, blood and brain matter splashing on the passenger side window.

"Target down," Lamar stated. "That makes two."

"Alright," Roger said. "I'm getting bored of this shit. Let's move in."

Shane stopped Roger mid-stride, grabbing him by his tactical vest as he began to push forward.

"You positive, boss?" Shane asked. "We still don't know how many are in there."

"What other choice do we have? If he doesn't show his face again, we have to go in and get his ass."

"You're right," Shane added. "I just don't like going in without intel."

"Roger is right," said Frank. "I think we've gained just about all the intel we're going to get, man. Besides, we have a good sense."

"Alright," continued Shane. "I trust your instincts. After all, you've saved our asses enough times in combat.

But, if this goes sideways, I'm going to be really pissed."

"Don't worry, Shane," Lamar said. "We've got you. I'll stay here on overwatch, and you guys go ahead."

Alright, then," Shane replied. "let's do this, gentleman."

The guys got down low to the ground and began to low crawl, weapons set across their folded arms, to the roadway a few hundred meters ahead. Once there, they would dash, one by one, across the road and position themselves against cover. Roger planned to clear that building like it was a Taliban stronghold.

"Stop," Roger whispered, noticing headlights nearing in their direction. "Somebody's coming."

A pickup truck entered the driveway, coming to a stop near the front walk.

"One, two three, four," he said, watching the occupants hop out of the vehicle through his ACOG. "Five. I count five."

"Let's hope they don't spot their dead friend, out there," Frank said.

"That has to be at least thirteen to fifteen guys," said Shane. "maybe more."

"And, I bet they've never been up against a group of angry special ops guys, either."

"Very true," added Shane. "Indeed."

After minutes of crawling, chins cool against the snow, the team finally made it to the edge of the road and prepared to make the leap.

"Alright, guys," Roger whispered. "Shane, you go first. "I'll go last. Stay low and take cover against that vehicle over there.

Roger patted Shane on his shoulder from behind.

"Go, go," he said in a low voice.

Shane traversed the slippery road, pinning himself hunched against the wheel well of the white sedan.

"Frank," Roger said. "Your move."

As he crossed over, his rifle and his body were a single unit. Frank twisted from side to side, examining his surroundings as he advanced. His body pausing against the cold metal, he spun around to cover the rear.

It was Roger's turn to move. He dipped low, swiftly pushing as he came to a stop in front of Shane, and facing his weapon forward.

"Ok, guys," Roger uttered. "Get ready to move again."

The men were prepared to bound forward when they heard Lamar's voice in their earpieces.

"Freeze!" Lamar told them. "There's a tango coming your way," over. "He's alone."

"Shh," Roger said," peeking his head partly out of the side of the vehicle.

Seizing his combat knife from the side of his vest, Roger positioned himself to engage the lone figure.

As the man made his way to the front of the drive, Roger got ready to spring from the shadows. He silently moved behind the man. Getting close enough to touch him, Roger wrapped his arm as tightly as he could around his neck, his hand covering the man's mouth so he couldn't squeal.

"Hey, asshole," Roger said, before inserting the blade into his chest and watching blood stream out of the gaping wound. "Remember me?"

Roger watched his life slipping away as he collapsed to the earth, lifeless. He felt no guilt for any of those guys, after what they had done to him. Roger picked the man up, hoisting his dead body over his shoulders and flinging him into the back seat of the unlocked vehicle.

"Cross another one off the list."

"Good kill," Lamar said to him.

"Where to now, boss?" Shane asked Roger.

"I think we should take up a position at the side of the house," Roger answered. "It's dark over there. I want to stay in cover for as long as possible. Or, at least until we can't, anymore."

"After you," said Frank.

"Follow me."

Roger led his team to the middle of the front yard, Noiselessly leaping, one at a time over the low fence rail and making their way to the right-hand side of the place. Heads held against the wall siding, the men could vaguely make out the bustle and talking going on inside through the bedroom window overhead.

"Sounds like Paul," Frank said.

"Yep," Roger replied. "That's him. I could recognize his loud voice anyplace."

SIX HUNDRED METERS from their position, Lamar was studying the perimeter, eyes peeled for any stragglers. He was yearning to drop as many of them as he possibly could. But, Lamar knew that he couldn't risk giving them away if the target was in a well-lit area, close to the home. For a while, he would remain, steadily in his sniper's nest, watching and waiting for Roger to give the team the order to push in on Paul and his associates.

CHAPTER 29
THE STORM

JAMES ROLLED THE WINDOW up as the snowdrift picked up and started to sweep forcefully over the roadway and into the vehicle. The blast was whisking dramatically, and poor visibility was becoming a pressing issue. Fighting to stay in the right lane, he switched the car radio on and caught reports of a harsh winter storm on the way.

"It could very well be the worst blizzard to hit the region in over thirty years," the voice on the radio announced.

"Shit," James said to himself. "That's not good."

A COUPLE OF MILES behind him, the U.S.. Marshals and State Police were gaining some ground on James. But, the impending storm was stalling them drastically. Marshal Jones was now assured that the police chopper wouldn't be able to make it to the scene.

"Marshal. This is Eagle 33," the pilot said into his radio. "This weather has caused us to have to land. We are grounded for the time being."

"Damn it!" Jones shouted sharply.

"Very sorry, Marshal," the pilot added. "Good luck."

Two words had never rung truer.

The pursuers had just lost their tactical advantage. They weren't just up against an elusive fugitive. They were now also facing the harsh unpredictability of winter weather in Montana. Still, the Marshal wasn't about to give up now. He was so close this time, he could feel it.

AHEAD, James was doing his utmost to keep from smashing the old car into the snow bank. He only had a few more miles left to go. But, a few more miles in that type of weather could prove to be disastrous, if the man wasn't careful. Nonetheless, if he didn't continue pushing on, he feared the cops catching up to him, and ultimately, what they would do once they had him. James kept his foot tightly against the accelerator, rubbing his muggy eyes and trying his best to keep it between the lines.

"Come on, James," he grumbled to himself, straining to see the road in front of him. "Damn. I can't see a God damned thing!"

While he strove to maintain a steady speed, the car started to slip and slide across the slippery, Montana highway as James fought to regain control.

"Shit!"

The whirlwind was massing so heavily now, that the whole area was desperately close to a complete whiteout.

IN CLYDE PARK, Lamar's plan of providing his team continuous overwatch had been thwarted as the storm quickly moved into town, covering everything in sight, including his sniper rifle. He was no longer able to recognize the ground through his high-powered scope, let alone the house across the roadway.

"Damn it!" He roared aloud.

"Guys," he continued into his radio mic. "I can't see anything from here. I'm coming to you."

"Roger that," Roger remarked. "Hurry, we can't see anything over here. We're at a standstill."

Lamar grasped the AR-15 from his side, wiping it down the best he could, and strapped his .338 rifle to his back. But, as he worked to creep forward against the prevailing wind, he detected what appeared to be headlights swaying from side to side and scarcely gleaming through the blustering snowfall.

"What the hell?"

It looked as though the vehicle was speeding towards their location, going way too fast for conditions all around. As Lamar kept watch, the car resumed moving closer and closer, and it seemed as if the driver was beginning to lose control.

"Stand by," he said into his mic. "We got a situation out here."

"What's wrong?" Roger asked. "Talk to me."

Lamar wiped the frosted flakes from his face as he advanced a little closer to the roadway.

"I got a vehicle approaching," he replied. "Hold one."

The black Thunderbird flew across the town limits on almost bald tires, skidding abruptly across the highway.

"Oh, damn," said Lamar. "He's coming right for us. Who the fuck is this guy?"

While the make of the car became more prominent the nearer it got to Lamar, James was steadily losing his grip on the vehicle. He started to spin uncontrollably, slamming into the bank in front of Paul's house. James began to flip violently onto the roof, gliding across the terrain and coming to a rest in the field in front of Lamar.

"Holy shit!" Lamar yelled! "Guys, you need to get away from that house, quick!"

Lamar carefully neared the wreckage, not totally positive if he was one of Paul's goons or not.

IN THE CAR, James was trying to free himself through the broken door. His left arm was in severe pain, having jammed violently into the steering wheel, and was most likely broken.

"Ahhh!" He screamed in agony, trying to push himself through the broken windshield.

As Lamar moved in near to the driver's side, rifle at the ready, he could hardly believe what he was seeing.

"Oh, shit," Lamar said. "You're Walter's brother, aren't you?"

"Yeah," he responded, wailing in anguish. "Give me a hand, will you?"

"I'm supposed to want to kill you, mister," Lamar added, aiming his weapon at the man's head. "Give me a reason why I shouldn't."

Roger and the rest of the crew came to Lamar's aid. But, as they surrounded the torn up vehicle, Roger's eyes got wider.

"James?" Roger asked. "Oh, you have been a naughty boy. What are the chances you'd land right here at our feet? Your bro sends his regards!"

"Please, don't shoot!"

Roger walked up closer to James, thrusting the barrel

of his rifle firmly against his temple.

"Why not?" Roger inquired. "You have put your brother through hell. Now he's in the damn hospital!"

"I'm sorry!" James yelled. "I'm not a threat to you guys. And, whatever you and my brother have been through, let's settle it today, right here, together!"

Roger glimpsed over at Lamar for a brief instant to read his mind. But, before they could respond back, shooting erupted from the house across the way.

"Shit! Get down!" Roger yelled. "They've spotted us!"

"I guess stealth is out the window, now!" Said Frank.

"Come on. Get me out of here, mister," James pleaded. "I can help you!"

"Fine," Roger stated. "But, if you cross me, I'll forgo the law and execute you right here!"

"I'm getting too old to be fighting young bucks like you," James said.

Roger began to pull James from the wreckage as shots sailed overhead and pinged off of the damaged car. The men could barely make out the outlines that were advancing for them and started to return fire. Three of Paul's associates crossed the roadway, firing their Uzi sub-machine guns rapidly at Roger's team. Using the car as cover, Roger and Frank sent 5.56 bullets into each of their bodies, dropping them into two feet of bloodstained snow.

"Fuck you guys!" Frank screamed. "We are coming for your ass!"

The team started advancing forward, James trailing closely behind them, sending a hail of bullets into Paul's drug house as his men began to exit the home and dart across the driveway, straight for Roger and his buddies.

"Paul!" Roger roared. "Get out here and fight like a man!"

The chaos around them and the fog of battle sustained as both parties sent rounds flying toward one another. Lamar spun his rifle right to left, squeezing the trigger with dead-on accuracy.

"Got 'em," he said.

Except, as they made their way to the front fence, a bullet hurled past Roger's head, and he heard the piercing wail of intense pain.

"Shit!" Frank said. "Shane is hit!"

"God, that fucking hurts!" Shane squealed as he sank to his side.

"It's ok, partner," Frank said, setting his body across the ground and pushing his hand hard to stop the bleeding. "I think it just missed your heart by a few inches. No sucking chest wound. You'll be alright, man!"

Frank snagged the first aid pouch from Shane's vest and wrapped the dressing tightly around the wound.

"Frank," Roger called out. "Stay with him, ok? We'll finish it. Just cover us from out here. And keep your eye on Shane. Don't let them near him."

"You sure?"

"Yes," Roger replied. "I'm sure."

"Alright. Roger that."

"Ok, Shane," Frank asserted, while Roger and the rest aimed their sights at the task at hand. "Just you and me, buddy. We'll get you out of here, soon. Just stay awake."

Though, while the team and James sprang closer to the exterior of the house, Swirling blue lights could be seen through the dense squall, reaching ever so near to their location.

"Damn," said James. "They're here for me."

"Just stay with us for now," Roger stated. "It isn't over yet."

OUT IN THE ROADWAY, Marshal Jones had spotted the wreck somewhat through the barrage of snow. He hit the brakes hard and skimmed to a stop right in front of Paul's drive.

"Could that be the same vehicle?"

"I believe it is, boss," Ferguson remarked.

"Damn. Where the hell is he, then?"

Peeping over to his left, Jones noticed Frank, leaned over Shane's body to keep him warm. Darting from the unmarked car, he and Ferguson hurried in to lend a hand.

"What happened to him?" Jones asked.

"He was shot."

"Alright," Jones replied. "Hang on, I'll get help."

The Marshal grabbed his mic to call EMS. As Ferguson and Frank carried Shane across to his government vehicle, shots started to pound his car, destroying the driver's window and blowing gaping holes all over the doors.

"Come on," said the Marshal. "We need to move him."

They quickly sprawled Shane's body to cover on the other side and opened fire back into the residence. State Trooper Barry had pulled up behind the car a short time later, and hastened out, taking cover behind his opened door.

IN THE SIDE YARD, Roger and Lamar were moving as a single unit, preparing to enter the house at any second, James tagging right behind them. Training weapons straight forward through iron sights, they were shedding Paul's goons left and right, as soon as they appeared out of the white background, and watching them fall motionlessly to the ground.

"How many was that?"

"I lost count!" Lamar said.

"You shot our friend, assholes!" Roger shouted. "There is no escaping for any of you!"

As Roger, Lamar, and James surged around the corner for the back door, two more men hurried out, shooting AK-47's and just missing Roger's head.

"Shit," he said as the three men squatted down and exchanged fire.

"Got one," James stated, discharging his stolen .45 caliber pistol.

Roger and Lamar commenced spraying bullets, and riddled the other two men, causing them to topple forward off the back porch.

"Is that all of 'em?" Lamar asked. "Should be damn near close."

"I hope so," Roger replied as Marshal Jones and his new partner rushed in beside them. "But, Paul is still in there, somewhere."

James knew that the Marshal's were there to capture him. He didn't actually care anymore. He was still breathing. So, at least that was something. For the moment, however, his interests were aligned with Roger and his buddies. Even if he were sent back to prison, at the least, he would do whatever he could to help get rid of this problem, once and for all, and for everyone affected by them.

The guys proceeded to the back door of the residence, Marshals in tow. Roger intended to bust into that run down, meth house and pull Paul out by his fucking throat. However, as they got somewhat closer to the entrance, Paul ran through the opened doorway and began running right for the hills and away from them.

"He's escaping!" Shouted Roger. "Let's get 'em!"

Roger and Lamar began the chase, quickly gaining on Paul as he attempted to get away.

"Why you running, you fucking pussy?" Lamar asked him. "Your men aren't here to protect your ass?"

Lamar caught up with him, and tackled him head first to the earth, causing Paul to roll forward in the snow.

"Come on, you racist prick!" Lamar sounded. "Let's end this, now!"

"Alright," Paul said as he rose to his feet, pulling a blade from his plaid shirt pocket. "Come on, monkey!"

As he prepared to fight Paul to the end, Roger put his hand across Lamar's chest.

"He's mine," Roger informed him. "We have a complicated history."

Lamar shrugged his shoulders and backed away, giving Roger ample room.

"Come on, punk," Roger stated. "You like punishing the weak, kidnapping the weak? Raping people's wives? Come on, you bastard!"

Paul bounded at Roger, and he moved to the side, kneeing him in his jaw and causing Paul to scrunch forward.

"That all you got?" Roger asked.

"I'm going to kill you, fucker," said Paul.

"Well, I'm right here!" Said, Roger.

Lamar tossed Roger a tactical knife, and he got into a fighting stance.

"Get his ass, man!" Lamar said.

The two men swiped their knives at each other, dodging and zigzagging to avoid being sliced. Roger started to ridicule Paul. He wanted to make him angry.

"Come get me," he said to him. "Can't fight someone your own size?"

Roger waited for Paul to come at him one more time. As he lurched forward at Roger, he sidestepped, guiding the tip of his blade up to Paul's windpipe and jolting it into his neck with a powerful thrust. As Paul skimmed downwards and hit his knees, the only noise that was heard was a gurgling sound, blood spilling from the large hole in his throat.

The men all stood there as Paul grappled with fighting the excessive loss of blood spilling all over him. Shadows were the only thing his eyes could see. He was faint and would slip into unconsciousness at any moment. But, James, determined to get the last shot, strolled over to Paul and held his pistol tight upon the man's forehead.

"This is for my brother, you son of a bitch," James said, squeezing the trigger and watching half of Paul's head blow out as the strength of the blast launched his body on it's back.

James spits on the man's corpse, and dropped the magazine from his handgun, hurling it onto Paul's chest.

"Have fun in hell," he added.

"Everybody ok?" Marshal Jones asked.

"Yeah," Roger replied. "Let's go check on Shane. I can't believe that asshole is finally dead."

The men departed back to the Marshal's vehicle as EMS had lastly arrived. They loaded Shane into the back, and Roger left the others and jumped into the ambulance with him.

"Roger," James called out just before they shut the ambulance doors. "Tell my brother I'm sorry, will you, please? For everything."

"Sure thing," Roger answered, nodding to him as they finally left the scene.

Frank and Lamar jumped into his pickup to follow Shane and Roger to the hospital as Marshal Jones neared to James, holding cuffs in his hands.

"You understand, I still have to take you in, right?"

James wasn't at all startled by the question. He knew it would come, eventually.

"Yes, sir," James answered. "I did what I came here to do. I'm ready to go now."

While the Marshals escorted James back to his bullet-riddled car, there appeared to be a new calmness in the air. The storm was beginning to wane. It was almost as if God had revealed the heavens, in agreement with them for sending more sinful souls to hell. Four men seemed to pull off the impossible; relieving their community of the scum that was the Aryan Brotherhood.

Now, maybe Roger could finally continue on with his original plan, giving his loving family the winter trip of a lifetime—what's left of it. A new era was on the horizon. Roger would nevermore take them for granted. Nor would he ever disregard the bond that he had with his band of brothers, a relationship that would remain for their entire lives.

As for his late grandfather, Roger knew that man was now smiling down on him from Heaven, proud of his braveness and the man he had become. He would never neglect the many lessons that were taught to him— lessons which undoubtedly saved him and his loved one's lives that winter.

Leaving Shane and Walter in the doctor's care, he was comfortable that they were in good hands, and would check on them later. For now, his family was the number one priority. As they returned to the cabin that he and grandpa shared so many fond memories within, there was a new appreciation for life, a life that would never be the same again. Maybe, someday, Roger would be called upon to assist others in need. Until that time arrived, he would remain willing and able to march into the line of fire to liberate the defenseless.

While Roger and Kate prepared for bed, he prayed for a quick recovery for both Shane and Walter. With his newly found freedom, maybe Walter would once again live in peace. As for James, he seemed to become a man who had resigned to his fate. Maybe he'd finally given in to circumstance and wanted to make things right, in the end.

With the Christmas holiday upon Roger and his loved ones, he would keep the promise of giving his children memories to last a lifetime—Never disregarding how lucky he was for the remainder of his days. Grandfather would have definitely been honored to see the way of life that he so cherished being taught to his grandchildren.

As both Roger and Kate embraced each other, the kids finally asleep in the next room, Roger couldn't help but grin as he switched the light off.

"You ok, hun?" Kate asked, pulling the covers up over them.

"I am now, babe," he replied, wrapping his arm tightly around her and gently kissing her forehead. "I am now."

THE END

AUTHOR'S NOTE

I sincerely thank you for taking the time to read my work. If you enjoyed the book, a short Amazon review would be greatly appreciated as it helps me, as an author, write more books for you to enjoy. It's readers like you who make this possible and extremely rewarding. Also, don't forget to visit my website and subscribe to be instantly notified when new books are released. This is the first in a four-book series. Stay tuned!

ABOUT THE AUTHOR

John Etterlee is a thriller author and retired U.S. Army combat Veteran. Born in Augusta, Georgia, he joined the United States Army in 2001, shortly after the attacks of September 11th, and served three tours overseas before being medically retired in 2013. Having been to many countries, the Army really opened his eyes to different cultures around the world and inspired many of the books that he has in the works.

John now lives in North Carolina with his wife Elizabeth, whom he met while stationed at Joint Base Lewis-McChord in Washington State in 2011, along with a few furry kids. He studies the German language, and enjoys traveling, especially to Europe, and meeting new and interesting people. Feel free to drop him a line anytime! Vielen Dank!

Follow thriller author, John Etterlee on Facebook at

https://www.facebook.com/jbetterlee

Or Twitter at

https://twitter.com/JEtterleeWrites

www.johnetterleebooks.com

john@johnetterleebooks.com

P.S. If you take a picture of you holding the book, with a short sentence or two and email it to John, you might just end up on his website!

Made in the USA
Coppell, TX
13 July 2022

79872740R10204